Ravage

Iain Rob Wright

SalGad Publishing Group
Worcestershire, UK

SalGad Publishing Group
Redditch, Worcestershire/UK
www.iainrobwright.com

Publisher's Note: This is a work of fiction. Names, characters, places, and incidents are a product of the author's imagination. Locales and public names are sometimes used for atmospheric purposes. Any resemblance to actual people, living or dead, or to businesses, companies, events, institutions, or locales is completely coincidental.

Book Layout & Design ©2015 - BookDesignTemplates.com

Ordering Information:
Quantity sales. Special discounts are available on quantity purchases by corporations, associations, and others. For details, contact the "Special Sales Department" at the address above.

Ravage/ Iain Rob Wright. -- 2nd ed.
ISBN 978-1490311197

BOOKS BY IAIN ROB WRIGHT

Animal Kingdom
2389
Holes in the Ground (with J.A.Konrath)
Sam
ASBO
The Final Winter
The Housemates
Sea Sick
Ravage
Savage
The Picture Frame
Wings of Sorrow
The Gates
Tar
Soft Target
Hot Zone
End Play

For my children

the beloved horrors of my life

"I used to lie in bed in my flat and imagine what would happen if there was a zombie attack."

–Simon Pegg

Terrorist attack suspected of killing up to 1500 people as commercial cruise liner, SPIRIT OF KIRKPATRICK, sinks due to massive explosion.

Joint relief efforts are underway today in the Mediterranean Sea by France, Italy, UK, and Egypt, as they to attempt to salvage the ill-fated cruise liner, Spirit of Kirkpatrick. No survivors have yet been identified and it is thought that an explosion inside the engine compartment is what caused the 33,000 tonne vessel to sink beneath the waves.

No terrorist groups have yet come forward to claim responsibility for an attack, but owners of the doomed cruise liner, Black Remedy Corporation, have claimed that, with the stringent safety measures present on all of their public passenger ships, there is no other possible cause for the disaster aside from an act of terrorism.

The company has previously been targeted by eco-terrorists and religious groups because of its reputation for operating unethically in the 3rd world, and for allegations of corruption and sabotage. While the vast, multi-national corporation has made great efforts in the last decade to conduct its affairs to a better moral standard, it is thought that there may still be groups and individuals who wish to target it.

NATO Secretary, General Able Rasmussen, condemned the suspected suicide attack as 'despicable.'

CHAPTER 1

"**T**HE TOWN IS dead," Paul said, re-entering the phone shop with a bored shuffling of his feet.

Nick sighed as his gaze fell upon the shopping centre's vacant seating and deserted walkways. The Boots megastore directly opposite – usually teeming with customers – was devoid of a single shopper today. Its staff pottered around the shelves aimlessly.

Likewise, the small mobile phone shop that Nick managed was deserted. It'd been two hours since the last customer left. Each minute felt like hours.

He yawned, then said, "I wonder why it's so quiet. Are England playing football or something?"

Paul shrugged and shook his bald head. "I'm Sikh. I only know when there's cricket on."

Nick chuckled but still felt frustrated. With no customers, how could they possibly expect to meet the day's sales targets? He needed to earn his bonus this month to cover the deposit he'd already paid on a new car. "All the other shops are just as quiet? You checked?"

Paul fingered the edge of his turban and nodded. "I spoke to Chris at Game Traders and he said they haven't had a customer since eleven. They've been playing Call of Duty in the back."

Nick rubbed at the dull stubble on his chin and stifled another yawn. Slow days weren't uncommon, especially with the recession still in full swing, but this was one of the worst footfalls he could remember.

Paul browsed the Internet while Nick stood around with his hands in his pockets. "Check if something's going on today that we don't know about," he told his colleague. "Find me an excuse to give the area manager later. An outbreak of plague would be ideal."

"No problem, governor." Paul typed away with his gold-ringed fingers.

Just then, Chelsea, another of Nick's salespeople exited the back and came back onto the shop floor. She looked at the empty shop floor and then gave Nick a look. "Maybe I should have taken a longer break."

"I know, I know. If it stays like this much longer, I'll probably send you home. No point the three of us being here."

No point even one of them being there, at this rate.

Nick was about to go for a break himself when, finally, a customer entered the store. "Hallelujah," he said under his breath.

"He's mine," said Chelsea.

"Go get him," Nick said. "We need to get a contract out of him or I'm screwed on the conference call later."

"No sweat!" Chelsea flicked her long blonde hair over her shoulder and tottered forward on her heels. She gave the customer her best smile, but the man didn't seem to even notice her.

"Hello, there," Chelsea said.

Instead of responding, the man slumped against the central display where the live demo-phones were lined up on a desk.

"Are you okay, sir?" Chelsea asked the man, somewhat tersely. "What kind of phone are you using at the moment?"

The man remained hunched over as if he hadn't heard her. He let out a low moan.

"I said, are you okay there, mate? Can I help you?" Chelsea had become irritable.

Nick eased the girl aside and took over. "Buddy, I'm afraid you can't sleep it off here."

The man still did not respond.

Nick reached out to the man, getting impatient. "You'll have to go someplace else."

The man shot upright like an uncoiling spring. He turned to Nick with swollen, bloodshot eyes. A thin strand of saliva hung pendulously from his lower lip.

Nick stumbled backwards. "Wow! What's wrong with you?"

The man swayed on his feet and groaned unintelligibly. He seemed to concentrate for a moment and managed to spit his words out slowly. "I...I'm not...feeling...well." His voice was thick, like he was speaking with a swollen tongue.

Paul gave Nick a queasy glance before looking back at the man. "You look rough, mate. Hope it's not catching."

"I...I don't think I can make it...home. W-will you call my wife for me...please?"

Nick stared for a moment, speechless. The stink coming off the man was foul, even worse than the sickly sight of him. Nick managed to find his voice, though, and do the right thing. "Yes, yes, of course," he said. "Chelsea, will you grab my mobile, please?"

Chelsea hurried over to the sales desk, then handed over Nick's phone gingerly, keeping her distance from the sickly man.

Nick held the phone up in front of him and looked at the man. "What's the number for your wife?"

The man's eyes rolled to the back of his head and it seemed like he was going to pass out. Eventually, he managed to reply. "It's... it's – one moment. It's 07...0798...07985..."

It took sixty seconds before the man managed to give out the full phone number. When Nick dialled it, a woman picked up immediately and asked who was calling.

"This is Nick Adams. I'm calling from Touch Pad, one of the phone shops in town. I have your husband here with me. I'm afraid he's not feeling well. He needs someone to come and collect him."

Nick clutched the phone to his ear while the woman informed him that she could be at the store in twenty minutes. The thought of having to babysit the sick man wasn't something he relished, but what worried him more was that the man's wife also sounded sick.

"Okay," Nick uttered into the phone. "See you soon." He slid the phone into his pocket and smiled at his sickly guest. "Your wife is on her way. She won't be long. Perhaps you should take a seat while you wait."

"I'll make the poor sod a cuppa," Paul said, already wandering towards the back. "Looks like he could use one."

Nick led the sick man over to the carpeted sales area. As the man sat, Nick was forced to turn away as the man's humid body odour made his eyes water.

"Should I do anything?" Chelsea asked, turning her head away and looking nauseous.

Nick waved a hand. "Just go, Chelsea. Paul and I will be okay."

Her shoulders loosened with relief. "You sure, boss?"

"Yeah, I'll see you when you're next in."

Chelsea hurried to get her things while Paul returned with three mugs of piping hot tea. He passed one to their sickly guest. "Here ya go, fella. Drink up."

"Thank you," the man replied weakly. He seemed a little better since sitting down, but still looked decidedly unwell as he sipped from the promotional coffee mug that Samsung had sent them. "I'm sorry to put you all out like this," he said. "I just felt like I was going to pass out. I just...I just headed into the nearest shop for help. My name is George, by the way. Thank you for taking care of me."

"So you're not interested in getting yourself a shiny new phone then?" Paul chuckled.

The man didn't laugh.

"So, any idea what you've come down with, George?" Nick pried, wondering if he should be covering his mouth.

George shook his head, spattering the desk with gobs of spittle. "I-I don't know. I've been feeling under the weather since yesterday morning – a lot of the lads on the lorries have been feeling low. I work at a distribution warehouse. I started feeling really bad this afternoon. I think I must have the flu or something."

Nick smiled reassuringly. "Probably just flu. Might be worth getting yourself down to see the doctor."

"Soon as my wife picks me up, I'll be heading right there, don't you worry."

"Your wife sounded pretty poorly, too," Nick mentioned.

George nodded slowly. "She has whatever I have, but she only started feeling ill this morning. Must have caught it from me. I feel terribly guilty if she feels half as bad as I do."

Nick sipped his tea and tried to ignore the smell of wet fart that was continuously drifting from the other side of the table. "I hope you get well soon, George. Then you can come back and buy a phone from Paul."

Paul chuckled.

George slumped over the desk, his head hitting the laminated wood with a thud!

Paul and Nick exchanged worried glances.

Fifteen minutes later, when George's wife arrived, he was still face down on the sales desk, snoring loudly. His wife tottered into the shop looking almost as bad as her husband did. Her bloodshot eyes bulged the same way.

"Hi!" Nick greeted her, but kept his distance.

"I'm here to take George home," she said, then sneezed three times in quick succession.

"He's here." Nick pointed to the desk. "I think he's napping."

George's wife staggered forward, her steps uncoordinated and clumsy. Her husband managed to lift his head as she approached, almost as if he sensed her. Perhaps it was a skill all men adopted after enough years of matrimony.

Paul placed one of his thick hands on George's shoulder and shook him tenderly. "The missus will get you to the doctors now, fella. You'll be right as rain."

Like a thrashing animal, George snapped his teeth. Paul yelled out, pulling his hand free and clutching it against his chest. He cursed in his native Punjabi. "Haram Jada!"

George looked frightened, as if he had no idea what he'd just done. "I...I'm so sorry. I..."

"George!" cried his wife. "What the bloody hell are you playing at?"

George looked tiny and afraid. "I'm so sorry," he gushed at Paul. "I don't know what came over me."

"No problem, fella," said Paul, bewildered. "I'll just put it down to the fever."

Nick frowned at George's wife. "Maybe you should get your husband to a doctor."

She nodded, looking as anxious as she did embarrassed as she hurriedly ushered her husband away.

Once they were gone, Nick and Paul looked at one another in confusion. "The fuck just happened?" Paul said. "The guy bit me like he was a vampire or something."

"Is your hand okay?"

Paul was still clutching it to his chest. "Hurts like a mother. Gandoo broke the skin. I probably got rabies or something."

"Then you best stay away from me. I don't want to start frothing at the mouth and biting people. That guy was a mess."

"You're telling me. He said his workmates were ill, too. Maybe something is going around."

Nick shook his head and rubbed his temples. He felt a huge headache coming on, vibrating like rails before an approaching passenger train. "Screw it," he said. "I've had enough of this. Let's just cash up and get out of here. I'll do the conference call at home and pretend I'm still here. If I get found out I'll just say that someone tried to eat you."

Paul nodded, rubbing at his hand and wincing. "Sounds good to me, governor. I'm sure things will be better tomorrow."

Nick huffed. "They couldn't be any worse."

CHAPTER 2

THE ROADS WERE quiet on the journey home. He had left early enough to avoid rush hour and the only vehicle he encountered was a rushing ambulance, its sirens blaring.

By ten-to-five he was walking into his house.

It was nice to be home an hour early. He began to think about what he could do with the extra time. Perhaps he would take Deana and James out for a nice meal. It'd been a while since they'd treated themselves and it'd be a nice way to put the day behind him. Maybe he'd forget that tomorrow he'd have to endure it all over again.

Deana was standing barefoot in the hallway when he walked through the front door, obviously surprised to see him. "What are you doing back?" Her dark Moroccan eyes were suspicious beneath her choppy black fringe. "Everything okay?"

Nick hooked his woollen coat onto one of the porch hangers and sighed. "We had three customers all day and then some weirdo came in and attacked Paul – he's okay. In the end I decided it wasn't even worth the trouble of being open."

"Won't you get in trouble?"

"I'll take the conference call in the bedroom. I'm sure no one will even know. You fancy going out for dinner tonight, oh dear wife of mine?"

Surprisingly Deana didn't seem enthused. "I don't know, honey," she said. "James is feeling a bit under the weather. I don't know if it's wise taking him out, and I don't want to get a babysitter."

Nick raised an eyebrow. "What is it with people getting sick today? I swear something must be going around. What's wrong with him?"

"He's just a little bunged-up with a headache. Probably just needs an early night. He's in the living room watching Family Guy."

Nick sighed. "I told you not to let him watch that show, Deana. It's not like The Simpsons."

"It's alright. He doesn't understand the adult jokes. Go check on him. He'll be glad to see you."

"Okay." He gave her a peck on the cheek and headed for the living room. His mop-haired son lay curled on the beige corner sofa, squinting and blinking as if something was irritating his eyes.

"You okay, little dude? Mommy says you're not feeling very well."

"I have a headache," he said pitifully.

Nick sat on the end of the sofa and pulled his son's bare feet onto his lap. They were cold and sweaty. "I'll get Mommy to cook you something nice and then you can get an early night. You'll feel all better tomorrow."

"Do I have to go to school?"

Nick laughed and tickled his son's foot, but James didn't react, which was strange because he was usually very sensitive to tickle-torture. "We'll see how you're feeling tonight, buddy, and then decide. So, what's happening in Family Guy?"

"Brian and Stewie are trapped inside a bank and Brian just ate Stewie's nappy."

Nick screwed his face up in disgust. "Lovely. Well, you can carry on watching until dinner, but then it's going off, okay?"

He was about to get back up again, but paused when he spotted the thick Beano plaster on his son's finger.

"Hey, buddy, what happened to your finger?"

"Jordan bit me at school. I didn't even call him a name or nothing. He got in lots of trouble with Mrs Tanner, though, so it's okay. Mommy had to kiss it better for me and put a Dennis the Menace on it."

Nick didn't like the coincidence. Paul had been bitten, too. But what did it mean? Surely an unruly child biting his son was nothing to worry about and in no way related to the man who bit Paul. Still, it was weird. "Jordan bit you? Were you feeling ill before that, or afterwards?"

James shook his head. "I didn't feel poorly until Mommy picked me up. I started to feel sick in the car and got a headache."

Nick patted his son on the leg and gave him a reassuring smile. "Okay," he said. "You just rest here and I'll call you when dinner's ready. Anything in particular you'd like?"

"Fish fingers."

"Anything else?"

"Fish fingers."

"Fish fingers it is then."

Nick got up from the sofa and headed into the hallway. Deana was in the kitchen, already starting dinner.

"His lord requires fish fingers," he said as he approached from behind and squeezed her hips.

"Right-o," she said, already rummaging around the fridge freezer. She set Cod sticks down on the breakfast table next to a basket of laundry and brushed off a layer of frost. "Did he ask for anything else?"

"Just fish fingers with a side of fish fingers. I suppose you could force him to accept some chips and beans with them."

"That wouldn't be because you want chips and beans, would it? You've got fillet steak in the fridge, you numpty."

"I know I have." He perched back against the table. "But I'm too tired to eat it tonight. I'll just have whatever James is having."

Deana moved closer to him, tiptoeing up on the tiles, and gave him a kiss. "You're not coming down with something as well, are you, babe? Because I can't be doing with nursing you both back to health. I'm in no mood for man-flu."

Nick shook his head. "I'm fine, just tired. Really, really, really tired. I don't know how much longer I can take working at that wretched place."

"Find something else, then. I don't want you to be miserable all the time."

"I'm not miserable. Just...unfulfilled. Anyway, don't worry about it for now. I'm just glad to be home early for a change. Shame we can't go out, but never mind."

"James show you his battle wound?" Deana asked.

"His finger? Yeah. What happened? Some kid bit him?"

"Yeah, during break time. It wasn't too bad, but it was still bleeding a little when he got home so I put a new plaster on it."

"And kissed it better?"

"Of course," she winked at him.

Nick chuckled and checked his watch. It was almost half-five. "I need to get ready for the conference call," he said. "I'll try to get away quickly."

Deana smiled. "I'll bring you a coffee up."

Nick hurried upstairs to his and Deana's bedroom and lay himself down on the freshly made bed, dumping his keys and wallet onto the glass side-table first. The duvet cover was the blue Egyptian cotton one he liked. The soft thread immediately relaxed him.

The conference call would commence at five-thirty sharp, but the managers of the other stores would usually get on early to check the lay of the land. How did your store do today? What was footfall like? Did you meet your insurance quota? What mood is the area manager in?

Nick picked up the phone and dialled, then tapped in the login pin number. There was a brief silence while the automated service connected him.

When he heard the static of the open line, Nick introduced himself. "Nick Adams, Solihull, Touchwood."

There were no replies. He must have been the first one there. Great, he thought to himself. Everyone else had had such a busy day that they were struggling to get away.

Nick took a deep breath and released it slowly, letting it echo in the receiver. He rubbed at his forehead and closed his eyes while he waited. He really hated conference calls.

There was nothing he could do, though. He wouldn't get paid as much anywhere else in retail. Most people hated their jobs just as much as he did. At least his family was secure, even if it meant he was miserable fifty hours a week.

It was now 5:32. "Hello," Nick said into the receiver. "Hello, is anyone else here?"

A second later, the line crackled and another voice came on.

"Hey," Nick said tentatively. "Who's there?"

"It's Paul."

"Paul, what are you doing on the call?"

"I figured you'd need backup after the day we had."

Nick smiled. It was good of Paul to go down in flames with him. "Thanks, man. I appreciate it. It's just me and you so far, though."

"Yeah, I think there're a couple managers who are reluctant to get on here. I phoned around on the way home and found out that other stores were deserted as well. Evesham only did two contracts and Tewkesbury did none, so don't worry too much."

Nick sighed relief. "That's good to know. Least I won't be the only one getting torn a new one."

Paul started coughing into the phone.

"You okay, buddy?"

"Just a cold coming on, I think. Probably from that doodi that bit me earlier."

"You best not be calling in sick tomorrow, dude."

"'Course not. Can't leave all the sales to Chelsea, can I?"

There was a crackle on the line and another voice entered the conversation. It was the distinctive Australian twang of the area manager. It grated at Nick's nerves every time he heard it.

"Who's on the call?" the area manager asked in his usual pissy tone.

"Just me and Paul," answered Nick.

"Who might me and Paul be?"

"Nick Adams and Paul Patel from Solihull. No one else is on the call yet."

"Yes, I know. I've had a lot of managers call in sick today, so there will be no call tonight."

The line clicked and the area manager was gone.

"Prick," said Paul.

Nick laughed. "I'd wet myself if he hadn't actually gone yet."

Paul tutted. "Gandoo don't scare me."

"You find it weird?" Nick asked. "I mean, what he said about all the managers calling in sick?"

"Maybe they all went on a bender and planned a mass sickie. You know us family men are never in the loop about staff get-togethers. This is a young man's game, fella."

"Yeah, maybe. I just find it weird how town was so quiet today. Everyone seems to be getting sick; that guy who came in at the end of the day was a total mess. There must be something really bad going around."

"Yeah, the bloody lergy, and I have it," Paul said, clearing his throat of phlegm with a wet grunt. "I got to go now, governor. Think a night in the pub is in order if I'm going to be feeling rough all night."

"Just don't come in with a hangover."

"Ha! I'm Sikh. We don't get drunk. There's no beer in the world strong enough." With that Paul hung up.

Nick laughed and went downstairs to spend the evening with his family, hoping that whatever was going around, he wouldn't catch.

CHAPTER 3

THE EVENING WENT by quickly. A dinner of fish fingers was followed by a few hours of innocuous reality television. Then it was time to go to bed. Nick had intended to put James down right after dinner, but he'd become so feverish and fitful that Nick decided to keep a close eye on him. Deana had started to feel grim, too. She'd spent the evening with the tissue box in her lap. Nick assumed it was only a matter of time before he succumbed to the dreaded 'lergy' himself.

Just after ten o'clock, Deana carried James upstairs – he remained asleep in her arms – and joined Nick in their bedroom a few minutes later. She took a handful of flu capsules from the bedside drawer and dry swallowed them, then dragged herself into her 'no-sex' frumpy pyjamas and was snoring loudly within minutes.

Nick was left staring at the ceiling alone. He was dreading another workday like the one he'd just had. The minutes had seemed like hours and the stress of not meeting target had been constant. He was nothing but a glorified salesman, really, but his area manager made his job far more stressful than it needed to be. Targets, working weekends, opening evenings, Nick was expected to live, eat, and breathe the phone industry. The truth was, though, that he didn't give two shits about selling phones or the company he worked for. It was a paycheque, nothing more, and he hated every minute he spent there.

He'd always told himself that one day he'd do something different, one day he'd start a career he enjoyed, but before he knew it he was thirty years old with a wife and child. Now, there was never going to be a 'one day.'

Nick sighed and closed his eyes, trying to ignore the beastly snores of his slumbering wife. God, he loved her, but sometimes she sounded like an asthmatic camel – especially when she was ill. Thankfully, before long, slumber finally befell him too.

* * *

When Nick opened his eyes again, the bedside clock read 5:03AM. It was almost dawn.

And there were noises downstairs.

Nick glanced at Deana, checking to see if she was awake also, but she was silent and still, no longer even snoring.

The noises downstairs were consistent and regular, like they were following a rhythm. It sounded like someone was shuffling around in the kitchen. Nick was sure he heard the breakfast bar stools dragging across the granite floor tiles.

Goddamn it. Nick had to be up in a couple hours and some git was trying to rob him.

He slid out from beneath the bed covers and headed for the door in his boxer shorts. The noises continued. If it was a burglar, it was the most negligent criminal ever. Either that, or crazy enough not to care if they're discovered.

Nick crept barefoot across the landing, wishing he had a baseball bat stashed upstairs. He'd never worried about being burgled before, but now he felt stupid for it. He started down the staircase, trying to see through the shadows. With each step he took downwards, his stomach churned a little harder. When he finally reached the bottom and padded into the hallway, he felt positively sick. From there it became clear that the stranger was definitely inside the kitchen. Not only could Nick hear them shuffling around, but he could see light coming from beneath the door.

Nick started to plan. Was he just going to burst in, wearing nothing but his boxer shorts, hoping to frighten the intruder away?

What if the intruder was armed? He decided he'd rather prevent a confrontation than create one, so he decided to give the burglar a chance to flee. He rapped his knuckles against the kitchen door and said, "Hey, whoever you are, get the hell out of my house. Right now!"

Silence.

"I've already called the police, so just get out of here while you still can."

Silence.

Nick didn't know what to do. Walking into the kitchen was probably the stupid thing, but he couldn't think of anything else to do. Despite his fear, he was pissed off and angry.

He pushed open the door, ready for action.

The kitchen was dark. The light Nick had seen creeping beneath the door was coming from the open fridge-freezer. The person standing in front of the appliance was a featureless silhouette.

"Hey, what the hell are you playing at? Get the fuck out of my house."

The person didn't answer or react.

As his eyesight continued to adjust, Nick could see that the figure wasn't facing him. However, slowly...gradually...the stranger was turning around.

Nick's breath caught in his chest. "James? What are you doing down here?" He trailed off as he saw what James was doing. Hanging from his son's mouth was a large hunk of fillet steak, still raw and dripping. Nick didn't understand what he was looking at. Why was James down here in the middle of the night, tearing into raw meat like a feral dog?

He raised a hand toward his son. "James, put the meat down, honey. It'll make your tummy bad. Put it down and come here."

James lowered his head, unblinking eyes trained on his father. His thin lips trembled into a snarl. Then he lunged at Nick, his delicate hands outstretched like claws. His sallow, naked chest was soaked with the steak blood and as he collided with Nick, the hunk of meat fell from his chomping mouth.

Nick wrapped his arms around his son and wrestled with him. "James! James, what's gotten into you? It's daddy. Calm down, daddy's got you. Just stop fighting me."

But it was no good. James continued to claw and bite, thrashing to get free. His bloodstained teeth snapped wildly at the air. Nick assumed his son was hallucinating from the fever, and if he could just turn the lights on, maybe he would be less confused.

Nick squeezed James tightly and sidestepped towards the light switch with the boy in his arms. James' relentless squirming made every step a battle of determination.

Nick's bare foot came down on something slippery. As his leg went out from under him, he realised it was the raw fillet steak, dropped from his son's jaws. He fell sideways with the full weight of his son still in his arms. Nick's head hit the tiles with a crack, and then there was another sound, meaty and wet.

Nick couldn't sit up as his vision spun and a roiling wave of sickness crashed against his stomach. He lay there for a few seconds, trying to catch his breath. After a while, he pushed himself up on his elbows and looked around.

James was lying nearby, his small body unmoving.

"Oh, Jesus. Oh Jesus, no!" Nick scurried across the floor on his hands and knees, until he could place a hand beneath James' head and lift it up. He withdrew his fingers when they touched something hot and tacky. Even in the dim light from the fridge, Nick could see the dark blood on his hands.

"No, no, no, no." On Nick's left, a matted clump of hair covered the corner of the breakfast bar. James's head had struck it on the way down

"James. No. No. Help me! Somebody help. Somebody fucking help me. God help me, what have I done?"

Nick leapt up from the floor and almost fell down again when his legs failed to work. His entire body was trembling, his vision spinning. He had to do something. Had to do something right now.

He could use the phone in the bed and wake up Deana at the same time. He needed Deana. He needed help. He couldn't do this alone.

Nick bolted out the kitchen, up the stairs, and burst into the bedroom, shouting at the top of his lungs for Deana to wake up.

His wife's body shifted beneath the sheets, but she didn't respond. "Deana, please wake up. I need you."

Nothing. Just a tired moan.

Nick cursed under his breath and grabbed the phone. There was no time to waste. He dialled 999.

"Emergency Services are currently dealing with a very high number of calls. Please leave your name, address, and situation, and help will arrive shortly. Please remain calm while waiting for assistance. Leave your details after the beep."

Beep!

999 was too busy to answer his call? That was bullshit.

He turned to Deana and knelt on the bed, shoving her hard. "Deana, wake up, wake up. I need your help. Something terrible has happened."

She stirred with a low moan and rolled out of bed.

"Thank God." Nick switched on the bedside lamp and started re-dialling 999. "Deana, James is hurt. He was in the kitchen and I...I..."

Deana's eyes glared at him. Their lower lids hung slack while the bloodshot orbs rattled around inside their sockets. A slick trail of blood covered her chin.

Before Nick had chance to think, Deana leapt at him.

Nick dodged sideways and stumbled against the foot of the bed. He almost fell down but managed to remain standing. "Deana, what the hell are you doing?"

Deana clambered over the bed towards him, leaving bloody hand-prints on the sheets and snarling at him like a rabid wolf. She glared at him balefully, her jaws grinding back and forth like saw blades.

"Deana? Please, say something."

Deana opened her mouth wide, let out a high-pitched screech, then leapt from the bed.

Nick managed to shove Deana aside as she took flight, sending her hurtling into the mahogany chest of drawers that her mother had bought them as a wedding gift. Instinctively, he went to help her, but Deana was right back on her feet.

Nick rushed out of the bedroom and slammed the door behind him. Deana crashed against the other side, shaking the wood on its hinges. She let out another ear-piercing shriek. Nick didn't know why she didn't just use the door handle, but was thankful for her lack of common sense. He used the opportunity to flee.

He needed to get help. His son and wife needed help now.

Deana continued battering the bedroom door, and all Nick could do to get away from the torturous sound was go downstairs. He sprinted back into the kitchen where he was once again faced with his son's body.

I'm in Hell. This is the Abyss.

Looking down at James, Nick knew his young son was dead. No ambulance or doctor could help him. James' face was the co-lour of chalk, except for his closed eyelids, which were the black of charcoal.

Nick stumbled to the kitchen sink and immediately vomited. He splashed cold water onto his face from the tap until his cheeks were freezing and numb. "I need to put some clothes on," he muttered to himself. Hearing his own voice calmed him slightly.

Deana still banged on the door upstairs, still letting out that terrible screeching. He couldn't go back into the bedroom with his wife the way she was, so he rummaged through the laundry basket on the breakfast table to find some clothes, pulling out a crinkled grey t-shirt and a pair of jeans. One of James' Pokémon socks clung to one of the legs.

He began to sob.

Nick didn't allow himself the luxury of crying for longer than a few seconds, not while his son lay dead at his feet and his wife flung herself against the bedroom door like a mental patient. He had to get out of the house and find help.

Nick got dressed quickly and exited the kitchen. As he did so, an almighty crash sounded from the bedroom.

Nick stopped at the bottom of the staircase, staring up at the first-floor landing.

Deana appeared, half-naked and snarling.

"Deana, just stay right where you are, okay? I'm going to get help"

She ran down the steps towards him.

Nick leapt inside the front porch and slammed the door behind him just in time. Deana's face smashed against the window panel, splitting the delicate flesh of her cheeks and smearing blood on the glass. Nick slid his feet into the first pair of trainers he could find and pulled on his long woollen overcoat. He had to get out of there. His wife was acting like she was possessed by a demon. He needed to drive to the nearest hospital or police station or...

He realised his car keys were in the bedroom.

He wouldn't get anywhere without a car.

Nick turned back to face the inner porch door. The glass panels were caked in bloody chunks of flesh, but Deana was nowhere to be seen. The hallway was dim and shadowy, but there was no sign of his wife anywhere.

She was inside somewhere, though. She hadn't just disappeared.

Nick placed his hand on the door handle carefully and turned it. With every inch the door opened, he paused, anticipating an attack from Deana.

He looked left, right. All was clear.

Where the hell did you go, Deana?

Nick pushed open the door and slid through the gap. He placed a foot on the first step on the staircase and listened. Then he took the second step, the third and the fourth. He reached the hallway upstairs and all was still clear. He felt his heart beating in his chest.

Darkness seemed to close around him like a blanket. The bedroom was just up ahead, the door hanging wide open. Out of habit, Nick went for the light switch as soon as he entered the room, but he managed to stop himself. It would be better to remain hidden in the dark.

He headed for the bedside table where he knew he'd left his wallet and keys. Sure enough, even in the dark, he saw them and shoved them into his coat pocket.

Now to get out of there fast.

When Nick turned to leave, Deana was right there in front of him, standing so close that he could smell the blood on her face. Her hands immediately went for his throat, choking him with a strength he didn't know she possessed. He tried to fight her off, to force her backwards, but she was unrelenting. She tried to bite him. Each snap of her teeth sent hot dribbles of bloody saliva down her chin.

Nick's vision began to crackle with spots and stars as he struggled to take a breath. He twisted in the vice-like grip of his wife's hands and lifted his knee to try and create space between them. Just when he was sure he was about to lose consciousness, he managed to thread both his arms between Deana's elbows and forced them outwards.

Deana's hold broke. The sudden, automatic intake of breath left Nick momentarily paralysed.

Deana was back on. All he could manage to do was to deliver a swift kick at his wife's knees.

Deana stumbled to the floor, snarling. Nick took his chance and made a run for it, heading out of the bedroom and down the corridor at full pelt. He could hear Deana give chase right behind him. He took the staircase three steps at a time, half-running, half-tumbling down them. Deana gained on him, leaping down the stairs with no fear for her own safety. She collided with him at the bottom, clinging to his shoulders like a piggybacking child. Nick felt her teeth clamp down on his shoulder and anticipated a sharp pang of agony as she tore his skin away, but he was relieved to find that Deana had only sunk her teeth into the thick woollen collar of his coat.

Nick stumbled back against the wall, crushing Deana, who clung to his back. Her jaws tore loose from his collar and he was suddenly free of her weight again. He made for the porch so quickly that his foot struck the lip of the doorway and he went crashing to the stone floor. With the wind knocked out of him, he saw Deana coming at him like a hungry hyena. She let out another of those high-pitched screeches and leapt at him.

Nick kicked out with both legs, catching Deana in the stomach and forcing her backwards. Before she had chance to regain her balance, he leapt up and slammed the porch door shut. Just like before, Deana crashed into the other side and shoved her face up against the glass, glaring at him with utter hatred. Nick doubled-over, gasping for breath. He barely recognising the woman he'd married. No longer was she his beautiful, exotic wife of seven years. She was a motherfucking zombie.

"I'm sorry, Deana," he said to her through the blood-smeared glass. "I'm going to find help right now – if there is any. I love you."

Nick's world was falling apart. He unlocked the front door and stepped outside into the cold, grey, approaching dawn.

CHAPTER 4

THE FIRST THING Nick noticed when he stepped outside was the orange glow of the horizon. The sun slowly crept above the roofs of the houses. The second thing he noticed was that his quiet cul-de-sac was unusually active for so early in the morning. Several of his neighbour's windows were illuminated and silhouetted figures rushed around inside.

Nick wasted no time, heading past Deana's sky-blue Peugeot parked on the driveway, and making towards his own car parked on the curb. He pressed the fob on his keychain; the lights flashed, the locks disengaged. He was just about to head around to the driver's side when he heard someone yelling from across the road.

"Help me! Somebody, please!"

Nick saw a woman racing across her lawn. He recognised her as the middle-aged blonde that lived opposite. He'd rarely spoken to her, but he was pretty certain her name was Lara.

Now she was staggering towards him with a looming spectre of a man – possibly her husband – close behind her.

Nick watched in confusion. "What's wrong, Lara? Are you okay?"

But it was clear she was not okay. Her eyes were bloated with fear. A ragged gash ruined the left side of her face. It looked like a bite mark.

"My...my husband. He's trying to kill me. Please, you have to help m—"

Lara's husband charged into the back of her, crushing her against the car. Nick watched in stunned silence as a domestic assault commenced right in front of him.

He raced around the side of his car to help Lara. Her husband had her pinned over the bonnet and was clawing at her neck and face. She screamed and writhed, battling him as best she could, but it was a battle she was losing. Her husband was twice her size.

Nick managed to shove Lara's husband away. "What the hell are you playing at?" he demanded of the man. "You ought to be bleeding locked up."

The man didn't reply. He threw himself at Nick, squashing him against the car. The bodywork crumpled and Nick cried out in pain. Lara's husband was half-a-foot taller than him and managed to bring his snarling face right up close to his.

The nutcase was trying to bite him. Just like Deana had.

Lara had a bite mark on her face, too. Nick looked down at the weeping woman and watched her scurry away on her rump. He shouted at her for help, but she shook her head and kept on backing away.

Thanks for nothing.

With no other obvious option, Nick, for the first time in his life, threw a head-butt. His forehead connected firmly with the other man's nose. There was a loud crack but Lara's husband did not release his grip. His face was a mashed-up canvas, but he didn't seem to care.

"Let go of me," Nick pleaded, knowing it would do no good. Jagged teeth snapped mere inches from his face. The smell of rancid breath was nauseating. Just when Nick expected to feel the agonising crunch of human teeth sinking into his face, the weight in his arms suddenly fell away.

"You can't mess around with these people," came a voice. Nick looked up to see it was the cankerous old man who lived in the detached bungalow at the end of the road. "You got to beat 'em down, right away," the pensioner said, "before they get their teeth into you."

Nick was doubled over and gasping for breath. He noticed the flesh-coated golf club clutched in the old man's gnarled fists and gagged. "Y-you just caved his skull in. Are you mad?"

"You naïve fool. These people aren't sick. They can't be helped. They're goddamn zomb—"

The pensioner lurched forward, golf club clattering to the tarmac. Nick hopped out of the way just in time to see that two more of his neighbours had appeared from out of the shadows. They took the old man down like animals.

Nick stepped back, unable to look away as his neighbours tore each other apart. How was this possible? How had everybody gone insane?

The pensioner stopped screaming as his two attackers hunched over his body. Nick gagged again.

Christ, they're eating him.

Nick shook away his revulsion and grabbed the driver's side door of the car, swinging it open as hard as he could. It caught one of the crazed neighbour the head and sent her reeling.

Nick leapt behind the steering wheel, slammed the door shut, and engaged the central locking.

His two neighbours rose to their feet, discarding the remains of the old man and beating their bloody fists against the car's windows instead. The vehicle rocked on its springs as Nick keyed the ignition and put the engine in gear. The automatic headlights flicked on immediately and it was then the full-scale of the horror affecting the neighbourhood became apparent.

Ten-feet ahead, a woman lay mangled in the middle of the road. Several feet beyond was a man doing battle with a group of attackers. They clawed and bit at him, tearing chunks of flesh from his flailing arms and wrists. One of the nearby houses billowed thick black smoke and muffled screams came from inside. In fact, there were screams coming from everywhere.

Nick sat in his car, frozen. There was too much to take in. Too much horror. Stumbling down the road towards him was a young boy, not much older than James. He wasn't crazed like the other neighbours; he was slower and clumsier, acting almost like he was drunk. When the boy stepped into the cone of the car's headlights, Nick saw that his intestines were dragging along behind him. Every couple of steps the boy would tread on them and stumble.

Nick couldn't take any more. He gear-changed into reverse and shot the car backwards. He kept on going until the shadows reclaimed the nightmarish child and the chaos of the street. Once there was nothing else left to see, he stamped on the brake, then sat there again, hyperventilating. For a brief moment, he almost convinced himself that it was all over and that he was the one who was sick, hallucinating the entire thing.

But he knew that wasn't true.

He shifted back into first gear and floored it, picking up speed quickly. The sooner he found help, the better. Somewhere, there would be people dealing with the situation. Somewhere, there would be answers and—

Nick stamped on the brake. "Goddamn it!" he shouted, more out of fright than anger.

It was Lara. She banged on the windscreen with her bloody palms. "Let me in, please!"

Nick shook his head. He didn't have time for this, nor did he owe the woman anything after she'd left him to fend off her husband. She was bitten and injured. Who was to say she wouldn't turn violent like everybody else

He brought the clutch back up, ready to take off. Crazed neighbours homed in on him from every direction.

"Please," Lara begged him. It would be only seconds before she was attacked again.

Nick cursed, disengaged the locks. "Get in the back. Quickly!"

Lara nodded and made for the rear passenger door, but some-one grabbed her from behind and dragged her back into the shad-ows. Nick waited a few seconds before deciding that Lara was a lost cause. He couldn't help her.

He looked forward and prepared to put his foot down.

Lara reappeared and ran for the car. She yanked open the rear door and threw herself across the back seat. She was bleeding bad-ly from several places. "G-go," she spluttered at him, pulling the door closed behind her. "Get the fuck out of here."

"You don't have to tell me twice." Nick took off as quickly as the car would accelerate. He had to steer erratically to avoid hitting his wandering neighbours, but he managed to make it to the end of the road without crashing. Screams filled the air behind him.

Nick steered onto the main road and left the nightmare of his street behind him. He let loose a sigh of relief. It felt good to be on the road, moving fast. "Are you okay?" he asked his passenger, glancing back over his shoulder.

Lara nodded but her skin had lost all colour. Her clothing was soaked with dark blood. Nick focused on the road. The sun had risen and the world seemed to be coming alive.

But it had awoken to panic.

Travelling down the highway in the opposite direction was a speeding police car, its sirens blaring, lights flashing. A fire truck hurtled along right behind it.

"This is nuts," Nick said. "What is happening? Did I miss a ter-rorist attack or something?"

"M...my husband. He just went crazy. I woke up in bed and he was on top of me, biting me."

"It's not just him, Lara. Everyone is acting the same way. My wife...my son. I don't know why. I don't know what's wrong."

"He...he's never tried to hurt me before. He was biting me."

Lara wasn't listening to him. "Your husband is sick," he said. "He wasn't in control of himself. Maybe he can be helped. Maybe everyone can. I don't know the answers. That's why we need to find people who do. My son is dead. Somebody needs to fucking pay for this."

More cars entered the highway, creating a steady stream of traffic. All of the drivers exceeded the speed limit, some outrageously so. Nick had only been on the road twenty minutes when he witnessed a turquoise Vauxhall Astra hurtle into a ditch. The vehicle flipped over, crunching up like an accordion. The chances of survival seemed pretty unlikely. Nick didn't stop to help.

One thing had become very clear: what had happened in Nick's neighbourhood was not an isolated incident. People everywhere were fleeing. To where exactly, Nick didn't know. He didn't know where he himself was going, so he just headed where everybody else seemed to be going.

A pile-up up ahead caused the traffic to slow down. A biker took it as an opportunity to overtake, but was quickly forced to decelerate as well when he found the highway's exit choked up by an overturned lorry and a crumpled police car. There was no room to get past, but the guy on the motorbike seemed like he was going to give it a good try.

Nick pulled on the handbrake and waited. He watched the biker trying to manoeuvre through the twisted wreckage and wished him luck. If Nick could find a path through he would take it too. But just when it looked like the biker might get clear of the highway, a female police officer sprinted out at him from behind the upturned lorry. She tackled him clean off his bike and dragged him to the ground. The biker screamed as more people appeared from the wreckage and began tearing him apart.

Nick backed his car up as much as possible before coming up against the other vehicles queuing behind him. He was blocked. The bloody policewoman started heading towards the traffic.

"Fuck this." Nick shunted the car behind him and made space. He ignored the angry beeping and spun the steering wheel before jolting forwards and out of the queue, heading in the wrong direction in the overtaking lane. As soon as he was able, he dodged through oncoming traffic and took the first junction he came across, spinning back around in the opposite direction in order to take it. It brought him onto a country road. Instead of housing estates and shops there was woodland and private cottages. The properties seemed undisturbed compared to the chaos of Nick's neighbourhood. The middle-class families who lived there were likely still sleeping soundly, while everywhere else had spun into madness.

Nick took the opportunity to check on Lara. "I'm going to try and head for the hospital, okay? You need help. So does my wife."

Lara answered with a moan.

A van pulled out of a nearby brickyard and Nick had to slow down to avoid crashing into it. Unbelievably, the driver nodded a polite 'thank you' as he passed. The man would get the shock of his life when he entered the main roads. Part of Nick considered warning him, but by that time the van had already passed.

Up ahead, Nick encountered another vehicular collision. This time two cars blocked the centre of the road, but there was still enough room to get around them. It still required Nick to slow right down.

He glanced around at the backseat. Lara was lying facedown now and having some kind of seizure. Her blood coated everything and the metallic odour filled the car. "Hey," he shouted. "Hey, Lara, are you okay? I'm going to get you some help, but you need to stay with me until I get there. Don't die on me."

Or turn into one of those psychopaths, he almost added.

Lara managed to lift her head as her seizures gradually stopped. She was still with him for the moment.

Nick faced the road and kept his speed steady as he approached the wreckage. The smashed cars were close enough now to see that both were unoccupied.

Nick turned around to face the backseat again. "Everything is going to be alright, Lara. Just hold—"

Lara lunged forward between the seats. Nick's feet slipped from the pedals as he found himself shoved up against the steering wheel and battered from behind. Lara screeched and clawed at him, trying to climb into the front of the car. Nick was unable to fight back in such close confines and strapped in by his seatbelt.

The car continued rolling forward, losing speed as the engine idled.

Nick leant over the steering wheel, trying to stay out of Lara's clutches. With his left hand he fiddled and tried to find his the belt release. He was relieved when his muscle-memory took his fingertips right to it. He pressed the release and slumped forward a little further as the seatbelt loosened its grip on him.

Lara grabbed a handful of his hair and yanked his head back. Then she brought her mouth to his neck.

Nick threw himself sideways into the door, pulling the handle and falling half out of the car. He hung by his legs, the rushing gravel only inches from his face. Lara grabbed at his ankle and twisted, making him yell out in pain. He kicked and wiggled, trying to untangle himself from his seatbelt and free himself from Lara's grip. He tried to reach up, but his own flailing weight was too heavy to do anything other than hang. He kicked out with all he had, scissoring his legs back forth like a child having a tantrum.

Then he was free.

Nick hit the road hard, cracking his elbow and grazing his face along the gravel. He rolled and rolled, every second filled with agony and whirling vision.

When his flailing body eventually came to a stop, Nick lay still at the side of the road, quietly staring up at the sky. His vision was muddled, but as he craned his neck he watched his car carry on without him at a speed just about fast enough to kill a small dog. Eventually it came to stop up against the two wrecks in the middle of the road.

Once Nick was sure he could still move, he rose gingerly to his feet. His right cheek was on fire. The wound stung ferociously. Nick was thankful he'd been wearing his thick woollen coat or he might have grazed his entire body. His elbow also ached like hell.

He had no clue what to do next. His car would still be drivable, the collision with the other cars not much more than a clumsy bump. Problem was, he was so shaken-up from what had just happened that he didn't feel safe getting behind the wheel right away. He needed time to calm his nerves.

The country road was deserted, surrounded on both sides by untended fields. There was, however, a small garden centre fifty yards ahead. There was a good chance someone might be there, and right now it seemed like a good idea to try and find other people in the same boat as he was.

He started forward, the loose gravel crunching beneath his feet. He started to think about Lara. She had attacked him in the car. Would she come at him again as he passed by on his way to the garden centre?

Whatever was making people crazy had gotten into her; probably when her husband bit her. Was that how it transmitted from person to person? Bites?

Nick was confused as to whether the sick people needed help or if they were completely beyond it. Each time he'd tried to assist anyone they ended up attacking him. Even Deana had seemingly wanted him dead. James too. It hurt too much to even think about right now.

Nick stepped carefully as he approached his car. He could see that Lara was still inside and mobile. She was hanging out of the driver's side door, the same way he had before leaping clear. The airbags were deployed and squashed her torso up against the seat. She was scrabbling at the gravel and reaching towards Nick with a hungry expression, but it didn't seem like she was going anywhere.

Once he got closer, Nick could see what was keeping Lara inside the car. Her legs were tangled in the seatbelt. The more she tried to crawl away, the tighter the strap became around her ankles. She wasn't going anywhere. Still, Nick trod carefully, steering clear of her clawing fingernails and bloody jaws. Before he was totally away from the wreckage, he examined his injured neighbour closely. He wasn't sure why he asked the question, "Can you hear me, Lara?" followed by, "Are you okay?" because both answers were obvious.

Of course Lara gave no response. She just kept on trying to get at him like a rabid fox. Nick shook his head, wishing he could understand what was happening; wishing he could do something about it, but he had no choice but to leave his concerns behind for the moment. His primary focus right now was finding somewhere safe.

The garden centre looked deserted, but there were a couple of cars in its pebbled car park, which made Nick hopeful. He climbed the nearby embankment and crossed over onto the pebbled parking area, heading for the main entrance up ahead. He was surprised when the glass doors slid open for him. Considering the early hour – 7:15 according to his watch – Nick had assumed the place would be closed.

The first part of the garden centre consisted of indoor planting, incense burners, and greeting cards. Nick almost jumped out of his skin when he brushed past a set of tinkling aluminium pipes, but got a hold on himself when he realised it was just a wind chime. The smell inside the building was one of musky perfumes mixed with soil and plants. In contrast to the many heady odours, his ears detected nothing except the diminishing clinks of the wind chime.

"Hello," Nick called out. "Hello, is anybody here?" Someone must be there, considering the automatic doors had allowed him access.

An alcove lay ahead, with an overhead banner reading: AQUAR-IUM. The space was full of wall-to-wall fish tanks, all of them glowing with soft blue light. The smell in the room was musky.

Nick spotted the girl in the corner peeking out from a storage closet and jumped out of his skin. She yelped and yanked the closet door closed with her inside.

"Hey," Nick shouted after her. "You frightened the life of me, there. I need help. I've been in an accident."

The girl said nothing. The closet remained closed.

"Please. I've been through hell this morning. I just need some help."

"Go away!"

Nick frowned. "Why won't you come out?"

"Go away," the girl repeated, "before they hear you."

"Before who hears me?"

"The owners. They've gone...mad."

Nick swallowed. Oh no, not here as well.

"There's no one around," he said, more in hope than anything else. "They've gone. You can come out."

"No. They're out there somewhere and I'm not coming out. No way."

Nick contemplated yanking the girl from the cupboard, but decided that would be counterproductive. It was no way to make a friend. His only option was to try to reason with her.

The sound of raspy breathing.

Nick sensed a presence behind him, but before he had chance to turn around, someone pummelled him in the spine and sent him reeling forwards onto his hands and knees.

Nick twisted around and saw a hunched-over old man in an olive-coloured cardigan. Flakes of scalp and grey dandruff covered the woollen garment. He wore the same insane, animalistic expression of the other sick people Nick had seen.

Nick scampered back just in time to dodge an attack from the old man. He hopped to his feet and ran to the corner of the aquarium, searching for an escape. But there was none.

Nick found himself cornered.

The old man approached, like a lion stalking a baby gazelle.

With nowhere to run and no other choice, Nick met the old man's charge head on, grabbing a fistful of grimy cardigan and using his attacker's momentum as a weapon. He twisted sideways, threw out his arms and flung the old man headfirst into the fish tanks.

Water exploded and flooded the ground.

The old man's head had impacted with a tank full of neon tetras and was now lodged between the jagged edges of the broken glass. The jutting shards tore at the wrinkled flesh around his neck and any attempt to get free only opened the wound up wider.

Nick staggered away, dizzy and confused.

Blood mixed with the remaining water at the bottom of the broken fish tanks as the old man continued squirming; the gash on his neck opened up further, eventually spouting thick arterial blood. His sandaled feet twitched a few moments then went still.

Nick slumped to the floor, breathing heavily. The urge to scream was growing. He just wanted it all to stop.

"What's happening? What's going on out there?"

Nick looked towards the closed closet. "I think I just met the owner. I don't recommend his customer service. Are you going to come out now?"

"No."

"Stop hiding like a child. You need to get a grip. Come on," he said. "I'm not going to hurt you."

Slowly the closet door creaked open and the girl peered out at him. "First sign of danger," she said, "and I'm back in the closet."

Nick nodded wearily and tried to smile. The girl was just a teenager, maybe early twenties. She was a dark-featured, big brown eyes full of trepidation and fear. She eyed Nick with suspicion and with an expression that suggested her morning hadn't been much better than his.

"What happened here?" Nick asked her.

"I'm still waiting for someone to tell me. I got here early because Mr Curtis wanted to set up a new display, but when I got here the place was deserted. I went round back to the cottage – that's where Mr Curtis and his wife live – and I found the front door wide open. Next thing I know, Mr Curtis and his wife are running at me like lunatics, trying to bite me. I ran back into the store, but I didn't know what to do so I ended up hiding in the closet. That's when you came along." She looked down at Mr Curtis's body, his head still trapped inside the fish tank. "I don't get it," she said. "He was so nice. I don't know why he would suddenly want to hurt me."

"It's not just him," Nick explained. "People have been losing their shit all over town. My wife...my son." He didn't want to think about James, so he turned his mind to something proactive. "We should try to get some help. Do you have a phone here? Or Internet access?"

The girl nodded. "Yeah, we have both in the office, but there's a problem."

"What?"

The girl nodded toward Mr Curtis. "Well, I'm looking at Mr Curtis, but where's his Mrs Curtis?"

As if to punctuate her point, a far-off crash caused them both to look towards the aquarium's exit.

"Close by, would be my guess," Nick said. The young girl started back towards the cupboard, but he grabbed her arm. "Hey, you're not going back into hiding. We need to deal with this."

"You deal with it. I'm going to sit down on the vacuum cleaner with the door closed."

"And then what? Stay there till it gets dark?"

The girl sighed and shook her head resignedly. "Fine, but can we at least get something to defend ourselves with?"

Nick nodded. "Sounds good to me."

* * *

They found what they needed in the storage closet. Nick removed the head from a broom handle and the girl found herself a hammer.

"What's your name, by the way?"

"Eve."

"Nice to meet you, Eve. My name is Nick."

"What's with your face?"

Nick suddenly remembered his bad graze and fingered it tenderly. "I had a car accident. Hurts like hell. My insurance is going to go up." He chuckled, not sure why he was thinking of such insignificant things.

Eve grunted. "Can we just get this over with?"

"Sure thing."

They headed out of the aquarium and into the main store. "What's through that archway?" Nick asked, pointing clear across the store.

"The café and checkouts. The office is near there."

"Then that's where we're heading."

Nick crept forwards, broom handle raised over his shoulder like a baseball bat. The area ahead was cloaked in shadow, lit only by the weak morning sunshine filtering in through the skylights. Through the archway and to the left was a cosy tearoom. To his immediate right was the store's checkout area. The STAFF ONLY door to the office was right behind.

He looked back at Eve and raised an eyebrow in concern. "Be careful," he told her. "Mrs Curtis could be hiding anywhere. These sick people have a habit of blindsiding you."

Eve didn't reply, but hung back and kept her distance.

The cash-tills were set into a booth with two long desks about four feet high. Behind the tills was the store's exit, leading back out to the parking lot.

"Hello," Nick said in a raised voice, deciding it would be better to alert Mrs Curtis and see her coming than to have her sneak up on them. "Mrs Curtis, are you here?"

"What are you doing, dumbass?" Eve hissed.

"Trying to flush her out. Better than her getting the drop on us."

Sure enough, Nick's calls were met by the sounds of someone shuffling behind the tills. A bloody hand clung to the surface of one of the desks.

"There!" Eve said. "There's someone over there.

Like a cat, Mrs Curtis sprang from behind the tills and landed on the counter, staring right at them. A stringy ribbon of flesh hung from her lower jaw.

"She always this friendly?" Nick asked.

"No," Eve said. "That's not Mrs Curtis."

"Then who the hell is it?"

"I have no fucking idea."

A hungry growl spun them both around. An old lady in a frilly blue dress glared at them from inside the café, face pressed up against the glass.

"Now that's Mrs Curtis," Eve said.

Mrs Curtis threw herself through the glass window of the café and rose to her feet on the other side, glittering shards covering her like confetti.

Nick and Eve were flanked from both sides.

"Run," Nick shouted, dropping the broom handle when he realised its uselessness. Eve hurried after him. They ran back into the main shopping area where Nick clattered into a chiminea. He only just managed to keep his balance.

As they reached the entrance's automatic sliding door, they quickly realised they were on the wrong side of the sensors and it wasn't going to open from inside the building.

"Damn it," Nick shouted.

The two crazed women clattered towards them, smashing apart everything in their path.

Eve pointed. "This way."

She dragged him by one of his coat cuffs and got him moving deeper into the store. Up ahead, she skidded to a halt. Nick almost slammed right into the back of her.

"What the hell are you doing?" Nick looked back over his shoulders at their pursuers. The only thing keeping them away was their clumsiness and staggered movement. "We need to move."

"Look!" Eve pointed.

Nick's jaw fell open.

Mr Curtis was back on his feet. The old man's neck wound was so deep that his head now hung to one side. He moaned at them hungrily, crept towards them with shuffling feet.

Nick took a step back. "There's no way he could still be alive."

"I don't think he is."

Nick didn't have time to ask what Eve meant. Mrs Curtis came crashing through a colourful display of hydrangeas and barrelled right into Eve, who immediately screamed and tried to escape.

Nick was just about to help her when the other crazed woman fell upon him. She grabbed for his throat, just the way Deana had only hours ago. This time Nick was ready. He took the brakes off his inhibitions and threw a solid punch. He felt a crack as the woman's bony nose turned sideways. As she staggered back, Nick reared up and aimed a massive kick to her knee. There was a crunching snap and the woman collapsed to the floor.

"Help me," Eve screamed.

Nick's path to Eve was blocked by Mr Curtis, who had finally made it over. He was much slower than his wife, frail and lethargic, so much so that Nick was able to step right around him and rugby-tackle Mrs Curtis just as the old lady was about to have a chomp on Eve's neck. Eve fell free and Nick and Mrs Curtis went down to the floor.

Nick was straight back up and running, shouting for Eve to get after him. They made it all the way to the far end of the garden centre before a heavy glass door marked FIRE EXIT stopped them. Eve didn't let it deter her and threw herself against the push-bar, shoving the door open and stumbling out into the car park. Nick followed and, together, they put their backs against the other side of the door and started shoving it closed. It was a typical fire door, built to close slowly and not cause a draft.

Nick felt himself going red in the face as he strained. Come on, come on. Close goddamnit!

Mrs Curtis threw herself against the other side. Nick and Eve both yelled out, startled by the sudden and unexpected strength of the old woman.

Eve moaned. "How is she so strong? Mrs Curtis is almost eighty."

"I...don't...know," Nick pushed as hard as he could, "but we need to get this door closed, right...sodding...now. Look!"

A man stumbled in their direction, all bloody and broken. His head craned when he spotted them and he let out a moan, before heading towards them across the crunching pea gravel of the car park.

"I'm slipping," Eve cried out. "I can't hold it much longer."

"I can't either," Nick admitted. "We're going to have to make a run for it. After three, you ready?"

"No."

"Okay. One...two..."

"...three!"

Nick and Eve made a mad dash across the car park, gravel flying up behind them as they sprinted like their lives were on the line. They cut a wide arc around the bloody man ambling in front of them and headed for the road. There was a chance Lara might have got free and was now lying in wait somewhere up ahead, but that would also mean it would be safe to get back inside Nick's car and drive the hell out of there. However, as Nick leapt down the embankment, he saw that Lara was still tangled up in the seatbelts and was going nowhere. The car was a no go.

"Where do we go?" Eve said.

Nick gritted his teeth, looked around. Then said, "Anywhere but here."

Eve pointed to a sharp bend in the road up ahead. "Maybe we can lose them around there!"

Mrs Curtis was now hunting around the car park, sniffing the air like a wolf; but so far she seemed unable to locate Nick and Eve's location at the foot of the embankment.

"Okay," Nick said. "Let's move."

They pounded the road, heading for the sharp bend. Nick's breaths were ragged and painful, but there was no other choice but to keep on running.

Just as Nick thought they might make it, a piercing screech filled the air, coming from the direction of the car park. They'd been spotted.

Eve's eyes went wide. "Mrs Curtis is coming."

"I know. Just keep runni—"

There was a noise. Right behind them.

A rumbling.

A screeching.

Nick spun around and managed to dive aside just in time to avoid getting hit by the skidding bus. Eve hit the dirt right beside him, their faces both buried in the dirt. There was a stretched-out moment where it seemed like death would descend upon on them any second, but it eventually passed, leaving behind nothing but a tense silence.

Nick lifted his face up out of the dirt.

The bus had come to a stop, its bulky rear tyres resting less than a metre from Nick's outstretched legs.

The vehicle's pneumatic doors hissed open.

"Get in!" screamed the driver.

CHAPTER 5

NICK HELPED EVE onto the bus then flung himself in after her. He sighed with relief when the doors hissed shut behind him.

The bus rattled and groaned, then got moving with a jolt. Nick and Eve stumbled into the aisle. Eve staggered to the nearest seat, clutching her chest as she tried to catch her breath.

Nick grabbed a rail and stayed where he was, noticing the other people on the bus. He nodded at them all politely, but then turned away to face his saviour: the bus driver.

If the man hadn't come along when he did...

The man behind the wheel was rotund, with thinning black hair that was grey at the sides. Both of his narrow, unblinking eyes were glued to the road with intense focus.

"There's a car wreck up ahead," Nick warned him.

The driver nodded and slowed up a little.

Mrs Curtis ran towards the bus, racing down the centre of the road like she was a bull charging a flag.

The driver shot Nick a quick glance. "Friends of yours?"

"More like acquaintance. She's one of them."

The driver narrowed his eyes and concentrated on the road. For a moment it looked like he intended to run Mrs Curtis down, but at the last minute he swerved and went round her.

"I'm Dave, by the way," the driver told him, once they were safely back on the main roads.

"Good to meet you, Dave. I'm Nick, and the girl with me is Eve. What made you pick us up?"

"You looked like you needed a lift, way you was running down the road like a flaming monkey. There have been quite a few people in need this morning, but I can only pick up so many."

Nick glanced back at the other passengers. All of them appeared weary, shell-shocked. Some sat silently, stony-faced, while others wept to themselves quietly.

"You rescued all these people?" Nick asked.

Dave shrugged. "Some of them, I did. I'd already picked up a few on my normal run before things went potty. After all hell broke loose I managed to collect a few more people, here and there. I dropped most of 'em off near their homes wherever I could; tried to get 'em home to their families where they might be safe. People've gone bad in the head, you know? Like wild animals."

Nick nodded. "I think it's some kind of...sickness."

"I was pretty much thinking the same thing. Seen a lot of sick people these last few days on my morning runs. Flu, colds, fevers; people sneezing and coughing from the moment I picked 'em up till the moment I dropped 'em off. Something bad has got inside people."

"I'm pretty sure I owe you my life," Nick said. "Thank you."

Dave shrugged again. "We ain't out the woods yet, I'm afraid. I got no clear destination and only half a tank of petrol."

Nick thought about Deana. "We should go the hospital. Find help."

"Hospital was the first place I checked."

Nick raised his eyebrows. "And?"

"No good. There were sick people everywhere, bleeding and half-naked, making those terrible screeching sounds they make. It was a bloodbath. I left no sooner than I'd got there. In fact, there's a bird named Pauline I picked up from near there - just in time, too. She had a group of crazies right on her heels, legging her down the highway. I got to her, though. She'll tell you herself that heading for the hospital is suicide."

Nick felt defeated. People were sick and even the hospital couldn't help. How was the situation ever going to get better when there was nowhere to go, no one to take control or offer assistance? Maybe there was no getting better. Perhaps this was it. The end.

"How about a police station?" Nick asked, grasping at straws.

Dave shook his head. "The cop shop's in the town centre and the main roads to town are all snarled with traffic."

Nick groaned. "Then where? Where the hell is safe?"

Dave answered him calmly. "One of the folks I picked up earlier had the idea of finding an Army base. They tend to be out in the countryside where things might not be so bad. Big fences, too."

Nick nodded. It was a good idea. "If anyone can deal with a shit storm like this, it's the military. Where's the nearest base?"

"That's the problem. No one has any idea, and the guy who suggested it took off to find his family. So, keep an eye out for any road signs that might help us. I'm going to head towards Nottingham, see if I can find the Sherwood Foresters or, at the very least, a rural petrol station that isn't overrun."

Nick looked at the road ahead and was glad to see that it was clear for the time being. There might finally be chance to take a breather...to think.

James.

Deana.

Nick blinked and shook away his thoughts. "You mind if I take a seat, Dave? I'm dead on my feet."

"Take a load off, mate. If I need something, I'll let you know."

Nick took the seat beside Eve who was leaning against the window and watching the scenery rush by.

"I'm filthy," she muttered.

Nick stared at her. "What?"

She stretched out her legs to show the mud covering her jeans. "Look at me. I need a shower. Need to wash my hair. It's disgusting."

Nick was surprised that cleanliness was her biggest concern. "Big picture, Eve. People are dead. You can clean yourself up later."

"Don't talk to me like that."

"Like what?"

"Like you're my dad or something."

"I'm not trying to be your dad," Nick grunted. "My son died this morning on my goddamn kitchen floor, so trust me the last thing I want to be is your dad. Especially when all you can do is whine about some dirt under your nails."

Eve folded her arms, showing that she had no interest in talking with him unless he was ready to indulge her complaints; so Nick moved to the other side of the bus. He took a seat in front of a middle-aged woman wearing the tattered remnants of a grey blouse. A colourful scarf lay on the seat beside her. It was caked in blood.

"Hello," she said to him while failing to blink even once. "Welcome to the hell bus."

Nick chuckled, but it held no mirth - a mere social instinct. "Well, I for one am glad to be a passenger. Beats being where I was before Dave picked me up."

"It's not the bus that's hell. It's everything outside of it."

Nick stared out the window and saw nothing but autumn leaves and muddy fields. It was a pleasant view for the time being, but he could imagine the things the woman had likely seen on the main roads.

"I know what you mean," he said. "I haven't had the greatest of mornings either."

"I was at the hospital," she said, staring out the window blankly, "to pick up my sister. We live together and her car isn't running.

She was working the night shift – she's a nurse...was a nurse. I was supposed to pick her up this morning."

"I'm sorry." Nick remembered the sight of his son lying on the kitchen floor. "I've lost people, too. I think a lot of people have."

The woman carried on talking as if she hadn't even heard him. "She was always a bit of a mess, my sister. Never could seem to get her life in order, always sponging off me and wasting her ability. I always figured she'd find her way eventually, once she'd grown up a little. Now she won't ever get the chance."

Nick remained silent for a while before he said: "Dave told me he picked you up near the hospital. Your name's Pauline?"

"Pauline Cummings. Wish I could say it's a pleasure, but...well, you know."

Nick tried to smile. While he'd been running around on adrenaline for the past couple hours, too panicked to properly grieve his losses, this woman had been sitting on the bus, alone with her grief. The reality of the situation was crushing her now and Nick knew that once he took time to slow down, his own grief would crush him too. He looked around the bus at the other passengers, trying not to dwell on things that could wait for later. There was a grimy-looking man in navy-blue work overalls at the rear of the bus, taking up the long seat. He had thick brown dreadlocks and was staring at the floor while picking at his calloused hands. A couple rows in front of dreadlocks sat a teenager in a bulbous yellow puffer jacket. He was staring down at a mobile phone in front of him.

Lastly, there were two older ladies sitting together in the middle rows, nattering to one another as if they were on an ordinary journey on an ordinary day - the stiff upper lip of the older generation.

The vibrations of the engine started to lull Nick into a restful daze. Now that he was finally safe, his entire body began to throb. His bladder felt heavy and his hearing seemed to be on high alert. He felt the blood pulsing in his veins. He buzzed.

Through the window, Nick watched the countryside break apart as the bus passed through an industrial estate. The various factories and workshops were all dormant, their workers unable to make it in today. Or likely for the foreseeable future.

"Looks like things are going to get a tad rough up ahead," Dave shouted back at them. "Everybody hold on to their arses."

Nick got up and clambered his way to the front, wanting to see what they were coming up against.

More car wrecks littered the road and pedestrians were everywhere. A motorway service station lay just off the upcoming island and it was currently ablaze. Nick could only assume what had happened there was another outbreak – of whatever was making people crazy. Weary commuters hoping to grab a quick pasty or make use of the restroom would have got more than they bargained for.

The whole scene was a disaster-zone. The healthy fought desperately against the sick. Burning husks of automobiles piled up in the road. Fires seemed to catch all over the place.

Nick swallowed the lump in his throat. "Think we can make it through?"

"I don't know," Dave said. "The motorway is totally blocked but I might be able to stay on the island and get round onto the A road."

"If we get stalled then we won't be able to get moving again. Those crazies will be all over us."

"Thanks for that, Nick. Very comforting." Dave took a deep breath and held it; then he stamped down on the accelerator, choosing speed over caution. He quickly steered to the right as a body flew out in front of the bus, arms flailing. Nick couldn't tell if it was one of the crazies or someone normal pleading to be picked up. It was too late to find out when their bodies fell under the wheels.

There was a woman at the side of the road clutching a bloody arm against her chest. As they passed her, Nick noticed the arm was missing a hand. She screamed at the bus to stop and help her, but there was no hope of doing anything for her, especially when a mob of infected people engulfed her.

"Holy shit!" Eve said. She had crept silently to join Nick at the front of the bus. "They're like a pack of piranha."

Dave steered through a gap between an abandoned minibus, an overturned Land Rover, and a Union Jack roofed Mini Cooper. The bus scraped the Mini and exchanged paintwork, but it didn't slow them down or alert the owner. Nick figured the ding was the least of anybody's concerns right now.

The bus jolted suddenly.

"What was that?" Nick asked. "What did we just run over?"

Dave stared straight ahead. "You don't want to know."

Halfway around the roundabout, the road opened up a little. Mangled bodies littered the verges, but there was no one alive walking around. The amount of car wrecks also lessened.

"I think we're through the worst of it," Nick said.

Dave put his foot down in reply and the bus accelerated. While Nick couldn't be sure, he had a feeling that the guy's unflappable manner was actually masking a great deal of fear; fear that was currently manifesting as a heavy right foot.

"Hey, Dave, slow down a little."

"It's fine, we're clear."

"I know, but we don't know what's around the next bend."

"Hey, this is my bus. I picked you up, remember?"

"Okay, okay. I just don't want us to have an accident."

"Yeah, of course...sorry."

Nick waved his hand. "Don't worry ab-"

The bus hit something. Hard.

Dave slammed on the brakes. The bus fishtailed, back tyres slipping. Everybody screamed, louder when the entire left side of the bus rose up off the road. Nick tumbled into the aisle. Eve landed on top of him, her elbow catching him in the ribs.

Nick was sure the bus was going to tip over.

But it didn't.

The wheels came back down onto the road and the bus came to a sudden stop with the pained screeching of its tyres. Everybody onboard stopped screaming and fell into silence.

Nick climbed gingerly to his feet, rubbing at his ribs. Dave was still staring straight ahead. He'd gone deathly pale.

"Are you okay?" Nick asked the man.

"I...I'm fine. We hit something."

"I don't think it matters," Nick said. He pointed. "Look!"

A group of ten or twelve infected people stood in the road, glaring at the bus like an army of savages. They let out a single, collective screech, then rushed towards the bus.

The first body to collide with the bus was a child. The small girl had pigtails dripping with blood. She leapt up onto the windscreen and began beating and clawing at the glass. The rest of the mob hit the bus from every direction. From inside, it sounded like a hailstorm, but the view from the windows betrayed the true horror of the situation. Blood-shot eyes peered in at the bus passengers from all sides. Swollen and smashed faces smeared themselves against the glass, leaving filthy streaks that blotted out the sun. The weak strip lighting overhead flickered as the bus rocked back and forth on its axles. The passengers inside were sheep ready to be slaughtered.

Nick turned to Dave, determined to act. "Can we still move?" When there was no answer, he shook the driver. "I said, can we still move?"

Dave snapped out of his daze and blinked his eyes rapidly. "I-I don't know." He reached shakily for the ignition key. "Let me try."

The engine grumbled back to life happily and Nick sighed relief.

Dave worked the clutch, kicked the accelerator. The bus lurched forward.

"We're moving," Dave said, "but I can't see a damn thing."

Nick patted his shoulder encouragingly. "Just keep her moving forward."

Bodies continued to leap and climb at the bus's sides, but only the little girl managed to hold on at the front, clinging to the windscreen defiantly. She stared in at them with unblinking red eyes.

Then the little girl began to beat her forehead against the glass. Again and again and again.

The little girl's face broke apart, flesh splitting open wider with each slam of her head. After a while, she no longer even resembled a child, just a gore-soaked skull with dripping pigtails.

Dave sped up, knocking loose several climbers from the bus's flanks; but the little girl still held on at the front, continued smashing her skull against the glass.

The windscreen started to give way, a small crack quickly growing into many tributaries.

"Shit!" Dave groaned.

"Just keep moving," Nick said. "If we stop now we'll never get going again."

The little girl kept smashing her skull against the glass and more cracks began to spread. At the sides of the bus, the remaining infected people also started bashing at the glass, trying to get inside.

Nick squeezed Dave hard on the shoulder. "Step on it."

"I can't see where I'm going! There's blood everywhere."

The little girl struck her skull against the glass one last time and the windscreen finally gave way. It fell out in a single cracked sheet and landed in the aisle, the girl came tumbling in after it. The only stroke of luck was, that as the bus picked up speed, the bodies on the flanks finally slipped free. Some fell beneath the wheels like morbid speed bumps. Nick lost his balance as the floor lurched beneath him.

The little girl thrashed on the floor like a barracuda stranded on deck. She was attempting to claw her way to her feet.

Dave took his eyes off the road long enough to give the girl a worried glance. "What do I do?"

"Just keep driving," Nick said. "Don't slow down."

He braced himself as the little girl rose to her feet. As soon as she was up she launched an immediate attack, barrelling into Nick with so much force that it felt like her bones were made of bricks. Staggering backwards, Nick's ankle clipped the bolted-down leg of one of the passenger benches. He stumbled into the aisle and fell at the feet of the teenager in the yellow puffer coat.

The teenager reached down to help, but as he did so, the girl pounced on him and sunk her bloody teeth into his hand. He cried out in agony and pushed her away.

The little girl fell backwards but attacked again immediately. Nick tried desperately to get back to his feet in time to defend himself, but then she bundled into him and knocked him onto his side. The teenager recovered and grabbed the girl around her waist before she could leap on top of Nick. He held her there, wrestling with her from behind.

"What should I do?" he cried out in the high-pitched tones of panic. "She's gunna take another chunk out of me in a minute."

Nick looked around for inspiration and quickly found it. "Pauline!" he shouted. The woman was already watching him, a terrified expression contorting her face. He clicked his fingers at her. "Pauline, throw me your scarf."

For a split second she looked at him like she didn't understand, but then grabbed it and balled it up. She threw it in Nick's direction, but it fell to the floor a foot short.

Nick stretched for the scarf, and once he managed to grab it, he shouted to the teenager. "Hold her as still."

"Fine, but whatever you're doing, mate, you better do it quick."

Nick got up and approached the young girl. Her face was a mess, her gums and cheekbones exposed. She growled at him like a demon and looked like she had come to them straight from Hell. But she was alive. The light in her eyes told him so.

Nick thrust the scarf over the girl's mangled face and quickly wrapped it around her head, trying to cover her bleeding eyes and the ruined mouth that snapped at him. After wrapping the scarf as tightly as he could, Nick tied a double knot with the two frayed ends.

The little girl stopped thrashing.

The teenager frowned. "She...she's stopped fighting me."

It was as if the little girl had shut down. Her attack mode had switched off.

"Everything alright back there?" Dave shouted.

"Yeah," Nick said. "I think so."

Nick's intention had only been to calm disorientate her, but as he waved a hand in front of the girl's face now, trying to tempt a reaction, there was none.

After thinking for a few moments, Nick came up with a suggestion. "Try letting her go."

The teenager balked. "What? No way."

"It's okay. I'm ready to grab her again if she tries anything. Go on, just let go of her, slowly."

The teenager eventually obliged, slowly pulling his arms away from the little girl until he was no longer holding her.

She stood there motionless. Everyone on the bus let out a collective sigh of relief. The girl's hands hung limply at her sides, fingernails caked in blood. One of those fingers pointed outward at an unnatural angle, suggesting a break or dislocation, but it didn't seem to bother her. She was also missing a shoe; dirt and stones were imbedded in her bare foot. Looking at the girl, one thing was clear: she needed help they could not provide her.

"How we looking, Dave?" Nick shouted toward the front.

"I got us back onto the main road, but there are pile-ups everywhere. It's like the whole country started trying to get somewhere in a hurry but forgot how to drive. I can't say how long until we get into difficulty again."

"Is it safe to stop for a second?"

"Safer than it was earlier."

Nick looked at the little girl with sadness. "Okay. Stop the bus. We're dropping off a passenger."

The bus slowed. Nick took hold of the little girl's arm and pulled her towards the front of the bus.

"What are you going to do?" Pauline asked him.

"Free her."

"We can't leave her, she's just a little girl."

Pauline was right of course, but Nick knew they couldn't keep her. "It's not safe," he said. "She's...infected, for want of a better word. We can't risk having her near us. She's acting like a zombie or a demon or...god, I don't know what, but I know you understand what I am saying."

Pauline was shaking her head. "We can't just leave her outside alone and blindfolded. She'll get hit by a car. She's just a little girl."

"A little girl that almost took my bastard thumb off," said the teenager from the rear of the bus.

Pauline could see she was fighting a lost battle, but continued pleading anyway. "Still, we should do something."

"I'll take off her blindfold," conceded Nick. It was the only compromise he could think of.

The teenager shook his head. "What? No way. She'll come right at you again."

"I'll do it outside. I'll do it quick."

"Your funeral, mate."

The bus stopped. The doors opened.

Nick guided the little girl out onto the road. She was completely docile, willing to go wherever he guided her.

"I'm sorry to do this," he whispered. "Whatever is happening to you, I hope it isn't permanent." Then he manoeuvred her into the treeline, hoping she would wander into the countryside rather than onto the motorway. He faced her away from him and then glanced back at the bus. The door was still hanging wide open for him, but he would still have to be quick.

He took a deep breath and yanked away the girl's blindfold.

The girl screeched at the top of her lungs.

Nick turned around, sprinted, and performed a running leap up the steps onto the bus, where he skidded into the aisle. He told Dave to "Step on it."

Dave didn't argue.

The doors closed and Nick watched the young girl turn around and snarl at them, but by that time they were already well on their way.

The bus picked up speed and the cold autumn air swept in through the broken windscreen. Nick slumped against the side of Dave's driver compartment and watched the road go by, eventually losing count of the numerous wrecked cars and fallen bodies he saw.

"We need a new plan," he said. "Driving around like this is just going to get us killed. Plus we can't drive around for ever."

Dave shrugged. "No argument here. So, what should we do?"

Nick thought for a second before giving his answer. The plan was simple. "We stop at the first safe place that will take us."

CHAPTER 6

ONE HOUR PASSED. The view from the bus's windows only got worse.

On the outskirts of Cannock, they witnessed an overturned petrol tanker and a dozen charred bodies. It seemed that the tanker's operator had decided to run right through a police barricade, disregarding the group of people gathered there. The explosion probably killed them all instantly.

Only minutes later, the bus entered a village called Alrewas only to find every resident dead. Their limbs and guts lined the concrete paths like Christmas decorations. A group of infected people milled around, eating the remains. Eve almost vomited and had been crying ever since. After everything they'd witnessed, the passengers were starting to realise that they weren't merely having a bad day. The situation wasn't going to be dealt with by the Ten O' Clock News. Things had fallen apart, totally and irreversibly. The country – maybe even the world – was under siege.

The bus's current heading was north on the A38, just past Derby. Nick still held a sliver of hope that they might chance upon a local army regiment or police force. His biggest hope was to simply to find some kind of authority. Once he was safe, he would finally find time to grieve his wife and son. Images of their smiling faces kept trying to burn their way into the forefront of his mind, but he kept pushing them into the pit of his stomach where he could deal with them later. Thinking about them now would be too much. He had to survive first.

The road they were currently on was one of the few that still flowed with traffic. Anyone lucky enough to still be on the road was now very careful, not wanting to add to the uncountable wrecks littering the landscape. Things moved along fairly well, but the problem was that most people didn't seem to know where they were going. Many cars were parked off on the verge; petrol tanks dry after miles and miles of aimless driving. Stragglers wandered the side of the road in small groups, trying to hitch a ride. Dave stopped for a couple of them whenever he could, but had no choice but to ignore most. Those he did pick up were eternally grateful. Those he ignored screamed obscenities.

In addition to the passengers they had started with, the bus now held Cassie, a twenty-something nail technician from Tamworth; Carl, a factory worker they picked up on the outskirts of blood-soaked Alrewas; and Kathryn, a supermarket manager from Birmingham. Kathryn kept mostly to herself, but had been kind enough to share her bottle of water with the teenager when he started to feel unwell. His hand had not yet stopped bleeding from when the little girl had bitten him.

Nick learned that the teenager's name was Jake, and that he was a Creative Writing student from Wolverhampton University. His hand was a mess - tough to even look at. The wound had blistered up and leaked a kind of mustardy pus. He was currently lying on the bus' back seat, after having applied a bandage Dave had given him from the bus's first aid kit. Nobody said it, but everybody worried that he had caught whatever the little girl had. All eyes gazed upon him with suspicion.

Dreadlocks, in the navy-blue overalls, was actually named Mark. He was a Jamaican-born mechanic with a thick accent who was currently living in Smethwick. Nick hadn't noticed Mark's leg was broken when he'd first spotted him on the bus, but the man's left leg sat inside a grubby white cast. Mark told Nick he'd desperately wanted to intervene when the little girl had attacked, but expected only to make things worse with his cumbersome leg getting in the way. Nick decided not to hold a grudge.

The two old ladies were Ethel and Margaret. They'd become sullen and voiceless in the last hour, a stark contrast to their earlier natterings. It seemed they'd only been able to take so much before losing their stiff upper lips.

"We're running on fumes," Dave informed Nick. "Every time we pass a petrol station, it's totally blocked up with car wrecks or swimming with sick people. We're going to have to pick somewhere to turn-in soon or we're going to come to a stop in the middle of the sodding road."

Nick patted the man's shoulder. "Okay. Let's get off the road as soon as we can. Maybe park off in the woods somewhere?"

Dave took the next slip road and headed west into a residential area full of Victorian semis and dusty shops. Nick eyed every road sign as they passed and, after a few minutes, he pointed. "There," he said. "Head for that."

Dave glanced at him. "Head for what?"

"The Ripley Heights Country Park. I bet we can hole up there. I just saw a sign for it, saying to head left. It's almost winter. The park has probably closed up for the season. It might be empty, safe."

Dave took the next turning. The bus entered onto a steep incline with woodland on either side and Nick was immediately pleased at the lack of buildings. If they found a rural enough area, they may just be able to sit tight somewhere until they could figure out what to do next. Or until help arrived.

While the bus continued to climb, Nick took a seat next to Eve. For some reason, he felt an attachment to her, perhaps because their relationship stretched back to before their presence on the bus. Perhaps because she was only there because of him.

"Hey," she said. "Any idea where we're going?"

"We're heading for a country park," he said. "We're hoping it'll be deserted enough that we can stop for a while. We're running low on petrol so it's not like we have a choice either way."

Eve stared out the window thoughtfully. "I wonder if my family are okay."

Nick thought about Deana and James. They certainly were not okay, but there could still be hope for other people. He knew he should try to care about that, regardless of how hard it was to think beyond his own losses. "I suppose it'll be a while before any of us find out how bad things are. I think Jake has a mobile phone if you want to call your parents."

"Already tried," she said. "My call wouldn't go through. Kathryn has a phone as well, but it wouldn't connect either."

"Just assume your family are okay, then," Nick urged her. "Anything else won't do you any good."

"I'm scared, Nick."

He went to put his arm around her, the same way he would whenever Deana was anxious, but stopped himself, remembering that he barely knew the girl. "I'm scared, too," he said. "I'm scared that even if we get through this, things will never be the same for any of us. We've all lost too much."

"Do you think terrorists did this?"

Nick hadn't thought much about it, but he considered it a possibility. "I don't think it's worth thinking about why this has happened, at least not for now. Leave that to the experts. All we need to focus on is sticking together and getting through the rest of the day in one piece."

"You think we'll manage to do that?"

"I think we're through the worst of it."

At least I hope so, Nick thought to himself as he looked out the window.

* * *

The bus came to a stop in a grassy picnic area inside a wooded clearing. There were no other vehicles in sight.

"Well done," Nick told Dave. "This place looks pretty deserted."

Dave switched off the engine and leant back in his chair, rubbed at his eyes with two meaty fists and blinked. "I'm just glad to take a break from driving. I would've gone cross-eyed after much longer."

"I'll bet," Nick said. "We all owe you for keeping us safe. I think we can stretch our legs for a while now and take a breather. Then perhaps we can check out the surrounding area."

"Sounds good to me." Dave pressed a button on the dashboard and the pneumatic doors opened. Everyone got to their feet and piled out. There were multiple sighs of relief as they each stretched and took deep whiffs of the country air. The temperature was a little low for comfort, so Nick fastened his coat before joining them all outside. He winced as the garment brushed his various injuries.

"You okay?" Eve asked him. "Your face still looks pretty bad."

"Just a little sore." He prodded at the slick wound on his cheek. "I'll live."

Mark limped off the bus behind Nick, his cast sinking into the mud as he hopped along awkwardly. "Hey," he said. "Do we have any water or snack food? I'm starting to feel lightheaded, mon."

"Me too," one of the old ladies added.

"We'll just have to make do for now," Dave told them, taking on an air of authority that he probably felt was rightfully his as driver of the bus. "We can see if there are any shops around here later, once we've all had a rest."

Pauline shook her head. "Bad idea. We're safer to just stay put."

Mark hopped on his one good leg to the side of the bus and leant up against a wheel arch. "We'll need to eat something eventually, lady. So how long do we plan on staying here?"

"I don't know," Dave said.

"Well, don't you think we should have a plan?" Pauline said.

Dave huffed. "If you have one, then I'm all ears. Until then, just keep quiet."

"Look," Nick said. "We don't know enough to make any sort of plan, which is why we just need to take things one step at a time. Let's just be glad that we're off the road at last."

Everyone grumbled in agreement before spreading out. The supermarket manager, Kathryn, sat on a nearby picnic table and began shaping her long red fingernails with a file. The two elderly women sat on another bench just a few feet away. Eve stood around aimlessly next to Dave, who had decided to check the oil level of the bus. Nick thought it was pointless, seeing as they were out of petrol anyway. Jake stayed on the bus, still feeling unwell. Carl chatted to Cassie nearby, and Mark remained leaning against the bus, taking the weight off his cast.

Nick chose to approach Cassie and Carl. He hadn't spoken to them much and thought it wise to know everyone he was with. "You folks okay?" he asked, approaching.

Carl sniffed. "As well as can be expected. Can't say I'm a big fan of sticking here indefinitely. We've got families to get home to."

"I know," Nick agreed, but deep down he knew that it was no longer true for him. "Ideally we'll be able to find help soon, but for now we just need to be safe. We all saw what's happening to people."

"It's like they've all gone crazy," Cassie uttered meekly.

Nick smiled at her but couldn't manage to get the expression returned. "I think it's some kind of virus. My son was feeling ill last night and then this morning..." He didn't need or want to finish the sentence. Everyone had been through his or her own specific torments, and that meant they all understood each other's losses without needing them explained. That they had all suffered was implicit.

"I don't know if it's something that can be cured," Nick added. "So, right now, our best bet is sticking together."

Carl sniffed again. "Safety in numbers, huh?"

"I'm glad you found me," Cassie said. "I don't know what I would've done if I hadn't been picked up. I watched my best friend get ripped to shreds by her own dad. Then she got up and came after me."

Nick scratched his chin. "She got up and came after you?"

Cassie nodded. "Yes, after her dad attacked her, Michelle and I managed to hole up in the bathroom together, but Michelle was hurt bad. Her neck and stomach were gushing and the floor tiles were covered in her blood. Then she just stopped breathing. I...I know she was dead, but two minutes later she was back on her feet and coming after me just like her dad had gone after her. Only she was different than her dad, she was..."

"Slower?" Nick finished for her, remembering how Mr Curtis had at first been fast and agile until his throat tore open on the fish tanks. After that he had moved very slowly, almost drunkenly.

"People don't come back from the dead," Carl scoffed. "It's crazy."

"Yeah, well," Nick said. "I think crazy got invited to the party today. Whatever people are infected with is doing something to them when they get badly injured. It still makes them want to kill us, but they get clumsy and slow."

"Like walking corpses?" Carl was shaking his head, apparently still too unwilling to accept such a concept. "You're talking about bloody zombies."

"Maybe it's something in their blood," Cassie suggested. "Maybe when they get injured and lose enough blood, the virus leaks out and makes them weaker." She shook her head and sighed. "Or maybe they really are just dead and this is the end of the world."

"You've been watching too many horror films," Carl told her. "We should just stay calm and wait for this whole thing to blow over. I guarantee this time next week we'll all be back at home, watching the news about whatever this is. It won't be that the dead are coming back to life to eat the living."

"I hope you're right," Nick said, moving away. "I really do."

He headed over to Mark next, nodding at him as he approached. "You doing okay, mon?"

"As well as can be expected. How's the leg?"

"Tis not too bad. Hurt it a few weeks ago at me old man's garage, ya know? Me own stupid fault. Tripped over a tyre, of all things, and me leg twisted like a screwdriver. Tain't hurting too much now tho. On its way."

"I wouldn't want to have to make a getaway with that thing," Nick said. "Good thing you're with us."

"For sure. I is blessed de good man, Dave, picked me up. A right calamity we is in right now, ya know?"

"Putting it mildly."

"Twill work itself out, mon."

Nick patted Mark on the shoulder. "I really hope so, Mark. Good to meet you anyway."

"Likewise. Think I'll go back on de bus. Take the weight off dis leg. See how the young lad is doing."

Nick nodded as Mark hobbled off. "I'll let you know if anything transpires," he shouted after him.

Eve was standing nearby. She was frowning. "You part of the morale squad or something?" she said. "Who made it your job to check up on everybody?"

"Just trying to keep myself busy."

"Why bother? We're all fucked. You keep going around like everything is going to be fine, though. We've got a bus with no petrol, a guy with a broken leg, and a pair of geriatric bingo warriors."

Nick let out an aggravated breath. "Being negative isn't going to do anybody any favours, is it? Should I have just left you in that closet?"

"Probably. It was safer than standing in the middle of a field, or letting that crazy little girl attack us."

"No one exactly let her do it, Eve. And that girl was sick, not crazy."

Eve flapped her arms. "Are you kidding me? The people we've seen don't need an aspirin. They're monsters. Mr Curtis was dead and he still came after us. They are all monsters."

"My son is not a monster. My wife is not a monster."

Eve sighed. "I was listening to what Cassie was saying and she's right. Soon as you put one of those crazies down, they get right back up again and stumble after you. They're zombies – walking dead people."

"I have trouble believing that, even with all that we've seen. Dead people don't rise. There must be some other explanation."

Eve flapped her arms. "Viruses don't usually turn people into bloodthirsty psychopaths, either, but hey, you know what, it happened anyway. Someone turned the crazy factor all the way up to eleven."

Nick closed his eyes for a second and thought. "Look, I don't know the answers any more than anybody else. I just don't think it's prudent to start assuming things like a zombie apocalypse. We all just need to stay calm and keep our heads about us."

"Who made you so important that you think you can manage everyone? What is wrong with you, man? Don't you see what's going on?"

"Eve, I'm just trying to help. What's gotten into you? Why are you so mad at me?"

Eve turned away from him, looking like she was hiding a bout of tears. "I just don't want to be here. I don't feel safe."

This time Nick decided to reach out and touch her. He placed a hand on her shoulder and rubbed. Eventually she began to turn back to face him.

A scream sounded from the bus.

Everybody in the field looked around as one, startled and afraid, nerves already close to cracking.

One of the bus's side windows cracked in the centre. It looked like someone's head had been pushed through it and then pulled back inside.

Eve had her hands clasped together in front of her face. "What the hell is happening now? I can't take any more."

Nick sprinted across the short patch of grass over to the bus and sprung up the steps into the aisle. What he saw confused him. Jake had Mark shoved up against the side of the bus, forcing his head against the broken window as he tried to bite a chunk out of his face. Mark tried to resist, but his bulbous cast was wedged beneath the seats, pinning him in place. Jake had hold on his dreadlocks.

Nick stumbled forward as Dave ran into the back of him. When the other man saw what was happening he swore loudly. "Shite! Jake is one of them."

Nick shook his head, but it quickly occurred to him what had happened. "The little girl bit Jake's hand. She infected him. Damn it!"

Mark screamed for help.

Nick broke from his stupor and started forward, but stopped when Mark's screams were cut short by Jake's teeth sinking deeply into his windpipe. Nick watched in horror as veins and cartilage were torn away like wet spaghetti.

Dave grabbed hold of his coat and pulled him back. "We're too late. Come on!"

But Nick was frozen. He couldn't take his eyes from what was happening in front of him. Two men who he had only just been chatting to were now soaked in blood before him.

Jake lifted his head from Mark's neck and spotted Nick standing at the front of the bus. He hissed through bloodstained teeth.

Nick leapt out of the bus and landed on the grass outside. Dave punched a big red button set beside the door and it quickly folded shut. Jake crashed up against the glass panel, glaring out at them with swollen, bloodshot eyes. Gory chunks of flesh hung from his teeth. Mark's flesh.

Jake screeched at the top of his lungs.

"Run!" Dave bellowed to everyone. "Jake is infected. Bloody move it!"

Everybody took off like kids in a playground, scattering at different speeds. Nick held up the back, trying to keep everybody moving in the same direction before they lost each other. He glanced back and watched as the bus shrunk away behind them, but then he saw Jake emerge from it, climbing through the hole where the windscreen used to be.

"Oh no!" Nick started coaxing the two old ladies to move faster. "Come on, come on," he shouted. "Ethel, Margaret, move, move, move."

Jake let out another piercing scream and the fleeing passengers managed to find another gear, picking up more speed, finding energy that only the fear of death could liberate. Eve and Cassie were at the front of the pack now, heading for the treeline.

Nick glanced back again, but it wasn't good. Jake would be on them long before they all made it to the treeline. He wasn't dead, not a shambling zombie. He was one of the crazed, adrenaline-fuelled members of the infected. Even if they did somehow make it into the woods, they still wouldn't be safe. Jake would just hunt for them.

Suddenly, Ethel stopped dead. She doubled over and clutched at her chest. Margaret stopped beside, putting an arm around her companion's shoulders. "Ethel! Ethel, now, we have to keep moving. Stop being a silly beggar."

Nick stopped and went back for them. They had only seconds to get moving again. Jake was sprinting after them at great speed.

"Come on," Nick urged the two old ladies. "We have to keep moving."

Ethel fell to her knees, wheezing. "M-my heart. I can't. I need to...stop. Just go."

"No," Margaret stated firmly. "I refuse to leave you here."

Nick grabbed Margaret's brittle forearm and tried to pull her away. "Come on, we have to go or we're all dead."

"Then you go." Margaret pulled her arm back with surprising strength. "I'm not leaving Ethel to face that monster alone."

Ethel managed to right herself on one knee. Her face had gone deep purple and she squinted in agony. Despite that, she grabbed Margaret by the hand and squeezed tightly. "Margaret Skinner, I am not letting you get hurt because of me. If you don't get moving right this very second, I will come back and haunt you. I swear it."

Margaret looked ready to burst into tears. Nick stared down the field. Jake was only metres away now, lolloping across the grass like a deranged ape.

Ethel fell down, rolling onto her side and clutching at her chest. She looked up at her friend and hissed. "Go."

Nick grabbed Margaret's arm and this time she didn't resist. They got moving again, leaving Ethel behind to her fate. Hopefully it would be the heart attack that claimed her and not Jake's savage teeth.

The last thing Nick heard before Ethel's screams filled the air was the old lady cursing at Jake. "I've taken shits harder than you, you fucking pussy."

The rest of the passengers entered the shadows of the treeline and didn't look back again.

CHAPTER 7

ICK AND THE group eventually stopped in a clearing about half a mile into the woods. Everyone was sweating, having run uphill most of the way. They managed to leave Jake behind as he stopped to maul Ethel, but Nick could still hear the infected teenager's animalistic shrieks in the distance. In her dying breaths, Margaret's old friend had bought the rest of them time to escape.

Dave slumped up against a tree and tried to catch his breath. Perspiration soaked his hair and matted it against his forehead. "I pray we never have to do that again. I think I left one of my lungs back there."

"Tell me about it," Nick said. He knelt on the ground and tried to catch his own breath. It was several minutes before he was able to stand again and ask the group a question. "Has anyone else been bitten?"

"Why?" Cassie asked.

"Because Jake was bitten by the little girl and now, a few hours later, he's infected. That's how this thing is spreading: an infected person bites a healthy person. I feel dumb for not realising it earlier, but it makes perfect sense. I just can't believe how quick it happens. I'd assumed a certain part of the population had become infected and that the rest of us were healthy, but that's not how it works. This thing is spreading person to person."

Carl spat at the ground. "So we could all end up like that?"

"If you get bitten, yes. Has anybody been bitten?"

Everyone shook their heads.

"Okay." Dave seemed to relax a little. "We all better be real careful from now on then. We come across someone infected, we run. No fighting with them like we did with that little girl."

"I agree," Nick said, feeling bad about Jake's fate now that he knew it involved him.

"We have to be more careful," Eve said. "I'm not ending up like one of those monsters."

"They're people," Nick grunted. "My wife and son were infected, and I'll be damned if I'm going to let you keep calling them monsters."

Eve folded her arms and lifted her chin. "I'm sorry, but as nice as people might once have been, if they've been infected, they're monsters."

Nick clenched his fists. But before he could shout his reply, Dave shushed them both. "Come on now. No point arguing over it. I think we all understand that people are sick – infected, if you like – but they're dangerous and we cannot forget that."

"I think some of them are dead," Cassie said, echoing her previous statements.

The group went silent. Nobody argued at first.

Then Carl spoke up. "This nonsense again," he muttered.

Eve was the first to speak in support of Cassie. "I think she's right. Nick killed an infected man when he rescued me. He got right back up and came after us again. He was messed up, slow and clumsy, but he was still walking around trying to eat us, even with most of his neck missing."

Nick couldn't contain his grief any longer. It had been building in the pit of his stomach like an ulcer and now it was ready to burst. What everyone was talking about was utter nonsense. And it offended him. "I killed my son," he said, feeling sick as he said it. "James was infected, but he didn't come back to life after I killed him. He stayed dead. He is dead. So your theory is bullshit."

"Well, that shoots Cassie's theory down once and for all then," Carl stated, obviously satisfied. "The dead are not getting up and walking around."

There was silence again. Everybody looked at Nick. The full weight of his confession suddenly dawned on him. He didn't want their judgment, their pity. They could never understand his loss or what had occurred in his kitchen.

Nick marched off deeper into the woods, leaving the others behind him – along with their unwanted pity. Far enough away, he slumped back against an old spruce tree and started bashing his head against the bark. He burst into tears, crying so hard he thought he might suffocate, so hard was his sobbing.

He wanted to die. He wanted it all to be over.

The nightmare was too much.

Eventually Nick's body became so weak that he couldn't sustain his own weight any longer and collapsed to the ground. He found himself staring up at the grey sky. Peculiarly he started to wonder if it might rain. Covered in dirt and blood, the thought of being cleansed by Mother Nature was surprisingly comforting.

A twig snapped nearby.

Nick's mind leapt back into focus. He sat up and searched in the direction of the noise.

"Hey," Eve said, coming and kneeling on the ground next to him. She stretched out her legs and then plonked herself down on her bum. "It's dangerous to be out her alone."

Nick sighed. "I honestly don't care."

"I do. Are you okay? I mean, considering the fact that the world has fallen apart."

"Yeah, I'm fine. Just getting some stuff out of my system."

Eve nodded as if she understood. "I'm sorry."

"What for?"

"The things I said. Actually, I'm pretty much sorry for everything I've said to you since we met. I know I've been a bit up and down. I'm hormonal at the best of times and this situation certainly isn't helping."

"You said I rescued you." Nick said, recalling the word Eve had used in their previous group conversation.

Eve looked down at her hands. "Yeah, well...that's because you did rescue me. I just don't like feeling like I owe anybody anything, I guess. Makes me defensive. I'm sorry I called your family monsters."

"It's okay," Nick said, managing to raise a tiny smile of forgiveness. "I just don't like to think of my wife as being beyond help. I keep trying to convince myself that this will all blow over and that Deana will be waiting for me when I get home. James too. Huh, stupid."

"James is your son?"

"He was my son. I killed him. I think there's probably a special kind of Hell for fathers who kill their sons."

"What happened?" Eve asked.

"He was sick, just like the others we've seen. He attacked me in the kitchen, like a wild animal, and I-I slipped. We both fell... His head hit the chair."

Eve sighed. Pity Nick didn't want. "He didn't come back like Mr Curtis?"

"No. I was in the house for another ten minutes and he was just...dead. Mr Curtis was back on his feet almost right away."

Eve propped her chin up with her hand and seemed to think for a moment. "Perhaps it has something to do with their injuries."

Nick frowned. "Dead is dead, isn't it? Why would it matter how they die?"

Another twig snapped.

"You have to go for the head," said a voice belonging to a stranger.

CHAPTER 8

NICK AND EVE leapt up. Three huge men, two black, one white, stood several metres away. One of the black men was bald with a pointed goatee, while the other was well groomed with short, cropped hair and light stubble. The white man was the biggest of the three – a mountain, six-and-a-half-feet for sure. His heavy beard was growing grey, giving him the appearance of a grimy Father Christmas. All three men wore the same grey tracksuits and white trainers.

"Who are you?" Nick demanded. Instinctively he placed Eve behind him.

The black man with the pointed goatee sucked at his teeth. "Could ask you the same thing, little man."

The towering white man put his hand up to silence his associate and then smiled at Nick. "My name is Jan. Janwin Banks. This is Rene," he motioned to the quiet man on his right. "The charmer on my left with the Fu Manchu is Dash. Don't ask what his real name is, though, because he won't tell you."

"You're prisoners," Nick said, noting their matching attire. He started backing away slowly, pulling Eve with him.

Jan held his palms out in peace. "Hey, brother, there's no need to fear us. We stepped in the same shit puddle you have. We're just trying to make it somewhere safe."

"How did you get free?" Eve asked from over Nick's shoulder.

"The fuck it got do wid you, sweetheart?" the one named Dash said.

Jan sighed and took a wary step forward. "Let's just say that we're the lucky victims of circumstance. The guards who were relocating us to a new bin in Nottingham are all dead."

Nick and Eve backed away more quickly.

Jan chuckled. "No, not because of us. There was an accident. Some imbecile driving a Land Rover went right into our minibus. Next thing I know, there's a bunch of lunatics tearing apart our P.O.s. We managed to cut our wrist ties on a piece of twisted metal on the banged-up Land Rover and ran for the hills. There were five of us to start with, but we didn't all make it. It appears things have changed a little recently. People aren't as friendly as I remember." He scratched his head. "Tell you the truth, I actually prefer it on the inside."

"There's some kind of virus infecting people, making everybody crazy," Eve said.

Jan nodded and scratched at his impressive beard. "Makes sense. People don't act like savages for no reason."

Nick thought about how the three men had introduced themselves. They could have snuck up, but instead Jan had spoken and given up his presence. "You said something about needing to go for the head?"

"Yeah," Dash told them enthusiastically. "It's the only sure way to put 'em down for keeps."

Jan nodded his agreement. "Don't know if you've noticed, but when one of these infected people dies they have a tendency to come back."

Nick stared at the man. "You know that for sure?"

"Like I said, there were five of us to begin with. I've seen enough to know the rules. The dead are getting up and walking. Hallelujah!"

"I told you," Eve said to Nick.

"When they come back," Jan continued, "they come back different. Clumsy, slow, and easy to deal with, but they tend to group together and come after you in a pack. If that happens you're in trouble. You can only drop them for good with a hefty blow to the head."

Eve glanced at Nick and he could tell what she was thinking. James hadn't come back because he struck his head on the chair when he fell.

"How do you know all this?" Nick asked.

"Because we saw that shit," Dash grunted. He obviously disapproved of having to explain himself. "We've been hiking it all the way from Nottingham. Seen some seriously wacky shit since then, blud."

"It wasn't too bad at first," Jan said, "but things quickly deteriorated. I don't even know the name of the last town we passed through, but there was no one left alive, all infected or dead. We managed to lay low and avoid them, but if they'd spotted us we would've been done for. That's why we made for the countryside. I suppose you both had the same idea?"

"There're half-a-dozen of us, actually," Nick said, wanting to let them know he had backup if he needed it. The spokesmen for the three men, Jan, seemed intelligent and rational, but there was no telling what the man was truly like.

"A bunch of us came here in a bus," Eve said, understanding Nick's strategy.

"Mind if we join up with you?" Jan asked bluntly.

Dash pulled a face. "You serious, J? We don't need to team up with this honkey and his bitch."

Nick clenched his fist and stepped forward. "I think you might want to learn to keep your mouth shut, blud. Let your associate do the talking. He's better at it."

Dash stepped forward to meet Nick. "You want a piece of me, honkey?"

Jan stepped between them, holding his fellow prisoner back. "Look, with all that's going on, I think safety in numbers is the only thing we've got going for us. If we join together we can figure something out and try to stay alive."

Nick felt uneasy about the situation. He wrung his hands together and took a few breaths as he thought it through. Three prisoners, at least one of them was a sure problem in Dash. The guy was an obvious loose cannon. Jan seemed reasonable enough, but the third man said not a word. He just stood there taking it all in silently.

"We don't know anything about you," Nick said.

Jan nodded. "True enough. We're criminals, and obviously that's a cause for concern for you. If what you say is true, though, you have a whole busload of people to keep an eye on us. It's not in our interests to harm you. We just want to find safety. I'm sure that's what you want to. If that's true then we have common ground."

Nick wavered, swayed from foot to foot as he wrestled with the right reply.

"What if I said, please?" Jan said. "And I promise to keep Dash on a tight leash. We're all beat, and pretty damn terrified to tell you the truth. If you allow us to join your group, I promise we'll pull our weight."

Nick sighed. Was it really a good idea to team up with bunch of criminals? But could he really turn his back on somebody asking for help? Jan was right about one thing: safety in numbers was the only thing any of them had going for them

"What were you in for?" Eve asked. It was the obvious question and Nick wondered why it hadn't occurred to him to ask.

"I tried to rob a bank," Jan replied, bluntly as ever.

Nick cleared his throat. "And your friends?"

Dash shrugged. "I'm innocent, blud."

"Sure you are," Jan said, patting him on the back. "Dash was in for dealing – he's a bit of a cliché. You'll have to excuse him. As for Rene, I honestly don't know. Fella doesn't talk none. Only reason I know his name is because I heard the guards use it before they bit the dust. He's an odd one, but no harm that I can tell."

Nick stared at Rene and found himself agreeing. The man was a picture of gentle calmness, almost smiling, but not quite. For some reason, Nick didn't feel in any danger at all around Rene. It was his two colleagues that were the bigger worry – Dash especially.

But what choice was there? It was a free country and Nick couldn't exactly stop the prisoners from tagging along. It would be better to extend the hand of friendship than to make an enemy, especially of a bunch of needy criminals lost in the woods.

"Okay," Nick said finally. "You can join us; but you keep to yourselves and don't upset anyone. These people have been through a lot already."

Jan nodded. "Understood and thank you. Lead the way, brother."

* * *

Nick emerged back into the clearing where everybody was waiting. When they saw the three newcomers they grew immediately apprehensive.

"Who are they?" Dave bristled.

Nick introduced the prisoners. "This is Jan, Rene, and Dash. They've had a similar day to ours."

"Why are they all wearing matching tracksuits?" Cassie asked timidly.

Nick decided on honesty. "Because they're prisoners. They're going to tag along with us for a while. There's safety in numbers."

"Are you shitting me?" Dave said. "They're supposed to be locked up, not roaming free. No way are they coming with us."

Jan, as was becoming standard, was the one to speak on behalf of the prisoners. "We are indeed supposed to be locked up, but right now there isn't really any authority to take charge of us. We were sprung free purely by accident and ever since we've just been trying to survive. We didn't escape by force or try to break out; we just suddenly found ourselves free in a very bad situation. What would you have us do?"

Dave sighed. "You better not be rapists or murderers."

Cassie whimpered.

Jan sniffed. "We are no such thing. We may not be angels, by any length of the imagination, but we are human beings and would very much like to survive. We don't want to become one of those things."

"Do you know what those things are?" Kathryn asked, before chewing anxiously at her fingernails.

"I don't know what they are, ma'am. I probably don't know any more than you folks do. Your man, Nick, thinks a virus did this and I'm inclined to agree, but the only thing I can say for sure is that I've seen dead bodies walking around and eating people. As for what could cause such a travesty of nature, I have no idea. I'm not a praying man, usually, but I would suggest asking our Lord take mercy on us right now, because it seems like he's pretty pissed off."

Carl scoffed. "You think it's the end of days?"

"Isn't it?" Jan asked. "You think this isn't the end of the world as we know it? Whether it was God, terrorists, or something else entirely, things have just taken one hell of a turn for the worse."

Cassie whimpered again. "We're all going to die. Eventually they'll get us."

Pauline tried to comfort her while the rest of the group exchanged nervous glances. Nick knew from his own mixed feelings that having the three prisoners tag along was as comforting as it was disconcerting. They were probably dangerous, but no more than anyone else was right now.

Kathryn broke the silence. She began to cough and splutter into her hands. Her legs wobbled like she was going to fall down.

Nick hurried over to her. "You okay?"

She caught her breath and nodded. "I-I'm fine. Just a frog in my throat."

Nick nodded and gave her some space.

"What's the plan then, folks?" Jan asked them all. "Is there a destination in mind?"

Dave shrugged and said, "Does anywhere count?"

"Better than nowhere, I guess." Jan turned and pointed in the direction they had met up with Nick. "Me and the boys came from the main roads beyond the woods. Things are pretty bad back in the towns, so I suggest we keep to the tress."

"This whole area is a country park, apparently," Nick said. "Maybe we'll find help somewhere up the hill. There might be a craft centre or a farm or something."

Jan clapped his meaty hands together. "Then we have somewhere to head for. We're happy to do whatever you folks think is best."

Dash rolled his eyes and grumbled. Being subservient obviously did not sit well with him.

"That okay with you?" Nick asked Dash, unwilling to deal with petulance from him any more than he would have from James. Not that James had been a particularly petulant little boy.

Dash smirked. "Yeah, honkey, I'm sound. Lead on."

Kathryn succumbed to another wracking cough. This time she seemed unable to stop it and began staggering around in a panic.

Dash eyeballed her suspiciously. "The fuck is wrong with that bitch?"

Jan marched over to Kathryn and grabbed her. He forced her chin up and stared into her eyes. Then he shoved her away so she could resume her coughing. "She's infected."

Nick baulked. "What? Impossible." Then he saw Kathryn's swollen, bloodshot eyes and knew it was true. "Oh no."

"We need to put her down," Jan said. The man seemed incapable of being anything other than blunt.

Kathryn managed to halt her coughing enough to stumble backwards with her hands outstretched. "No! No, I'm fine. Leave me alone, please. Just leave me alone."

Jan stalked after her. Nick grabbed the big man by his wrist, which was too thick to get a hand around. "Back off! No one's killing anybody. Are you insane?"

Jan looked at Nick like he was the one who was insane. "If we don't kill her now, she'll kill us later. I've seen it enough times to know."

"He's right," Dave said. "We've seen it too, with Jake."

Nick shook his head. "But she can't have it. She hasn't been bitten."

"We don't know that," Dave argued. "How can we be sure?"

"It was the water," Pauline said.

Nick turned on her. "What?"

"When we picked her up she had a bottle of water. Jake was feeling unwell so she shared it with him. Cross-contamination."

Carl groaned, then kicked at the dirt. "Are you fucking kidding me? What virus acts this fast?"

Nick thought about Deana and how she had kissed James's wounded finger before putting a Beano plaster on it. Had that been all it had taken for her to catch it? And, for that matter, was the kid who bit James's finger the one who passed it on to him?

Nick shook his head, feeling dizzy. "It can't be... It can't be that contagious."

"It is what it is," Jan said. "We need to put her out of her misery before she loses it and comes after us. It's a kindness, believe me."

"Fuck you," Kathryn shouted. "You're all fucking insane. You can't kill me. I'm fine—" More wracking coughs. She dropped to her knees, wheezing for breath. Blood spattered the crisp brown leaves in front of her.

Dash picked up a rock the size of his fist and handed it to Jan. "Turn her lights out, blud."

Jan didn't hesitate in taking the rock. He moved towards Kathryn with it in his hand.

Nick blocked his way. "Not going to happen."

"Move out of his way, Nick." Dave said. "There's no other way and you know it."

"Yeah." Carl added his voice to the argument. "We have to think about ourselves."

Nick shook his head in disbelief. "Do you all think this is the right way to behave? You think we should kill an innocent woman like it's nothing? Has it really taken less than a day to turn us into a bunch of savages?"

"All men are savages," Jan said. "Times like these when they really begin to show it."

"I'm not a man and I'm not a savage." It was Eve talking. She stood next to Nick. "I don't think this is okay."

"Me either," Pauline said. "It's barbaric."

"It's cowardly, is what it is," Margaret grumbled. "This is not the way people in Britain behave. We're not French."

Nick looked at Cassie, trying to swing a vote. "What about you, Cassie? What do you think?"

Cassie looked at her feet and eventually shrugged. "I don't want anyone to die."

Nick sighed with relief. "Thank you."

"But I don't want to be attacked again, either. I think...I think Kathryn is already dead if she has the virus."

Nick couldn't believe it. Of all people to advocate mob violence, shy and quiet Cassie seemed least likely.

"You can't do this." Nick was exasperated yet held himself firm in front of Jan's towering frame.

Jan stared down at Nick with his crystal-blue eyes. The shallow divots of widening crow's feet betrayed the man's age, but also his weathered toughness. It was the hard face of a hard man, but Jan's expression seemed to soften slightly as Nick stood his ground.

Jan let go of the rock and let it fall to the ground. "It's bad judgment, brother, but I promised to play things your way, so that's what I'm going to do. How do you want to proceed?"

Nick deflated and let his shoulders relax. For a moment there he thought he was about to be crushed by a giant.

"We send Kathryn in the opposite direction," Nick said. "By the time she turns – loses it, or whatever – we'll be a mile and half in the other direction. We don't need to kill—"

Thud! A sickening wet sound.

Nick spun around and tried to understand what he was seeing. "Dave? What the hell are you doing?"

Dave had just bludgeoned Kathryn with a meaty blow to the head with a rock even bigger than the one Jan had had. Already the left side of her face had swollen up like a balloon. Everybody watched in horror as the bus driver prepared to smash the rock down again into the struggling woman's face.

Kathryn moaned as Dave climbed on top of her. The pungent smell of urine wafted into the air as a dark stain appeared on the crotch of her work trousers. Dave was going to kill her.

Nick tackled him to the ground.

"What the hell are you doing, Nick? We have to do this. Get off me. GET OFF ME!"

Kathryn crawled away, weeping and moaning in the dirt.

Nick held Dave down by his wrists and shouted over his shoulder. "Run, Kathryn. Find someplace safe."

She glanced back at him like a rabbit in the headlights, her face a crimson mask of blood. She managed to scramble to her feet and then she was sprinting through the trees and into the distance.

Once she had disappeared, Nick let go of an irate Dave.

The bus driver hopped up, brushing twigs and dry leaves from his knees with aggressive swipes. "You fool! I was doing what needed to be done. I wasn't going to let her take a bite out of me or anyone else. Now she's running around in the wilderness, ready to become a monster. The people she kills will be on your head."

"You're out of your mind," Eve shouted, pointing her finger at Dave.

Pauline looked disgusted. "This isn't how people behave."

Dave spat at the ground. "It is now. If we want to stay alive."

Silence hung densely in the air. Eventually Jan shrugged and looked at Nick. "Can't change it now, brother. For better or worse, we need to get going."

"What? And just leave her out here alone?" Pauline said.

Dave grunted. "We'll alert the authorities when we can. You can even tell them what I did. I'll stand by it, don't you worry."

Nick was utterly shocked by Dave's actions and by the rage that had suddenly taken over him. Nick had read Dave all wrong. He thought Dave was a rescuer, a decent and brave man, but he was something else entirely.

Nick started walking. "Let's just get moving. Quicker we find help, quicker we can contact Kathryn's family and tell them you just tried to smash her brains in."

"It was more like he was trying to smash them out to be honest," Dash said, giggling.

Nick ignored the bad joke and sped up his pace, leaving the rest of the group several yards behind him, but after a while, Eve caught up to him. He wasn't about to admit it, but he was glad she was there.

CHAPTER 9

"SO WHAT DO you think we're going to find?" Eve asked as she and Nick trudged through the woods together. The rest of the group were trailing a dozen feet behind. Everyone seemed to be following Dave's lead for the most part – probably because he was constantly barking orders. Regardless of whether anybody condoned the bus driver's actions, his willingness to take charge and act cemented his place of authority. Nick tried not to think of poor Kathryn in the woods, alone, injured, and afraid.

"I don't know what we're going to find," he said. "I hope we can find somewhere with a nice big gate and a police sniper on the roof, but I'm pretty sure we won't get it."

Eve laughed. "I'm just wishing for a shower."

"You're not still bothered about being mucky, are you? Not after what happened to Kath—"

"Hey," she cut him off. "Don't give me grief. I'm just trying to focus on the small things. Creature comforts, you know?"

"Sorry. I'm just angry about what happened back there."

"Me too, but none of us really know each other. We have no power over the actions of Dave or anybody else. Nobody here is boss."

Nick huffed. "I'm not sure Dave would agree with you. I would've stopped him if I knew what he was going to do."

"I know you would have, but you didn't and you couldn't, so forgive yourself. At least Kathryn's still alive. She wouldn't be if you hadn't stepped in."

Nick remained silent, but took in what Eve was saying. There was no point in ruminating about things he couldn't change, and right now a lapse in concentration was surely a death sentence.

* * *

"We've been walking through these woods for more than two hours," Margaret complained. "I need to rest."

Nick and Eve were still a little further ahead than the others, but they stopped when they heard Margaret. Nick didn't know how long they'd been trudging through the woods, but two hours sounded about right.

"We keep moving," Dave told the old woman. "We can't afford to stop."

Eve frowned. "Why not? What's the harm in taking a ten minute rest?"

Dave stared at her and his top lip curled slightly upwards. "We need to find help, young lady, or have you forgotten that? The longer we stay in these woods, the bigger the risk we get attacked again."

Eve turned a slow circle, taking in their surroundings. "I think we'll be okay, old man. We're totally alone."

Dave shook his head. "We're not stopping."

"Who the hell put you in charge?" Nick said. "Margaret needs to rest, so we let her. There's no argument to be had about it. She's elderly. Show some compassion."

Margaret looked at Dave pleadingly. She seemed embarrassed that her age and weakness was causing a spat, but she seemed determined to get her own way.

Dave gritted his teeth then said, "Fine. She can have ten minutes, but then we're not stopping again until we find help. We can't afford to be stuck in these woods after dark."

Nick checked his watch. It was just after two. It wouldn't get dark until about 7PM, but Dave did have a point: they didn't want to be wondering through the woods in the dark.

Margaret eased herself down onto a fallen log. Pauline sat beside her and rubbed her back. Dave, Cassie, Carl, and the three prisoners huddled together between the trees, chatting.

"Dave is starting to get on my tits," Eve whispered to Nick. "Talk about a power trip. He thinks he's head boy scout or something. What the hell happened to him?"

"I don't know," Nick admitted. "I can't believe how quickly his attitude has changed. To think he was driving around rescuing people, and then to just attack Kathryn the way he did. I think driving us all to safety has made him feel entitled. On the bus he was his old self, doing what he does for a living. Since we got off, though, he's finding a new role for himself. Still trying to be the driver."

Eve picked up a fallen pinecone and ran her fingers over its ridges. "I think when we parked the bus, the reality of the situation finally dawned on everybody. It was a bit like being in a cocoon when we were driving around - just watching all the chaos but not really being a part of it. Now that we're on foot, I think we've all realised just how vulnerable we are and how much the normal rules don't apply. Dave is just doing what he thinks is right, in a screwed up way. Maybe Kathryn was dead already. I don't think Dave is bad. Just fucking annoying."

Nick leant back against a towering poplar tree and looked up at the sky. Birds fluttered overhead. "Are you doing okay?"

"Who, me? Yeah, why do you ask?"

"Just checking. You're a young girl. This whole thing must be pretty frightening."

"Twenty-two doesn't make me a child. It just makes me better looking than the rest of you."

Nick laughed. "You think so?"

"Absolutely. Me and Margaret are the hottest people here."

Nick laughed harder. "Well, I didn't want to say anything, but the old dear does have something about her."

Eve punched him in the arm and giggled loudly. Everyone looked over at them

"Stop," Nick said. "We shouldn't chat about people behind their backs. Especially not a nice old lady like Margaret."

"I agree. We should look after her. She reminds me of my gran. Except my gran didn't swear as much."

They said nothing else for the remainder of the break, just made the most of the quiet after so much chaos. Nearby, Dave checked his watch every thirty seconds, keeping exact time, with a constant look of irritation on his face. The three prisoners had stuck close to him since they all got going. Dash was constantly cracking crude jokes and laughing with Dave, while Jan mostly just looked disapproving. The third prisoner, Rene, stood was still to utter a single word, yet his eyes darted constantly, taking in the surroundings.

"Okay," Dave said five minutes later, checking his watch one last time. "Time to get moving again. I think if we carry on in this direction it'll only be a matter of time before we come out somewhere."

"And then what?" Pauline asked. "What if we get attacked again?"

"We'll remain in the treeline and check stuff out before we make any decisions, Pauline. We can send a scout if need be."

A scout, Nick thought to himself. Dave was beginning to act like a military commander.

There were no arguments, so everyone got moving again. This time, instead of moving on ahead, Nick stayed back amongst the group. This way, he could keep an eye on Margaret. She'd recently witnessed her friend being ripped apart and deserved their compassion, but right now she wasn't getting any of it from Dave. Nick would have to make sure she was looked after.

* * *

Another half-hour went by before the trees thinned out. Dave hurried to the front of the group and put his hand up to stop them.

"We have to be careful," he said. "We don't know what lies ahead. It's quiet, so I don't think it's a motorway or a road, but it could still be dangerous."

"We should send one person to check it out," Carl said. "No point risking everybody."

Dave nodded. "Agreed. Nick, go see what we're dealing with."

"Me?"

"Yes, what's the problem? Just stay low and keep out of sight."

"Why don't you do it?"

Dave pinched a roll of fat on his belly. "Because I'm not as light on my feet as you are."

Nick sighed. He didn't have a problem with going - it made sense. What he had a problem with was Dave thinking he had any right to give him orders.

Nick headed towards the edge of the clearing. "Fine. Everybody wait here."

The ground ahead was free of the roots and undergrowth that had made their progress so laborious over the last few hours and the mud was harder, more compact. It did indeed seem like there was something up ahead.

Nick crouched down and concentrated on what he could hear as well as what he could see, but there was total silence. He could only consider that a positive; the last thing he wanted to hear was the bloodthirsty screech of an infected person.

Beyond the treeline was something large and grey – something manmade. Something solid.

Well, I'll be damned.

The car park was vast and empty. Its several hundred white-lined parking spaces were vacant, the whole area a barren field of weathered concrete. At the near end was a long, single-story building backed up against the base of a very steep and wooded hill.

Nick left the woods and stepped cautiously onto the car park. In addition to the single-story building up ahead was something else that looked like some kind of cable car system. Its thick steel cords stretched from the base of the hill all the way to the lofty summit high above. The dozen or so carriage-cars, hanging from the stretched cables at regular intervals, were antiquated, small and rickety, with bright-red, peeling paintwork. They were also intact and seemingly operational.

A ticket office and embarkation platform had been erected at the foot of the hill. A large, suspended sign read: RIPLEY HEIGHTS AMUSEMENT PARK AND ZOO.

Nick scratched his chin and looked around again. The whole area was deserted. Safe.

Nick quickly headed back up the embankment and re-entered the woods. He needed to tell the others.

"What have we got?" Dave asked Nick when he returned.

"There's a car park and a building. Looks like a café or a fast food place. There's an amusement park nearby, I think, up a steep hill. I haven't seen a single soul and it looks pretty safe. There aren't even any cars in the car park."

"Good work!" Dave patted him on the back like an old buddy – or an obedient son. "Okay, people, let's be cautious and keep our eyes peeled. We may be able to find a phone inside that café. Maybe we can all manage to call home."

There was a muted cheer from the group.

They all headed out of the woods and stepped carefully down the embankment and onto the cracked pavement of the car park. "Ripley Heights," Eve said, almost gasping. "I haven't been here since I was a kid."

Nick looked at her. "You know this place?"

"Yeah, it's a kiddie park. You take the cable car up to the top and there's a petting zoo and some rides. It's all pretty lame, but as a kid I loved it. Surprised the place is still going. It was falling apart ten years ago."

"What's the building up ahead?" he asked her.

She giggled. "The Rainforest Café. Sit with the monkeys and stay all day; you're always welcome at the Rainforest Café. Ha! My dad used to make us all sit inside the café while he and Mom had a coffee. We used to moan because we wanted to go straight to the top and ride the rides. My sister and I hated having to sit patiently while my mum and dad drank that coffee. Kind of miss it now, though. My dad passed away a few years later. Heart disease." She sighed.

Nick knew Eve was wondering whether the rest of her family were alright, so he tried to distract her. "Let's go take a look around before Dave takes over."

The wooden sign for the Rainforest Café had become weathered and frayed and the outside bricks were lined with moss and other weeds. It fitted the buildings theme, however, and merely added to its charm.

Nick peered through the grimy windows and saw two-dozen fibreboard tables surrounded by plastic chairs. At one end of the building's interior was a fast food counter.

"There's no way for us to get inside," Eve said, "and no one inside to let us in."

"We'll break in," Dave said, approaching. "Unless Nick has a better idea."

Nick didn't find reason to object. With all the damage and destruction they'd witnessed on the road, breaking a window seemed little more than spitting in the ocean.

"What can we use?" Eve asked. "This whole place is pretty barren."

"Does anybody have anything hard on them?" Dave asked the group.

Nearby, Dash grabbed his crotch and snickered. "I certainly do, but I don't think you can break glass with it."

"That's gross." Cassie covered her mouth with her hand.

Dash sucked at his teeth. "Come on, darlin, quit playing coy. A fine piece of ass like you must have had her fair share of crotch rockets. If not, allow me to be the first."

Jan slammed a meaty palms into Dash's chest, knocking the smaller man back on his heels. "Take a cold shower or someone will cut it off."

Dash carried on snickering but kept his mouth shut.

"Okay," Dave said, clapping his hands together to get everyone's attention. "Everybody spread. We're looking for a brick or anything else that could help us get inside."

Everybody set off at once. Nick checked over by the cable car station, joined by Pauline, who seemed exhausted.

"How you holding up?" he asked her.

"Well, the only thing keeping me going is the chance that there might be food inside this building. I'm hoping something to eat might stop my stomach churning so much."

Nick hadn't considered the possibility of food, but he realised now that he, too, was famished. "I guess we could all do with an energy boost. What's your favourite food?"

Pauline looked at him. "Really?"

"Yeah, why not? Just making conversation. I can't stand silence. It's so tense that I feel like somebody might spontaneously combust."

Her lips cracked a smile for the first time since he'd met her. "I know what you mean. I don't really have a favourite meal, but if I did, I could guarantee you that I wouldn't find it inside that little burger bar. I like French food, cheese and red wine. Delicious."

Nick pulled a face. "No thank you. I like a big hunk of meat. Nice fat steak or a pork chop. Caveman-style."

He suddenly thought about the steak he was supposed to have eaten last night and felt his stomach roil. The sight of that bloody hunk of meat between his son's teeth...

Pauline noticed his discomfort. "You okay?"

"Yeah, fine. Hey, what's that over there?" He pointed to a pile of debris up ahead. He and Pauline hurried over and started sifting through the mess.

"They do a really bad job of looking after this place," Pauline said as she kicked aside some mushy cardboard.

"I'd guess this place is making a loss," Nick said. "Most places are nowadays."

He moved aside an old wooden pallet, completely rotten underneath. Spiders, woodlice, and other insects scurried from their uncovered hiding places.

Nick found exactly what they needed. He picked up the grubby rock and examined it. It was heavy in his hand, but light enough to throw.

"Perfect," he said, showing Pauline what he had found.

They headed back around to the front and joined up with Jan and the other two prisoners. Nick held the rock out in front of him.

Jan put his hand out to take it. "Give it here and I'll get us in."

Nick handed it over and stepped away. Jan stood in front of the Rainforest Café's window and wound up like an American baseball pitcher and let the rock fly.

The windowpane shattered instantly, showering the ground with shards of glass and making a noise like rain.

They all cringed as the alarm went off.

Dave came sprinting around from the far side of the building. "You stupid shits!" he shouted. "Who told you to do that? You should have waited until I gave the okay."

Nick threw his head back and cursed. "Piss off, Dave."

The bus driver got right in Nick's face. "Piss off? Who the hell do you think you are? You'd still be on the side of the road if it weren't for me."

"We don't have time for this," Pauline shouted over the din. "We have to turn that alarm off before it attracts attention. What if there are infected people nearby?"

"She's right," Jan said. "In one of the towns we passed through, I saw a bunch of infected people head right for a church when its bell started ringing. Attracted every one of them within a two-mile radius. We need to cut the noise right now or they'll be here within minutes."

"Don't worry. I got this." Dash leapt over the window ledge and disappeared inside.

Everyone stood around anxiously, eyeing the treeline. The alarm was loud enough to travel for miles.

"This is not good," Cassie said. "Not good at all."

Carl put an arm around her. "It'll be okay, luv."

Dave stomped back and forth furiously, clenching his fists and clenching his jaw. Jan and Rene were the calmest, waiting patiently and apparently at peace with whatever came.

Nick wished he could be so unflappable. They were all sitting ducks.

The alarm stopped.

Dash appeared at the broken window, holding what looked like a frying pan. He used it to knock loose the remaining shards of glass from the window frame and made it safe to climb through. "Come on in, people," he said with a proud grin.

"Something tells me you've done this before," Nick commented.

"I don't know what you mean, blud. I'm just a man that knows a few things."

"You did good," Dave said. "Is there any way you can get the doors open as well?"

Dash shook his head. "No can do. Any keys would be in the safe and I'm not hot enough to break the locks."

"Then pass us one of those plastic chairs to help us climb over."

Dash got a chair and passed it out to Dave, who set it on the pavement outside. "Okay," he said. "Ladies first."

They sent Margaret over to start. Nick helped her up and Dash helped her back down from inside. Then everybody else followed.

The Rainforest Café's interior was unlit, but not completely dark. The chairs and tables were all neatly stacked and the floors were clean. The place was still operational by the looks of things, although not open for business today.

"Wonder why there's no one here," Pauline said.

Nick answered. "Makes sense when you think about the time this all started. My wife and son were sick before dawn. I'd imagine some people probably took longer, but it's safe to assume that the situation was pretty bad most places by 8AM. The café probably doesn't open until nine or ten, so the staff wouldn't have even started their commute by the time the shit hit the fan."

"I think we can all count ourselves pretty lucky," Dave said. "All of us managed to escape before it got real bad."

"We owe you big time, Dave," Carl said. "I don't know what I would've done if you hadn't picked me up."

Dave puffed out his chest proudly. "Don't mention it."

"Do you think the power is still on?" Cassie asked.

Nick shrugged. "No reason it shouldn't be." He headed for the door that read STAFF ONLY. Beside it was a little incision in the wall. He sighed. "The lights are operated by one of those little fish key thingies."

"Anybody got a hair clip?" Jan asked.

Pauline pulled one from her ponytail and handed it over. Jan jammed it into the small slit and fiddled about. Eventually came an audible click!

The lights flicked on. Everybody cheered.

Dave grinned. "Excellent. Now, let's hunt down a phone."

"There's one through that door," Dash said. "It leads to an office and a staffroom. I saw it when I broke in."

"Excellent," Dave said again. "I'll see if I can reach somebody."

Nick was interested in Dave's plan, so he plonked himself down at one of the tables and slouched forward onto it with his elbows.

His left arm throbbed from multiple bruises and his face stung constantly, but it felt good to sit down indoors. He had been beginning to feel like a nomad, trekking through the land without a destination. It was good to finally stop.

Pauline took a seat next to him. "Hope that alarm didn't bring any attention. I don't think I can face being attacked again."

Nick looked across at the empty car park outside. "I think we got away with it. We might even be able to stay here until the authorities get a handle of things."

"You think they will?"

Nick wanted to be optimistic, but couldn't find the energy to kid himself. "I don't know. I don't even know what there is for them to get a handle on. If those sick people can't be helped...well, let's just say there will be a lot of funerals to arrange. I have some of my own to organise as soon as this is over."

Pauline looked like she was trying to hold back tears. "Oh, how could something like this happen, Nick? It makes no sense."

"Aliens," Carl muttered from the next table over.

Nick frowned. "What?"

"Maybe it was aliens. As good a theory as any. I read once on the Internet that they have this big hole someplace in America called the Spiral that's filled with all sorts of things we don't know about. I bet it was aliens."

Nick groaned. "Come up with something else."

Carl shrugged. "Terrorists, laboratory accident, evil corporations, Mother Nature fighting back. Meteor. God punishing us. What about that cruise ship that went down last month?"

"What about it?"

"Well, something sent that ship down. Maybe terrorists were testing out the virus before they used it on land."

"How do you even think up so many conspiracies?" Pauline asked.

"I watch a lot of films. My point is that something this big doesn't just happen. It's an insane scenario, so it would only make sense that there's an insane cause for it all."

"I guess you're right," Nick said, "but I'd rather keep my feet on the ground and my mind focused for now. No more talk of Aliens. It will just upset people."

"I know exactly what you mean," Carl said, tapping his nose sagely. He looked at Pauline. "You fancy helping me get the grills on, luv? I think everyone could do with some grub. Power's on so there should be no reason we can't get some chow on the go."

Pauline shot up from her seat. "Sounds good to me. I'm bleedin' starving."

Nick laughed and watched them wander off into the kitchen. His smile faded as he remembered all of the reasons not to be happy.

The staff door flew open with what sounded like a kick. Dave re-entered and was shaking his head, seeming right pissed off.

"What is it?" Nick asked him.

"The phones are completely dead. There's not even a dial tone."

Nick rubbed at his forehead and sighed. "I'm beginning to think there's no help to even call for."

"Nonsense! The police must be dealing with this. Probably the army, too. They'll come eventually."

Nick considered it. It was a possibility, but they had no way of knowing. "Maybe they'll come," he admitted, "but what do you plan on doing in the meantime?"

"We can stay here, keep trying the phones."

"Alright, then we should get that broken window covered up or we're all going to freeze tonight."

Dave nodded, his jowls wobbling. "Good idea. Please get right on that." Then he turned on his heel and marched away.

Nick snapped off a petulant salute. "Right, away, sir."

He got up and headed through the STAFF ONLY door at the back and started searching for materials. The tiled hallway smelt faintly of lemon and bleach and the chemical odour tickled Nick's sinuses almost into a sneeze.

On his right was an open door leading to a small staffroom and sofa. Straight ahead was a door marked MANAGER'S OFFICE. Nick entered that room and looked around. An old CRT monitor perched on a desk and a heavy safe took up the wall behind it. Beside the monitor was a telephone, which Nick picked up and held to his ear. Like Dave had said, the line was completely dead. He didn't know why he'd felt the need to double-check.

On one of the walls was a large corkboard. It was definitely big enough to cover the broken window in the restaurant. Nick pulled it down and took it outside. Five minutes later, with the help of Jan and Rene, the large corkboard covered the broken window, held snugly in place by a couple of tables stacked up against it.

"That should keep the wind out," Jan said.

Nick nodded. "Hopefully. It isn't the wind that worries me, though."

Jan patted him on the back with a meaty slap. "Long as we lay low, I can't see any danger."

"Long as nobody makes the mistake of sneezing or coughing, you mean? Else you and Dave will smash their skull in."

Jan gave Nick a look that suddenly made him feel threatened. "Listen, brother," Jan said to him. "I may be a lot of things, but I'm not a killer. That lady was already dead. I believe that truly. Poor Kathryn is probably wandering around in those woods right this second, a raving loony looking to kill. There was nothing any of us could do for her except ease her suffering. Dave was trying to do her a favour."

Nick huffed. "Funny, because it seemed to me like Kathryn was begging for her life. She didn't sound grateful for any favours."

Jan shoved Nick aside, sending him sprawling into the wall. "You seem to be forgetting I came around to your way of thinking in the end. Maybe next time I'll just go with my gut, whether you like it or not."

Jan stomped away like an angry giant leaving Nick to think about things. It was true that Jan had not been the one who had tried to kill Kathryn, but he was the one who had suggested it. He was a criminal when all was said and done. But he had sided with Nick when it counted, and Nick had chided him all the same. It felt like a big mistake.

CHAPTER 10

IT TURNED OUT that Carl and Pauline were able to rustle up quite the feast. A large freezer in the kitchen contained burger patties, hot dogs, mini-pizzas, and bags of frying chips. With a little bit of fiddling they'd managed to switch on the fat fryers and griddles, and within the hour everyone was eating more than they needed.

Nick felt bloated, but found that the act of eating cathartic. It allowed him to blank his mind of its troubles while he focused on a basic human need. At his table were Eve, Margaret, and Pauline. Carl, Cassie, and Rene sat at another table, while Jan, Dash, and Dave sat at a third. The women at Nick's table all looked deeply satisfied as they finished off their French fries. They also had a variety of soft drinks in front of them, which they slurped readily, except for Margaret who was drinking piping hot tea. It felt like luxury. The day had been undeniably long.

"Nothing seems as bad after a good brew," Margaret said. "It can get you through anything."

Eve wiped her mouth with a napkin. "I bet you've seen some things in your lifetime, Margaret."

"I have at that. Not nothing like this, though. This is Hell on Earth."

"You think it's the same everywhere?" Pauline asked, rubbing at her eyes and smudging her make-up.

Margaret nodded. "I do. There seems to be something very deliberate about all this. How could things degenerate so completely without being planned? Should we believe that there weren't any doctors who picked this up early? That the Government had no warning at all? If that's the case, this is either the work of very powerful enemies or a very angry God. And neither of those would release something this destructive solely on Britain."

"So you think it's happening in other countries, too?" Nick asked.

"At least in the Western world. If it were terrorists, as an example, they would have far more to gain by releasing this in America and mainland Europe as well as the UK. It would be a waste to focus it only on our tiny island. The spread of the disease would halt at our natural barriers – the coastline."

While Nick thought about Margaret's words, Dave took the opportunity to address everybody. He cleared his throat before he began. "Perhaps now would be a good opportunity for us to get some rest; see what tomorrow brings. We can turn off the lights and bed down wherever we can. Margaret, you can have the sofa in the staffroom."

"Thank you."

"We can hold a meeting in the morning to figure out what our next move will be, although I would suggest staying here until help finds us. Agreed?"

With no one taking exception, the group began shuffling around as they each tried to find somewhere soft to lie down. Margaret headed for the staffroom to claim her sofa while Dave claimed the tall-backed leather chair in the manager's office. Nick decided to roll up his coat as a pillow and just bed down on the restaurant floor. Eve and Pauline did the same, lying down a few feet from him. The two women were beginning to feel like his responsibility. Or maybe it was just friendship developing that made him feel that way.

The three prisoners huddled up in the corner of the restaurant, making a bed from some aprons they'd found in the kitchen. Carl and Cassie separated off to sleep in the kitchen. Nick wondered if they'd formed a relationship throughout the day's events, as they had become inseparable in the last hours. Carl was at least ten years older.

Nick lay back on his rolled-up coat and stared up at the suspended ceiling. The lights were off and moonlight spilled in through the windows. If it wasn't for all the bloodshed, one might even have described the night as beautiful. Deana would have found it romantic, bedding down on the floor beneath the moonlight.

I miss you, Deana...

Nick closed his eyes and listened to the silence for what seemed like hours until, finally, the silence was replaced by the dozing snores of his companions. The last thing he heard before sleep was a soft whimpering coming from Eve as she struggled with the unseen terrors of her dreams.

* * *

Nick was back home again, standing in his kitchen as if nothing had happened. Deana stood in front of the sink with her back to him. She was washing dishes. The cooker was on, a spitting steak cooking over the flames.

James lay on the tiles in the centre of the kitchen, staring up at the ceiling blankly.

Nick moved towards his son, tried to speak to him and tell him to get up, but no sound came out of his mouth. When Nick pressed his fingers to his own face he realised it was because he had no lips. Only coarse scar tissue lay where his mouth should have been.

Deana turned around and faced Nick and she too was mouthless. Her eyes were wet with blood and crimson tears stained her cheeks. She held a claw hammer, which she offered to him now.

Nick was powerless as he reached out and took it. He held the heavy hammer in his hand and stared at it. Then he turned involuntarily on his heels as if suspended by invisible wires.

He knelt beside James's body.

No, Nick wanted to shout, but could not.

James continued to stare up at the ceiling, blinking occasionally, but never moving.

Nick raised the hammer, staring into his son's eyes the entire time, and then brought it down with everything he had. The aluminium head struck James right between the eyes, caving in the front of his skull.

Nick vomited, but with no lips, he was forced to choke on it.

He raised the hammer again and this time struck James in the mouth, shattering his baby teeth into tiny shards.

James choked and spluttered. Nick hit him again and shattered his jaw.

Nick wanted to die.

But he raised the hammer again.

Over and over, Nick swung the hammer, spraying blood and bone fragments, until there was nothing left of his son's face but bloody pulp.

He looked over at Deana desperately, pleadingly. Deana looked at him. This time she held a carving knife. Powerless, Nick stood up and took it from her.

When he turned back around, James's face was back to normal, untouched by the vicious blows of the hammer. He continued staring up at the ceiling.

Nick knelt back down beside his son and got back to work.

* * *

Nick's eyes flew open. He was surrounded by darkness, a floating gloom. When he saw the moon through the windows, he remembered where he was – he remembered everything.

He sat up a little too quickly and thought he was going to throw up. Then he saw that the lights were on in the kitchen and could hear something too. Eve and Pauline were still sleeping nearby; their shapes clear even in the darkness.

Who was in the kitchen?

The sounds continued.

Nick got up quietly and crept towards the kitchen. He thought he heard someone weeping. He kept his footsteps careful and stepped behind the counter, sliding between the lined-up cookers and lengths of countertops. At the far end of the kitchen was an L-shaped corridor. The noises were coming from around the bend.

Nick sped up and rounded the corner quickly, not wanting to be too late to help if someone was in danger. He found Carl lying facedown on the floor. Then he spotted Jan standing over Cassie, who was cowering on the floor without her shirt.

Jan's eyes widened when he noticed Nick and he quickly raised his hands in submission. "This isn't what it looks like, brother."

Nick snarled. "You have no idea what this fucking looks like." He looked down at Cassie and shook his head in disgust. "Cassie, it's okay. Come over here to me."

For a second it looked like she might refuse, but then she clambered on her hands and knees until she was safely behind him.

Jan looked Cassie in the eyes, even as she cowered behind Nick. "You remember what we spoke about, sweetheart, okay?"

"You don't talk to her," Nick spat. "You don't say a word to her, you understand me?"

"You got this all wrong, brother."

"The only thing I got wrong was letting a bunch of criminals tag along with us. Soon as the sun's up, you're gone. When the others hear about this they're going to lynch you."

Jan laughed, his chest heaving. "Who is? You and Dave? Don't make me shit myself!"

Nick shoved Jan angrily, but found himself swatted aside like a measly fly. Jan punched Nick in the ribs and sent him to his knees, gasping for breath. His lungs felt like they might explode.

Jan shoved Nick backwards with his boot, before glaring right in his face. "We'll talk about this in the morning and we'll see who gets lynched."

Then the big man walked away, cursing under his breath.

Nick managed to catch a strangled breath a few moments later, followed by another. He rolled onto his side and shuddered in pain. He'd never felt so sure he would die, so impossible had it been to take a single breath.

After a while, Cassie helped Nick back to his feet. Her shirt was rolled up on the floor and she hastily put it back on and as she did so she seemed to remember that Carl was still facedown on the floor. She dropped to her knees beside him and patted his cheeks. "Carl, wake up. Carl..."

Carl moaned, his eyes fluttering open slowly. "W-what happened? My head feels like a Skoda parked on it."

"I think you got struck from behind," Nick explained. "It was Jan."

"Motherfu—"

"Don't worry about it for now," Cassie said soothingly. "We can talk about it tomorrow. Let's just get some sleep."

Together, Nick and Cassie picked Carl up off the floor. He was still pretty out of it, but was gradually regaining his senses.

"What the hell happened?" Nick whispered to Cassie, determined to get to the bottom of things.

She shook her head. "Nothing. Don't worry about it."

"Jesus, Cassie. Don't listen to that son of a bitch. He can't hurt you. It's okay, you're safe. You can tell me what happened."

Cassie huffed as they laid Carl on the floor beside the service counter. "None of us are safe anymore. We're all screwed."

Nick didn't want to argue and Cassie obviously didn't want to talk about what had happened, at least not yet. "Okay," he conceded. "Get some sleep, then, and we'll talk about it in the morning. Don't go wandering off anywhere, okay? Stay close."

Nick headed back to his spot between Eve and Pauline. He looked for Jan and the other prisoners and saw the three of them huddled together by the restaurant's exit doors. Jan seemed to be having a heated discussion with Dash, but both lowered their voices when they noticed Nick looking at them.

Nick looked away and settled back down at his spot on the floor. He winced as he lay back down on his coat. His breathing was still laboured after Jan's gut punch. The guy was big – huge – and if it came down to violence Nick wasn't confident what the outcome would be.

"Hey," Eve whispered to him. "What's going on?"

"Nothing," Nick lied. "I'll tell you about it in the morning. Just don't go anywhere in the night without letting me know first."

Eve shuffled across the floor so that she was only inches from him. "Okay," she said. "Same goes for you. No sneaking off again without telling me first."

"Deal."

Nick stared up at the ceiling and wondered what the morning would bring.

CHAPTER 11

THE ALARM WOKE everyone.

Nick leapt to his feet in an instant, spinning around, disorientated and confused. Panicked.

"What's happening?" Eve cried out.

"I don't know. Something tripped the alarms." Nick grabbed his coat from the floor and shoved it on quickly.

"I thought Dash turned them off," Pauline shouted.

Nick saw that Dash, Jan, and Rene were still huddled in the corner by the doors. They seemed just as confused as everybody else, but that didn't mean they knew nothing about what was happening.

He marched over to the prisoners and pointed his finger at them. "Did you do this?"

Dash shook his head. "Do what, honkey? Why would we set off the alarms?"

"I can't imagine why you do most of the things you do. Why is it going off again? I thought you disconnected it?"

"Nah, man. I just smashed up the console and shut off the intruder alert. The alarm is still intact. I just cut the link between the broken window and the siren. It was an ancient piece of shit. Piece of cake."

"So what set it off again?"

Dave stormed out of the 'STAFF ONLY' door, shouting and cursing. "Why is the alarm going off again? And why is the power off?"

"There's your answer," Dash said. "If the power went out, the security system probably went over to a battery system. It tripped the alarm all over again."

Nick sighed. "So what do we do?"

"Disconnect the battery power and the whole system will be dead."

"We need to do it quickly before any infected people find us."

"Nick?" Eve tapped him on the shoulder.

"Not now, Eve."

"Nick!"

He shot her an irritated glance. "What?"

"I think we should forget about the alarm."

Nick spun around to argue, but quickly found himself stunned.

Standing at the many windows of the café, peering in with their bloodshot, swollen eyes, were dozens of infected people. Hundreds of them.

Carl shook his head frantically. "What the fuck are we going to do now? Game over man! Game over."

The mob of infected burst through the windows as one. Their bodies tumbled over the ledge clumsily, embedding themselves with shards of glass and hitting the floor in piles. They were like ants crawling over one another.

The room was closing in.

"Everybody get out of here!" Nick screamed. "Run for it!"

Everybody bolted, but there was no way out of the restaurant – all the doors and windows were blocked by the infected – so they made instinctively for the only barrier they could find: the fast food service counter.

"Into the kitchen," Carl yelled. "There's a fire exit at the back. I saw it last night."

Everybody funnelled together and raced towards the back of the kitchen.

The infected screeched as they gave chase clambering over the counter behind them.

When Carl led the group around the bend to the fire exit, Jan leapt up in the air and kicked the push-bar across it and sent the door flying open.

The air rushed in from outside, crisp and cold.

"Everyone outside," Dave shouted.

Jan held the door open and ushered everyone passed him. The infected were teeming into the kitchen and coming right at them.

Nick held back and made sure everybody got out. He realised someone was missing.

"Shit!" he exclaimed. "I have to get Margaret. She'll still be in the staffroom."

"Leave her," Dave said. "You've got no way to reach her."

Nick stood, tempted to fight his way back through the restaurant, but the infected were everywhere and one bite was all it took.

Jan yanked Nick and tossed him through the door before Dave slammed it shut behind them. The infected mob clattered against the other side, beating at it furiously.

"We have to go," Dave said to everyone gathered around the back of the café,

Nick shook his head. "We can't just leave Margaret behind. She might still be alive in there."

"Don't be a fool. You can't risk your life for an old woman."

"She went back for her friend, Ethel. She deserves someone to go back for her."

"You do whatever you have to," Dave said, "but the rest of us are getting out of here while we still can."

Eve looked at Nick pleadingly. "He's right. We have to get out of here before they find us. You can't help Margaret."

Nick couldn't bear the thought of leaving the old woman behind. He had already gotten Jake killed when the lad had tried to help him. He had to do something to even the books. "You go with everyone else," he told Eve. "I'll catch up with you."

"No way, Nick. You have to come with us."

"I will. Just get going and I'll catch up. I promise." Eve started to argue but he cut her off. "Just go!"

The argument over with, everyone clambered up the hill behind the cafe, before heading for the woods they'd come from the day before. Nick watched them go, but was surprised to see that Jan did not go with them.

"What the hell are you doing? Get out of here, Jan."

"I figured you could use a hand."

"I'm not sure I trust you to help me."

"Well, maybe the old dear trapped inside would like my help. You selfish enough to turn me away when a woman's life is at stake?"

"Fine, let's just do this."

Nick pressed his back against the building. There was no way back inside the fire exit, and even if there was it was suicide, but the staffroom had a window. If Nick could find it, he might be able to get Margaret out. If she had stayed put inside.

Jan followed Nick as he moved cautiously around the building. The keening pitch of the security alarm was deafening, making it impossible to hear what was going on around the next corner.

"Be careful," Jan told him. "The infected people see you and they come at you like heat-seeking missiles."

"I know. I've seen enough of them."

Slowly, inch-by-inch, Nick leaned around the corner.

"Damn it!" he grunted. "There must be at least a dozen of them around there."

Jan scratched his beard. "I have an idea."

"What idea?"

Jan glanced up at the cafe's roof. "It's a single story," he said. "With a boost, I should be able to get up there and create a distraction for you."

"Yeah, great idea. How do you get down afterwards without them getting you?"

Jan shrugged. "One thing at a time, brother. You in?"

Nick shrugged. "If you're crazy enough to do it."

He threaded his fingers and made a platform for Jan to step on, then hoisted him up.

"Jesus Christ, you weigh the same as an elephant."

Jan dangled and then heaved himself up. "Only two things to do in prison," he said. "Educate one's mind and exercise one's body. You ready? I'll try to get them to follow me to the other end of the building."

Nick nodded. "You know we're still going to have to have that conversation about what happened to Cassie last night?"

"Looking forward to it," Jan said, then raced to the opposite side of the roof.

Nick waited for the distraction. Then got it.

"COME ON, YOU STINKING ARSEHOLES. COME GET IT!"

Nick peeked around the corner and saw the infected disappear as they rushed to the other side of the building. The coast was clear.

Nick hurried around the side of the building, peering inside each window as he passed. After looking into the kitchen and then into the manager's office, he found the window that led to the staffroom.

There was no sign of Margaret.

He tapped on the glass lightly. "Margaret! Margaret, are you in there?"

Margaret suddenly appeared from her hiding place behind the room's sofa.

Nick sighed with relief.

"They're inside," Margaret said to him through the glass. "I can hear them."

"I know, they're everywhere. Open the window and I'll get you out of here."

Margaret was white as a sheet, but she did as she was told. She fiddled with the window latch and managed to slide it upwards. Nick held his arms out to her and she clambered through. It was clearly a struggle but she managed to get herself into Nick's waiting arms.

Jan continued to heckle the infected from the rooftop. "COME ON, YOU PANSIES. YOU WANT A PIECE OF MY ASS; YOU NEED TO WORK FOR IT.

The coast remained clear.

Nick grabbed Margaret by the arm and hurried her to the back of the building before heading into the woods. When they were sufficiently far enough away from the café and car park, they stopped to catch their breath.

Jan still shouted curses from the rooftop. Nick wasn't sure he could've got Margaret out without the other man's help.

He placed a hand on Margaret's shoulder. "I need to find a way to get Jan off that roof in one piece. Can you wait here?"

"Of course, just make sure you come back in one piece, young man. I've grown rather fond of you."

Nick patted her shoulder gently and then headed back through the trees. Once at the treeline, he could see Jan still standing on top of the roof, waving his muscly arms above his head and hollering at the mob of infected below. Jan probably didn't even know that Nick and Margaret had already got away.

With the alarm still wailing, Nick could think of no subtle way to get Jan's attention, other than whistling. Luckily, Jan heard it and turned around.

Nick crouched in the bushes and waved a hand. Jan spotted him and gave a thumbs-up. The expression on his face was an obvious, now what? Nick had no clue. Getting Jan off the roof safely was not going to be easy.

He crept out of the bushes and headed for the rear of the building. The only way he could help Jan get down was if he took his turn distracting the mob, so he headed around the side of the building and went back to the open staffroom window. First checking that no infected people had found their way inside the room, he climbed through.

The only weapon he could find was an abandoned umbrella that wasn't even worth taking. He would have nothing with which to defend himself.

The alarm was muffled from inside the staffroom but Nick could make out the shuffling of infected feet in the corridor outside. If he opened the door, Nick would be face-to-face with a murderous horde.

Then, suddenly, Nick had an idea. He hopped up on the sofa and balanced on the backrest. From there he was able to push up against one of the foam ceiling tiles. They wouldn't be strong enough to hold his weight, but the metal railings fixing them in place might be.

He leapt up and grabbed at one of the rails and held on. It bent beneath his weight but then held firm. Kicking at the wall for leverage, Nick managed to clamber his way up into the ceiling space. It allowed unrestricted access from one end of the building to the other. It was a struggle to move along the railings, and the exertion was quickly exhausting, but Nick kept going. Inch by inch, he shuffled through the crawlspace until he was where he felt he wanted to be.

He pulled aside a tile and peeked through the gap. In the corridor below were half-a-dozen infected people. They milled about like hungry birds searching for insects, all twitchy movements and sudden flinches. They barely resembled human beings anymore. Yet they were not dead, only infected.

Nick carefully replaced the ceiling tile and continued along the railings. He had to keep his face down, chin-to-chest, as age-old insulation and dust swirled around him and threatened to make him choke or sneeze.

Eventually he stopped where he imagined the restaurant floor to be and carefully positioned himself astride two parallel rails. They groaned a little. He took a deep breath and prepared himself, then smashed his fist into one of the ceiling tiles and sent it plummeting to the floor. A couple of infected people immediately stared upwards and screeched.

"Hey!" Nick shouted through the gap in the ceiling. "Come and get it, you...you knobheads!"

The screech of the infected in the restaurant brought others near. They funnelled in from the corridors and kitchen areas, and even started pouring in through the windows from outside. It wasn't long before the Rainforest Café was once again packed with infected people. Eventually Nick was satisfied that he had them all. So many of them were now packed inside that their collective screeching was enough to drown out the alarm.

Nick pulled himself back up into the ceiling and swivelled around on the railings, ready to return to the staffroom.

He fell.

The railings bent beneath Nick bent and then sagged. The screech of the infected below grew more ravenous as he slipped towards them.

Nick grabbed hold of the sagging rails as best he could, wrapping his arms around them as he dangled perilously.

The rails continued to groan, but they ceased to bend any further. Nick started to pull himself back up. The infected directly beneath him leapt upwards, snatching at his ankles and trying to bring him down.

Nick felt his arms tire, his muscles freeze. He groaned as the effort became unbearable; but he did not stop until he had made it back up into the ceiling space. He quickly flattened himself across several rails and was sure that he was once again safe. A delirious giggle escaped his lips.

He quickly headed back to the staffroom, mindful to make as little noise as possible. His intention was for the infected to remain in the restaurant, glaring up at where they'd seen him last.

Nick dropped down into the staffroom and doubled-over with exhaustion, but there was no time to dawdle. He raced towards the open window and threw himself through it. As soon as his feet hit the ground, he let out another quick whistle, hoping to get Jan's attention.

Jan appeared at the back edge of the roof. "They've all gone back inside," he said.

Nick nodded. "Get down. We need to go."

Jan hopped down off the roof and the two of them raced into the treeline and headed towards the woods.

"D'you think the others will have waited?" Jan asked him as they cut a path along the base of the steep hill.

"I doubt it," Nick said. "Dave pretty much said that he wouldn't hang around. Damn it!"

Nick skidded to a halt.

Jan stopped too and looked worried. "What is it?"

"Margaret. I told her to wait here for me. Where is she?"

"I'm sure she's here somewhere."

Nick turned a circle, scanning the trees that surrounded them, but there was no sign of the old lady.

Crack!

"What was that?" Nick said.

Jan crouched down and grabbed a branch. "I don't know, brother. I think we should keep moving."

"Nick? Nick, are you okay?"

Nick couldn't help but grin. "Eve! What are you doing out here on your own?"

"I came to find you. The others are going to move on if you're not back in ten minutes."

"You need to stop coming to my rescue," Nick said, still smiling. "Where's the group now? Do they have Margaret?"

"Yes, she's with us."

"Thank God," Jan said.

"We should head up the hill," Nick said. "It might be safe up there."

"Dave said it would be a waste of energy climbing all the way up the hill. He's taking everyone back the way we came in."

Jan shrugged his giant shoulders. "Up, down, left, right, I don't care. Let's just catch up to them before they leave us behind."

They got moving, Eve leading the way. The screeches and wails of the infected stopped as the restaurant's security alarm finally died out and they eventually realised Nick was no longer there. Now the only sound was the pounding of feet, the panting of breath, and the snapping of twigs.

Eve pointed. "They're down there."

At the bottom of the hill, Dave and the others were gathered in a tight bunch. Margaret waved at Nick as they approached. "Thank Heaven's you're okay," she said once they were close enough.

Nick gave Margaret a quick hug.

Dave folded his arms impatiently. "We were just about to give up on you."

"Thanks for waiting," Jan said. "What's the plan?"

"We head back into the woods where we started out. We know it's clear of infected because it was clear when we came through."

"So was the car park," Carl said, "but it's had a few visitors since."

Dave glowered. "That was the alarm. It brought them to us overnight."

"But Dash managed to turn the alarm off after only a couple of minutes," Eve said. "Was that all it took?"

"They must have just kept heading in the same direction," Nick said. "Even once the alarm stopped."

"Damn, those sick fucks are relentless," Dash said.

"Let's just get moving," Jan said. "It's only a matter of time before one of them buggers stumbles on us. We're exposed out-"

Carl screamed.

So did everyone else.

"It's that bitch," Dave shouted in alarm.

"Oh hells no," Dash added.

Kathryn had Carl on the ground and was trying to sink her teeth into him. Her face was swollen with the bruises Dave had given her, but her eyes were now bulbous red orbs threatening to pop out of her skull. Blood poured from her mouth, so thickly that it was like her insides were melting.

"Help me!" Carl cried out from the floor. "Somebody get her off m—"

Kathryn's teeth sunk into Carl's throat and cut of his voice, ripping away his carotid artery and chewing on it like a length of sausage.

Cassie cried out. "Carl, no!"

She went to run to him, but Eve grabbed her and pulled her back. "He's already gone."

"Look out!" Dash shouted.

Several metres away, coming at them like a charging bull, was Jake.

"He must have heard the alarm," Nick said.

"Everybody run," Dave bellowed.

No one hesitated. They stampeded back onto the car park, bursting back out of the treeline and spilling onto the cracked concrete; but they skidded immediately to a halt.

Several of the infected had now exited the Rainforest Café and were now back outside. Jake and Kathryn's screeching had alerted them.

"There's nowhere to run," Eve cried. "We're surrounded."

Jake and Kathryn were coming up behind them. Dozens of infected people came at them from the front, more piling out of the rainforest café to join them.

Nick looked around desperately for an option. "There!" he pointed. "Head for the cable cars."

The group sprinted across the car park. The infected clattered across the pavement towards them. Nick didn't know if they had any chance of making it. They were running for their lives, so fast that he worried his legs might fail at any second. The infected would be on them any second.

"Quickly," he shouted. "Into the cable cars."

On the raised cement platform, only two cars were accessible. They were too small to accommodate the entire group, so they were forced to split up. Nick leapt into the nearest car, followed by Cassie and the three prisoners. The rest of the group were lagging further behind and barely managed to make their way inside the remaining car before the infected reached the platform.

Nick yanked the sliding door shut and watched through the plastic windows as Dave did the same in the other car. It was then that he realised something horrible: Margaret wasn't inside either car. Nick looked out across the car park and spotted the old lady stumbling across the pavement.

"You won't make it in time, brother," Jan told him. "Her nine lives are up."

"We only just saved her."

But it was definitely too late. The infected engulfed her like a swarm of flesh-eating locusts. They pulled her arms at unnatural angles, snapping her fragile bones and sinking their teeth into her tissue-paper skin. She came apart like freshly baked bread.

Nick closed his eyes.

The infected hit the cable cars like a storm, rocking the vehicles on their hooks and pinballing everyone inside.

"There's no way these cars are going to hold," Jan said, climbing up off his knees.

"We be screwed, honkey," Dash shouted at Nick. "Great plan."

The infected bashed their fists against the car's plastic windows, loosening them in their frames. One of the infected – a plump Asian man reminding Nick of his co-worker, Paul – got his fingers inside the sliding door and started to work it back and forth on its hinges.

The occupants of the other car were equally doomed. Eve stared over at Nick with pleading terror in her eyes, but he couldn't bear to look at her. If only he had left her in that cupboard. He hadn't rescued her, he'd doomed her.

Eve began to move. Not just Eve, but the entire cable car she was in. Nick stumbled and realised he was moving too. The cars were operational, climbing the cable up the hill.

Tears were streaming down Cassie's face. "What's happening? Why are we moving?"

"Someone switched on the cable cars," Nick could only assume. "They saved us."

They were climbing out of danger, rising up where the infected could not reach them.

Except for one.

The plump Asian hung from the cable car's door and had already managed to get one of his arms through the widening gap. He clawed at the passengers inside.

Nick kicked at the infected man's arm, but the blow had no effect. He just snarled at them and clawed even more furiously.

"Screw this," Jan said. He stood up against the far wall and then leapt forward, delivering a hefty kick to the centre of the cabin's metal door. Its rusty hinges gave way and the entire sheet of metal, along with its infected hanger-on, went plummeting to the treetops below.

Nick peered out the open doorway in shock and watched as the Asian man cartwheeled through the canopy of branches a hundred feet below, disappearing towards the ground.

"They don't give up, do they?" Nick said, more to himself than anyone else. "It's like they don't feel pain."

"Everything feels pain, honkey," Dash told him, sounding almost philosophical.

Nick didn't think that was true. The infected did not feel pain. They felt only rage and hunger and maybe hate. They were animals, monsters, demons...zombies. Nick finally accepted that the infected were beyond saving and that life had become about survival. No one could hope to make it through the days ahead and remain the people they were before. They would be forced to adapt, or they would die.

James and Deana were gone. Nick's entire life was gone. He wasn't sure what was left.

He gazed down at the treetops as the car leisurely climbed the hill. Now that the snarling mob at the bottom of the hill was out of sight, the view was actually quite beautiful. The woods went on forever; autumn-coloured leaves a never-ending swirl of orange and red. It was a peaceful moment, and Nick knew that it might just be his last peaceful moment he would ever have.

Something hit Nick from behind and he was thrown violently to the humming floor of the cable car.

He shook his head, dazed and confused. "What the hell?"

Jan and Dash stood over him as Cassie whimpered in the corner. "Time to die, honkey. Whatever this place is, it belongs to us."

Dash was about to kick Nick in the face, but was stopped short when Jan hammered him in the ribs with a fist, knocking the wind out of him in a startled wail.

Then Jan shoved Dash backwards, right through the open doorway, where he fell into thin air and was gone.

"What the hell did you just do?" Nick screamed, leaping up to his feet.

"Saved your life," Jan said. "Dash was about to send you on your merry way. Ask Cassie."

Nick looked at Cassie who was fidgeting on the bench. "He's telling the truth," she said. "He was going to push you out until Jan saved you."

"What? But why? Why would he want to kill me?"

Jan huffed as if the answer were obvious. "Because he tried to take liberties with Cassie last night and you weren't going to let it stand. In fact, he was planning to get rid of Dave, too."

"I don't understand," Nick said, moving away from the open doorway. "Weren't you his friend?"

"Dash? That gangbanging piece of shit? No way. I just got stuck with him when the prison guards were killed and our transport was sprung." He pointed at Rene, who was continued to remain silent. "Rene's not a problem, but Dash was a degenerate. I've seen him do some really reprehensible things the last forty-eight hours. Me and Rene were already looking to ditch him when we ran into you and Eve in the woods."

Nick looked at Cassie and frowned. "So, Jan didn't, you know, hurt you?"

She shook her head. "No. Carl and I were fooling around in the kitchen. He was on top of me when something hit him from behind. It was Dash. He came at me and tore off my shirt. Then Jan came and stopped him."

Jan said, "I saw Dash go to the kitchen. I knew he'd be up to no good so I went after him. Caught him red-handed trying to force himself on poor Cassie. I told him to get his ass back to the restaurant before I beat the living hell out of him. Usually he's not the type of guy to back down, but I think he understood I wasn't playing around. Then you turned up, brother, and got the wrong idea."

Nick stared at Cassie. "Why didn't you tell me at the time?"

"Jan told me he would deal with Dash, but I had to keep quiet, otherwise Dash would hurt more people."

"Dash was going to take you out before you had chance to bring it up," Jan said. "He planned to deal with Dave and Carl too eventually, so that he could hole up with the women at the restaurant and be top dog. He was no different in prison, only there were no women."

"You told him you'd help him kill me," Nick guessed. "Jesus."

"Of course I told him that, but I planned to take him out first, or at least try to ditch him someplace. Then the alarm went off and everything took on a life of its own. It wasn't until we started climbing this hill that an opportunity presented itself for Dash to kill you, so I intervened and killed him. You can thank me later."

"I'll thank you now," Nick said. "I owe you, Jan."

"Don't sweat it."

"No." Nick was adamant. "I judged you wrong. I treated you like a criminal and that was unfair."

"I am a criminal," Jan said. "It was perfectly rational. Truthfully, I was a rotten piece of shit for a good chunk of my life. Even my own son, Damien, didn't want anything to do with me. Haven't seen him in years and I don't want to reinsert myself into his life. I think losing the respect of my son was what made me finally decide to sort myself out – and that's exactly what I did. One day I'll find my boy and make things right. I'll tell him I'm proud of him for finding his own way.

"Prison changed you?" Nick said.

"After eight years inside, my intentions have been pure for at least the last five. I'm not the same man I was when they put me inside, but that's a story for a different day."

"I hope I get to hear it," Nick said honestly.

The cable car reached the final third of its ascent and Nick squinted up at the approaching summit. It was hard to be sure, but he thought he could see someone standing there, ready to receive them. That person must have been the one who had started the cable cars. The one who had saved their lives.

That person was their saviour.

But who the hell were they and what were they doing at the top of the hill?

28 HOURS EARLIER

ANNA WASHED HER hands in the steel sink and watched the blood drain away. The birth had been a success. Rita, one of the zoo's Clydesdale horses, had delivered a healthy 80lb foal and seemed to be recovering well. Now that it was over, she was looking forward to getting home and resuming sleep she'd been woken from at 3AM.

"That went really well, I thought," Bradley said to her. He was Ripley Height's resident veterinary nurse and it was he who'd called Anna when Rita went into labour.

Anna smiled at the boy and stifled a yawn. "Y-yes, completely by the book. Make sure Rita allows her foal to suckle, but other than that, nature should take care of itself."

Bradley beamed. "It was pretty bloody amazing, to tell the truth. It was my first birth."

"You'll see many more working at a zoo." She spotted a flake of blood beneath her nail. "It loses its charm."

"So...are you going home now?"

"Too blooming right I am. I'm exhausted. I'd only been in bed a few hours when I got your call."

"One of the downsides of being a vet on-call, huh?"

"I need my sleep. Always have."

"Sorry I had to wake you. I couldn't have done it without you, though. You were amazing."

"No problem." She gave her hands one last rinse in the sink and put on her cardigan. "I'll be back Wednesday to do a check-up. Will you be here?"

"I'll be around. As usual. Seven days a week, eighteen hours a day. I love the work."

Anna admired Bradley for living on the park's grounds – he was young and eager to gain experience – but she thought he'd be better off having some semblance of a life as well.

"You should get out more," she told him. "You'll end up working yourself to death before you're thirty. You need to find a balance between work and life."

He shrugged. "I enjoy it. Tell you the truth, I like spending time with animals more than I do people. Sad, huh?"

"Yeah, very sad, but I know what you mean." She really did understand the tranquillity being around animals brought. It was unhealthy to retreat from people entirely, though. "Get yourself out on the town. Grab a drink and a girl. Be irresponsible for a night."

"You fancy going with me?" Bradley asked, his cheeks instantly growing red.

Anna spluttered. "Me? I'm ten years older than you. You can find better company than an old woman like me."

"I don't think so. I'd like to get to know you better. Besides, you're like what...thirty-two."

Add another three years and you'd still be a year short, Anna thought to herself. She was surprised. She'd had no idea that Bradley thought of her in that way. She didn't know what to say or how to feel about it. It had been years since she'd dated.

"I...I'll think about it, Bradley," she said, and perhaps she would. The boy wasn't without charm or looks. "See you Wednesday."

Anna headed out of the stable's washroom and into the corridor that reeked of oiled leather and horse piss. Rita was lain down in her stall, cleaning her mewing foal with her probing tongue. The stallion, Cassius, was in the stall beside her.

The dawn chill pinched her cheeks and invigorated her a little, but it didn't stop her from rubbing at the fuzziness behind her eyelids. Her watch read 6AM. She was almost dead on her feet.

The real reason she'd gotten so little sleep wasn't the call-out, it was because she'd passed out drunk, alone in her flat, at 2AM. She hadn't even made it to the bed. It was the same way she ended most evenings. Especially when it was an anniversary.

She gave her shoulders a vigorous rub and got going. The sun balanced on the horizon, ready to leap into the sky. The various enclosures of the petting zoo were filled with sleeping animals that would soon wake or nocturnal creatures that would soon sleep. The silence of the night would soon give way to the snuffling of pigs and the bleating of goats.

Up ahead were the zoo's only truly exotic inhabitants: a small family of orang-utans. Anna imagined the park owners had seen them as a lucrative tourist attraction. It was an immoral way to view such magnificent creatures, but at least time and money had been spent ensuring they were given a suitable habitat. The half-acre plot at Ripley Heights was one of the best in the country and the original pair of apes had happily produced an infant, now one-year old.

The female, Lily, was already awake, cradling her sleeping boy in her arms. Anna waved and was moved when the orang-utan waved back. It wasn't so much a surprise, as Lily was often receptive to humans, but it was still remarkable.

Lily's mate, Brick, was sprawled out in the branches of the habitat's mangrove tree, sleeping soundly, his snores filling the air. Lily gave Anna a bemused look that suggested she was thinking something along the lines of: men, huh?

Annaliese grinned. I hear ya, sister.

Anna's Prius was in the staff car park up top, rather than the public one by the Rainforest Café down below. As she headed towards the park's Jacobean manor house, Ripley Hall, where the car park was located nearby, she spotted a pair of young lovers hiding amongst the lawn's sycamore trees. They'd obviously spilled out of the manor from some boozy, corporate function.

Half the money the Ripley Heights made was from hiring out the many rooms and facilities of it grand hall and grounds. There was a lot of profit to be made from supplying ample amounts of booze and warm beds for the night.

Anna cleared her throat loudly as she neared the two lovers, determined to let them know they'd been spotted. There was no way to avoid them on her way to her car and she was damned if she was going to be the one who felt uncomfortable.

However, the young lovers ignored Anna's presence. The man was really going for it, nuzzling at the woman's neck with animal-istic passion. You could hear the wet, slopping sounds from several feet away.

"Excuse me," she said. "Perhaps you should take that back inside. The park will be opening soon. Probably time to call it a night."

The couple continued necking.

"Hey! Time to wrap it up. Party's over."

Finally, Anna got a response. The man ceased his fevered nuz-zling of the woman's neck and looked at her.

Anna almost collapsed as her knees suddenly went weak.

The man's face was smeared with blood. A sliver of what looked like flesh hung from his cracked and splintered teeth. The young woman slumped to the ground, her neck torn open and gushing.

Anna stepped backwards, shaking her head and fighting the urge to vomit. Vet or not, she had never seen such a horrific sight in all her life.

"Back the hell away," she shouted at the approaching man. "Stay back."

The man kept coming.

Anna's heel caught on a root and she stumbled to the ground. Shooting pains ran up her spine, emanating from her coccyx.

The man was on her immediately, falling on top of her and clawing at her shirt. He was trying to bite her.

Anna let loose a scream as the weight on top of her seemed to grow. She pushed with all her might, but it was no use. The man was too strong. His jaws snapped mere centimetres in front of her face.

"Somebody help me! Help!"

"Anna?"

Anna craned her neck and saw Bradley racing towards her.

"Bradley, help me get this psychopath off me."

Bradley tackled the man, throwing him to the ground. Anna clambered back to her feet, panting and whining with fright. Bradley got up and immediately went to her, cradling her in his arms as she wept.

The man rose up off the ground. Bloody tears poured from his eyes, staining his cheeks red. His face was a picture of rage.

Bradley stood in front of Anna protectively and faced the man down. "What the hell is with this guy, Anna?"

"I don't know, but that woman is dead. He ripped her goddamn throat out with his teeth."

"Pissing hell!"

The man stumbled towards them, quick and determined, jaws chomping at thin air.

Bradley wound up a punch and let fly. His fist connected hard with the man's chin and made a sickening thup sound.

The man kept coming.

Anna was pretty sure the punch should have floored all but a professional boxer, but the man was unaffected and grabbed a hold of Bradley's collar. The two of them collapsed to the ground in a struggle.

Bradley yelled out in agony as the psychopath clamped his teeth down on his hand, grinding at the middle and ring fingers.

"Jesus, Bradley."

"Help me," he screamed.

Anna had to act fast. Her eyes fell upon a small picket sign, set into the ground by a short metal spike. She yanked it free and pointed it at the crazy man, her hands shaking. "Get off him now, or I'll drive this right through your goddamn eyeball."

The man ignored her threats and continued tearing at Bradley's fingers, moaning in ecstasy as torrents of blood spilled from the wound into his mouth.

"I'm warning you," Anna said.

"Just get him off me," Bradley yelled.

Anna saw no other option. The man clearly wasn't going to stop. It was as if some wild fever had taken over him, removing all powers of rationality. The man was a vicious animal.

Anna leapt forward and drove the metal spike into the man's shoulder. It sunk easily into the soft flesh and sinewy muscle.

The man didn't flinch.

Anna couldn't believe what was happening. The man felt no pain, even when stabbed. She stood stunned and disbelieving. Bradley's screams became a faraway echo as she tried to make sense of the situation.

"Anna...help."

Anna snapped out of her daze and rushed forward, yanking the spike from the man's shoulder and releasing a jet of blood into the air. At that same moment, Bradley's fingers finally came free of their knuckles, gristle and cartilage tearing and giving way. Bradley wailed as his two fingers disappeared into his tormentor's mouth.

Anna took her opportunity. The crazy man had lifted his head as he came away with Bradley's severed digits in his jaws. He chewed the severed fingers ecstatically, even as Anna lifted the spike into the air and brought it down hard against the top of his skull. The sharp metal fought against thick bone, but quickly delved deep into the soft tissue beyond.

The man's body went stiff. His chewing stopped and he toppled sideways onto the lawn.

Bradley shuffled away on his back, clambering as quickly as he could from his now-dead attacker. He held his injured hand in front of him as he stumbled to his feet, too much in shock to pay it much mind.

"Come on," Anna said to him. "We need to get you some help."

They took off towards Ripley Hall. There were several phone lines inside which they could use to call help.

Anna had to almost drag Bradley up the steps to the front doors. He was weak from shock and leaning on her for support. "Come on," she encouraged. "We just need to get you inside and then you can sit down."

She pushed on the door handle and shouldered open one of the two heavy wooden doors. A crystal chandelier and several wall sconces brightly lighted the foyer, but the reception area was entirely deserted.

To Anna's immediate right were Ripley Hall's grand dining room and the kitchens beyond. To her left were the function suites and bar. Straight ahead was the winding staircase that led to the two upper floors and bedrooms.

She headed for the vacant reception desk. Behind it was the door to the front office. She tried the handle and was disheartened to find it locked.

Bradley flopped down on a nearby swivel chair and closed his eyes as he fought against the pain. His finger stumps dripped slick trails of blood, which began to form sticky pools on the floor.

Anna banged on the office door. "Hello? Is anybody in there?"

No answer.

She turned and put her hand on Bradley's shoulder. "Just hold in there."

"N-no...problem."

She edged around the reception desk until she was back in front of it, then searched around. Shawcross was the manager of Ripley Hall and he would never usually allow the front desk to go unattended like this. She palmed the service bell and waited while its chime echoed off the walls.

Nobody came, even after ringing the bell several more times.

"This is ridiculous," she said. "Somebody always mans the front desk. Where the hell is Shawcross?"

Bradley tried to focus, but his eyes were red and irritated, like he had a bad case of hay fever. "He...he must be somewhere. The guy n-never leaves."

"A lot like you, then," Anna said with an impotent grin.

There were noises nearby. The sounds of shuffling feet.

Anna looked around at both the entrance to the function suites and the doorway leading to the dining room.

"Hello?" she shouted. "Hey, we need help here."

"I don't like this," Bradley said, his voice thick with phlegm. Anna examined him for a second and worried about his condition. He seemed far worse than he should have been.

Somebody appeared in the arched entrance of the function suites. It was one of the maids. Anna could tell from the woman's green tabard.

"Finally! I need to call an ambulance and get my colleague somewhere comfortable. Do you have a key to the office? I need to perform first aid immediately."

The maid said nothing. She just stared at Anna.

"Hey, can you answer me, please? I'm not messing around. Bradley is hurt."

The maid continued to stare at Anna curiously.

"Look, if you can't help me, can you at least get Shawcross? Where the hell is he?"

The maid took a step forward and Anna spotted the blood in her eyes.

The maid let out an animalistic screech and then launched herself towards Anna.

Anna wavered, but survival instinct soon took over, making her leap behind the reception desk.

"She's like that guy outside," Bradley shouted. "She's crazy."

Anna could make no sense of it, but she knew Bradley was right. Whatever had been wrong with the man outside was also wrong with the maid, who now leapt over the desk and reached out to grab hold of Anna. Without thinking, Anna picked up the keyboard from the desk's computer station and smashed it over the woman's head. Several keys came loose and a bloody wound opened on the back of the woman's skull. She grabbed a handful of the maid's tabard and pulled her across the desk then grabbed the shattered keyboard by its cord. Quickly she wound it around the maid's neck, pulled as tight as she could.

The maid tumbled from the desk and tried to straighten up, but was held back by the tangled wire around her throat. The more she pulled, the tighter the bonds became. She was unable to move more than a foot away from the desk.

Anna grabbed the back of Bradley's chair and started rolling him across the reception hall away from danger.

"What the hell is going on here?" she said. "Where the hell is everyone? And why the hell are people acting crazy?"

Several more bodies appeared in the entrance of the function suites. Anna could tell right away that the strangers were all dangerous.

The mob was a mixture of uniformed staff and assorted guests. They were each covered in blood and hanging chunks of flesh, perhaps their own, perhaps not. All at once, like a demonic choir, they screeched at the top of their lungs.

Anna became aware of more people behind her. She peeked over her shoulder and saw that another snarling mob flanked her.

Bradley was weeping and cradling his head in his hands. "We are so screwed."

The mobs charged from both sides.

Anna grabbed Bradley's chair and raced towards the only place she had left to run: the grand dining room.

The cavernous dining room was empty when she entered, yet its monolithic mahogany tables and delicate ornate chairs lay disturbed. Blood coated everything and Anna almost slipped in a puddle of it as she sprinted across the room. If not for Bradley's chair offering a handhold, she may have gone down on her face.

The mob pursued her. If not for their wild lack of coordination, Anna would already have been caught. It was likely still inevitable that she would be soon.

Ripley Hall's kitchen was up ahead, accessed via a pair of swinging oak doors. Anna raced towards them now, desperate for sanctuary, but the effort of pushing Bradley in his chair was starting to slow her down. The mad rush of bodies behind her was gaining. She wasn't going to make it.

The kitchen doors ahead of her suddenly opened. A face popped out from the gap.

"Come on," said a stranger, a woman. "Quickly! They're right behind you."

Anna summoned a final burst of strength and leant forward against Bradley's chair. She managed to pick up speed, but her attackers gained on her with every step. Eventually she exerted herself so hard that she was screeching at the top of her lungs just like them.

Anna hit the kitchen doors like a battering ram, using Bradley as an unwilling plough. He went sprawling onto the tiles and started to moan, while Anna's legs gave out and sent her tumbling to her knees.

People scurried around the kitchen, shouting at one another in panicked voices.

"Come on," said one of the strangers. "Get the table back up against the doors."

"I'm doing it, I'm doing it!"

"Damn, they're at the door. They're going to get in."

"No, no. We're fine. Just keep pushing."

"There, see. We're fine."

Anna peeled herself off the floor and crawled over to Bradley. His skin had gone alabaster and his finger stumps continued jetting blood onto the floor.

"Is he bitten?" asked a voice that she recognised. It was Shawcross, the manager of Ripley Hall.

Anna stared up at him, surprised by his wild ginger hair that was usually so neatly combed and his flush red face that was usually so pale.

She shook her head in confusion. "What?"

"Bradley," he said impatiently. "Did one of those things bite him?"

"Things?"

Shawcross smashed his fist against the wall. "Fuck sake, just answer the question, woman."

Anna didn't understand. She didn't know what was happening and she certainly didn't know what made Shawcross feel he had the right to talk to her like this. "I...I..."

"Yes, I'm bitten." Bradley uttered from the floor. He held up the mangled stumps where his fingers used to be. "I need help."

"You're beyond help, son." Shawcross shook his head and marched to one of the aluminium work counters. There, he picked a wooden meat tenderiser from a hanging set of utensils. Everyone in the room backed away and gave him space.

"What the hell are you doing?" Anna asked him, bewildered.

"What does it bloody well look like? We have to kill him."

"What?"

Bradley's eyes went wide and he tried to sit up. He couldn't manage it, though, and flopped back down onto his side. Anna stood over him protectively.

"Are you insane? You're not killing anybody, you lunatic."

"He's serious," said a nearby woman, who seemed anxious, but had a steely determination in her eyes. "Have you not seen what happens when someone gets bitten?"

Anna shook her head and held out a hand to keep Shawcross from advancing any further. "No, I haven't. I have no clue what's going on here. All I know is that there's a dead woman in the gardens and people keep attacking me. Can somebody here please explain things to me?"

Shawcross sighed and leant up against one of the kitchen counters. He lowered the meat tenderiser so that it hung less-threateningly by his thigh. "It started in the middle of the night," he began. "Everything just went to hell."

CHAPTER 12

ANNA MANAGED TO get Bradley back onto the swivel chair and fetched him a glass of water. She couldn't help but notice the way everybody in the room kept eyeballing him suspiciously, like he was a bomb ready to go off.

"Okay," she said to Shawcross, "let's hear it. I want to know exactly what's going on."

"Well, I'm afraid I will have to disappoint you there," Shawcross told her. "None of us can tell you exactly what is going on. We can only tell you what we know."

"Good enough."

"Okay then. Firstly, though, could you explain how you came to be here tonight, Anna?"

"I was on-call. Bradley needed assistance with a birth."

Shawcross nodded, uninterested. The zoo and amusement park were never his concern. He was the manager only of the manor and its grounds.

"Everything went okay, by the way," she told him. "I was just heading for my car to go home when I encountered a pair of strangers in the gardens."

Shawcross was interested again. "Who? What happened?"

"It was a man and a woman. The woman was dead – ripped apart by the man. Then he came at me like a lunatic. If it wasn't for Bradley coming to my rescue, I would be a goner."

"And Bradley got bit?"

Anna nodded. "Yes. I thought you were going to be the one explaining things, so why am I doing all the talking?"

Shawcross sighed. "Last night started out normally enough. We were hosting a corporate function, just like countless others. Drinks were flowing, bar tabs were rising, and not a single person had started a fight. It was as smooth as ever, but a few people were noticeably under the weather."

Anna frowned. "Under the weather?"

"Not everyone was ill," someone added. "Just a couple people from the office. Alex Reid from Accounting and Kim Hill from the Southampton branch were worst-off."

"There were about three or four sick people in total," Shawcross said. "Sneezing, coughing, sweating. None of them were getting involved with the rest of the party, barely drinking or chatting with other people. They just sat there looking like death warmed up."

"How is that connected to what's happening now?" Anna asked.

"They were the first to turn...nasty. I checked on them throughout the evening, of course – asking if they needed assistance or even just some Paracetamol – but they were barely responsive. By 1AM they looked like they were on death's door. One of them even had a nosebleed. They were bringing down the mood of the other guests, so I asked staff to escort them to their rooms."

"Should you not have called an ambulance?" Anna asked.

Shawcross shrugged. "They could have asked for one. I'm no one's carer. I left the sick people in the care of Antoine and Stephen."

Anna knew the two young men Shawcross was referring to. Antoine was a student from French Guyana and had an interest in animals, often stopping Anna to ask a question or two. Stephen was a typical English teenager earning a bit of pocket money while he decided what to do with the rest of his life.

"Where are Stephen and Antoine now?" Anna asked.

"The sick guests attacked them," Shawcross told her. "They...they just sprung to life like wild animals and took the poor lads down."

Anna remembered the man who had attacked her. Wild animals was as good a description as any.

Shawcross was staring at the floor, as if remembering something in vivid detail. "They tore out poor Stephen's throat before he even knew what was happening. I have no idea what I'll tell his family. No doubt they will hold me responsible."

"They just...attacked?" Anna confirmed. "It makes no sense."

"I reckon it's a virus or something," somebody muttered. "I bet terrorists were behind it, like the attack on that cruise ship not long ago."

"Or it could be some new kind of drug," added another voice. "Like that bath salts thing in America."

"Next thing we knew," Shawcross continued, ignoring the various conspiracy theories being bandied about, "half the guests were injured and bleeding. Or dead. Thirty guests ripped to pieces in minutes. The function suites are ruined."

Anna slumped back against one of the worktops. "Jesus wept."

"That's not the worst part," Shawcross said. "Those who were left of us managed to get the sick guests under control. We tied them up and locked them in the wine cellar. Some of us got bitten or scratched in the process, but no one was badly hurt. We thought we were safe again, that the whole thing was over..." He wiped the back of his hand against his clammy forehead and ran his fingers through his damp ginger hair. "I placed a call to the emergency services and those others left standing set about trying to help those who were not." He looked at Bradley and narrowed his eyes. "We have to deal with him right now, before it's too late."

Anna pushed away from the worktop and moved back between Bradley and Shawcross. "Nobody's doing anything until I understand what it is you're all afraid of."

"Isn't it obvious, you fool?" Shawcross almost shouted in her face. "He's going to become one of them. He's infected."

Anna moved over to the sink, filled a glass with water and swigged it in one gulp. It was only then that she noticed all the dried blood on the kitchen tiles.

"What the hell happened in here?"

"Follow me," Shawcross said. "The rest of you stay here, and be vigilant. Find something to tie Bradley up."

Anna followed Shawcross to the back of the kitchen. He led her to an industrial chiller and placed a hand on its long aluminium handle.

"You ready for this?" he asked her.

"I don't even know what this is."

"Well, you're about to find out." Shawcross yanked open the chiller door and a cold mist invaded Anna's lungs. It took a few moments for that mist to clear.

What she saw inside terrified her.

Shawcross explained what she was looking at. "These people were all injured when we first holed up in here. Just cuts and bruises mostly but, by the time we locked ourselves in this kitchen, we knew what would become of them. We had already seen it happen at the bar."

Anna stared at all the people tied up in the freezer with a mixture of curiosity and revulsion. They thrashed about, spitting and hissing in her direction, some of them making that horrible screeching sound they made. Ragged wounds covered many of them while others appeared entirely uninjured. All of them had the sickness, though, that much was clear. Their eyes swollen, blood smeared each of their orifices. Their skin was puffy and sore.

"What happened in the bar?" Anna needed to know. She needed to make some sense of what she was seeing.

Shawcross looked at her. "Like I said, we were helping the wounded. Some people were dead, their throats and stomachs ripped open, but others just had minor bites and scratches. We tried to patch up their wounds, but they deteriorated fast. One woman only had a bite on her wrist, yet she passed out unconscious. Many others fell unconscious as well. We assumed it was shock. I was feeling pretty weak myself, of course, but then they began to rise."

"Rise?"

"Men and women who we thought dead got up and started coming after us. Stephen's neck had been ripped to shreds, but he was back on his feet like nothing had happened, only he was clumsy now, stumbling around like a drunk. We assumed that we'd gotten it wrong, that the people hadn't been dead at all, but then one of us got too near...

"The dead came after us like something out of a horror movie; and when things were at their worst, the previously unconscious people snapped awake and came after us as well. They were different than the dead guests; they were quick and brutal. They came after us like predators, hunting us down in a pack. We were lucky any of us made it through alive at all. A group of us ended up in this kitchen, but half our number was badly injured and bleeding. It was too late for them."

Anna pointed at the people in the freezer. "Them?"

"Yes. We'd all seen what had happened to those who'd been injured. Our wounded became extremely ill before falling unconscious. We moved them all into the chiller before they could do any damage. One member of the group started feeling weak and volunteered to be restrained while he was still conscious. We secured him to the refrigeration racks and cranked up the thermostat. Then, one-by-one, all of the people in the chiller began to wake up.

Anna looked at the infected people with sadness now as she considered them being quarantined inside, condemned victims of some horrid plague.

"We need to call for help," she said.

"You're forgetting that I already did. I placed the call about..." he looked at his watch, "eight hours ago. Nobody's arrived yet. We've been waiting here all night, listening to those monsters outside tearing the place apart. To be quite frank, Anna, I thought it was a bad idea opening the doors for you, but Kimberly didn't feel it was right to leave you out there when we heard you shouting. It was she that opened the doors for you."

Anna patted him on the arm. Her usual opinion of Shawcross was that he was a stuffy, pedantic asshole, but she could tell that he was genuinely shaken. "You were just being pragmatic," she told him, "and that's good."

The infected people continued grasping at the air, trying to get at Anna and Shawcross. The screeching sounds they made were enough to send a person insane.

"They only make that noise when they can see people," Shawcross said. "I think it's how they let each other know they've found someone to attack. Fresh meat."

Anna cringed. She didn't like to think of herself as meat in any scenario.

"This is impossible," she said. "There's no known condition that could cause this kind of behaviour. Cannibalistic rage? It's insane, the stuff of fiction."

Shawcross slammed the chiller door shut. The screeching stopped.

"I can't make any more sense of this than you," he said, "but I have one last thing to show you that might make you accept what we're up against."

Anna fought against the rising sickness in her stomach. How much more could there be?

At the very back of the vast industrial kitchen was a door, which Shawcross now stood in front of. Anna assumed it was the pantry.

"What's inside there?" she asked.

"See for yourself." Shawcross twisted the door handle and pulled.

Inside, hanging from a light fixture by what appeared to be a bright red tie, was a man. He was kicking and wriggling as he hung by his neck.

"Just when I think things are screwed up enough," Anna said.

"James was one of the company managers," Shawcross explained. "He never owned up to having been bitten. None of us knew. He covered it up with his sleeve. While we were all distracted moving people into the freezer, James must have snuck off on his own. I found him hanging like this a few hours ago. He knew what was to become of him. I haven't told the others yet."

Anna watched the man swinging and kicking. "He's been like this for hours? That can't be. Nobody could—"

"Survive being hanged by their neck all this time? No, they could not. This man is categorically dead. Check his pulse if you don't believe me, but I would advise against getting close."

The purple ligature marks around the businessman's neck were proof enough that the blood supply and oxygen to his brain had been cut off long ago.

"We need to get out of here," she said. "We need to get every doctor and scientist in the country out here working this thing out. Whatever's happening must have some explanation."

Shawcross looked at her like she was mad. "We can't leave. There's no way."

"What? Of course there is. There's a door marked fire escape right over there." She pointed.

"It's locked. I know it shouldn't be, but I don't like the thought of leaving the kitchen unsecured at night. I always lock it once the cooks go home."

Anna shook her head and cursed. "Great idea. So how on earth do we get out of this bloody kitchen?"

"The only way out," he said, "is to go back through the house."

Before Anna had time to reply, a scream echoed through the kitchen.

CHAPTER 13

IT WAS KIMBERLY who was screaming. The woman's misty blue eyes were stretched wide as she fought desperately with Bradley, who had her up against the wall and was snapping his teeth at her. Slobber fell from his mouth and plastered his chin. His eyes were bleeding.

No one in the room was helping her. They stood back, frozen in fear. Anna ran over and shouted at Bradley to stop, but he wasn't listening. Kimberly was weakening. She needed help.

But it was already too late.

Bradley swatted aside Kimberley's arms and sunk his teeth into her windpipe. Her mouth filled with blood and she choked.

"I told you," Shawcross shouted in Anna's face. "I told you this would happen."

"I-I'm sorry."

Shawcross still held the meat tenderiser in his hand and he swung it now in a wild arc, leaping as he did so.

The first blow opened a wide divot in Bradley's skull and sent him staggering away from Kimberly, who was already still alive, yet badly wounded. The second blow dropped him, legs folding as he hit the floor in a crumpled heap.

Kimberly looked at Shawcross like he was her saviour. She even managed to smile at him. Shawcross smiled back, then smashed the mallet into the side of her skull, cracking open her temple and sending her to the floor alongside Bradley.

Anna threw up.

"S-she let me inside, saved me, and now she's dead."

Shawcross stared at Anna with bulging eyes. Blood spattered his face and streaked his ginger hair. "I told you this would happen, but I let you have your own way. I should have dealt with Bradley the moment you brought him in. A woman is dead because of my mistake."

Anna shook her head. "This wasn't your fault."

"No," he said, thrusting the bloody meat tenderiser in her face. "You're right. It's your fault."

Anna looked down at Kimberly and Bradley. Was it really her fault that this had happened? Was a kindly, courageous woman dead because of her?

"I want to get out of here," somebody said. "I'm going to lose my mind if I don't get some air. All this blood."

"We can't leave," Shawcross shouted, gesticulating furiously. "Those things are still out there. Soon as we step foot outside they'll be on us like a pack of bloody hyenas."

"But we can't stay in here forever," someone said.

"I'm leaving," said somebody else.

Shawcross fumed. "You'd rather die a horrible death than stay here a while until help arrives?"

Anna thought about the call to emergency services that Shawcross had made hours ago, and how help was still yet to arrive. She didn't like any plan that involved waiting around to be rescued because she wasn't sure any help was coming. They needed a better plan.

"How about causing a distraction?" she asked. Shawcross glared at her, but his silence suggested he was at least willing to listen. "Those things seem to operate on sight and sound more than anything else. Maybe if we can lead them away from this part of the manor, we can all sneak out."

"And go where?" Shawcross asked. "You said you were attacked in the gardens, so those things have obviously gotten outside too."

I only saw one guy and I dealt with him. I think the park and zoo would be a safe place to go. We could even make a break for our cars."

"Perhaps, but none of that makes any sense without a plan to get out of the kitchen. How on earth do we distract them?"

Anna stared down at Kimberly's dead body, then looked at the frightened faces of the others. "I'll go out. I'll try to lead them away so the rest of you can escape."

Shawcross frowned at her, but a slight twitch at the corner of his mouth suggested that he might actually be impressed by her suggestion. "That's insane. They'll rip you apart."

"Maybe, but these things have chased me once already. They're fast, yes, but they're also clumsy. If I know exactly where I'm heading, I can stay ahead of them."

"But what do you do once you've led them away? You can't run forever. Eventually you'll have to shake them off."

Anna thought for a moment. "Can't I slip inside one of the bedrooms and lock the door behind me? I could climb through a window and re-join you all outside."

"You'll never make it. Besides, I don't have my keys. I was cashing-up the bar when the first attacks happened. My keys are still in the till."

"I have my room card," a man said from over by the sinks. He had a bloody handprint on his light blue shirt but seemed in good shape otherwise. "You can take it to get into my room," he said.

"What's your name?"

"Mike. I'm a junior sales rep for...it doesn't matter, does it?"

Anna took the card and thanked him. "What number is your room, Mike?"

"Seven. It's just up the stairs on the right. It's not far."

"Great. I'm sure I'll be able to get there."

"You really want to do this?" Shawcross asked her.

"A woman is dead because of me. Least I can do is try to get you people out of here alive."

"Then you should take a weapon." He offered her the bloody meat tenderiser.

She waved it away. "It'll just slow me down. Plus, I still think these people are ill. I'm not about to bash somebody's skull in unless there's no other choice."

"Sometimes there isn't," he said.

"Wait," Mike said. "How will we know when the coast is clear?"

"You won't. Just come out five minutes after I leave and pray that they've all followed me."

"Any sign of danger and we will return back here to wait for help," Shawcross said. "But if everything is all clear, we head out the front doors and regroup at the zoo. Hopefully Anna is correct when she says it's safe out there."

"Like I said, there was just the man who attacked Bradley. I didn't see anybody else."

"Just be careful," Mike told her.

Anna smiled at the man. "I'll see you outside."

"My wallet is on the bedside table," he said. "It sounds a little crazy, but if you see it, could you grab it?"

Anna was confused, but agreed. "I don't think there's going to be much need for your credit cards, but I'll grab it if I see it."

"Shall we get this over with?" Shawcross said impatiently. He was standing next to the barricaded exit with his ear against the door. "I think they've wandered off. I can't hear them anymore, but who knows when they'll wander back."

Anna rubbed at her eyes. "Okay, I'm ready. I've had three hours sleep in the last thirty-six hours and I'm stuck in a low-budget horror movie, but I'm ready."

Shawcross slid the fridge away from the doors, slowly shuffling it so as not to make noise. Mike lent a hand and the two of them got the exit clear.

"You ready?" Shawcross asked her. "Things get too dangerous, you come right back here and we'll think of another way."

"There is no other way," she said. "We don't know when help will get here or how long we can stay safe inside this kitchen. We have to get outside."

Shawcross opened the door a crack and peered through the gap. "It seems all clear," he whispered. "When they lose sight of people, they wander away to look elsewhere."

"They're still out there somewhere, though," Mike said, "so be alert."

Anna slipped through the exit and re-entered the dining room. Bloody streaks and handprints covered the back of the kitchen doors where the mob had been battering to get inside, but it was all clear now. Although her ears picked up the slightest sound of movement. A rhythmic tapping.

She crept onwards, heading for the foyer, her wellington boots sticking to the tacky bloodstains that covered the entire floor.

Tap, tap.

Tap, tap.

There was an overturned chair up ahead, and the sound seemed to be coming from behind it. Anna felt her muscles tense up as she waited for someone to spot her. But no one did.

Tap, tap.

Anna approached the overturned chair, stepping closer and closer.

Tap, tap.

Finally, she spotted the source of the noise, and it was a sight she wished she could un-see.

Ten feet away, lying amongst a pile of broken chairs, was an infected person – one of the clumsy, slow ones. Dead if Shawcross was to be believed. It was lying on its back; face a half-eaten mess, only the chomping jaws left intact. The tapping sound came from its thrashing legs. They had been stripped clean of flesh from the knees downwards and the exposed bones of the foot and ankle were clicking against the stone floor. With each attempt to get up, the withered legs folded uselessly.

Tap, tap.

Tap.

The torn-apart beast spotted Anna and let out a hungry moan, like a plea for help, but she knew what would happen if she got too close. The body dragged itself across the floor towards her, but its progress was snail-like.

Anna ignored the corpse and crept onwards, trying to shake the disturbing images from her mind. The doorway to the reception hall was just up ahead and she could see the open front doors leading outside. A voice in her mind urged her to just make a break for it, to get outside on her own and run for help. Then she remembered that the others would be coming out in five minutes whatever she did. They were counting on her to clear the way for them.

She stepped out into the foyer, praying the space would be empty.

But that was not the case.

When Anna stepped into the reception area, a dozen infected people glared at her.

They screeched.

And then they came.

CHAPTER 14

ANNA WAS SURROUNDED on all sides. The only place left to run was towards the kitchen, but she knew she wouldn't make it. They had the jump on her.

A stocky man in a navy blue jumper came at Anna first. He collided with her so hard that she went hurtling back into the dining room. She stumbled, and when she looked down, she saw that the body with skeletal legs had managed to crawl up behind her. It now clawed at her leg, trying to bite down on her ankle. If not for her thick wellington boots, it might have succeeded.

The stocky man came at Anna again. She managed to kick her leg free just in time to move. Her attacker missed her and went crashing into the dining room.

More came.

Anna watched the horde of infected rushing into the room. Seeking the nearest barrier for protection, she leapt onto the mahogany dining table and clambered down it. She was counting on the erratic, uncoordinated movements of her pursuers to buy her some time and, sure enough, as they reached the table, they struggled to lift themselves up onto its polished surface.

Anna dodged candelabras and centrepieces as she made her way down the table. Only a couple of infected people had managed to clamber behind her, and they slid and toppled as they tried to keep balance. Most of the remaining mob pursued her from the ground, reaching up at her as they kept pace.

Pure survival instinct urged Anna onwards, but she was running out of table. She had to think fast.

She put on the brakes, skidding on her heels and turning. An infected girl sprinted towards her from atop the table. Anna met her charge head on and, at the last moment, skidded on her knees. The highly polished surface allowed her to glide, and she collided with the girl charging towards her and knocked her aside like a bowling pin.

Anna's rubber wellingtons got a grip and brought her to a stop. She hopped back to her feet and continued running, heading for the foyer. There was one more infected person on the table with her: a large man with an ample gut. She threw herself at his large belly, tucking in her shoulder and ramming him.

The man rocked backwards, lost his footing and fell off the table, leaving Anna free to sprint the rest of its length. Within seconds she'd reached the end and was leaping through the air. As she landed, she glanced back at the mob that was now behind her.

She had a brief chance to make it back to the safety of the kitchen, but she found herself heading for the reception foyer as originally intended. She picked up speed, the screeching mob giving chase pushing her to a level of effort she didn't know possible.

She reached the foyer and the only infected person in her way was the woman she'd tied up earlier with the keyboard and cord. Anna dodged right past her and rushed for the staircase, hoping there were no infected people on the second floor where she was headed.

The mob ran up the stairs after her.

Anna's heart threatened to burst in her chest. Her feet throbbed as they struck the cold stone steps one after the other, but she couldn't afford to stop. Death pursued her.

At the top of the staircase she turned right. The mob was still behind her, crashing into the walls and side tables as they hurtled along screeching.

As Anna passed Room 5, someone jumped out at her. The two people in front of her were both young and clearly not infected.

They stared at Anna with wide, terrified eyes as they quickly realised that she was in no position to help them. If they'd been hoping for rescue, they were going to be sorely disappointed.

The youngsters turned back to re-enter their room, but the
door had already closed behind them and locked them out. The
panic on their face was sudden and obvious.

"Run," Anna shouted at them, pulling the Room 7 key card from
her jeans pocket and getting it ready. The youngsters spun on their
heels and hurried after her.

The infected were right behind them.

Anna threw herself against the door to Room 7 and slid the
card into the magnetic reader. As she did so, the plastic card bent
and the reader flashed red. An irritated buzz sounded.

"Shit! Shit! Come on."

She looked left and saw two-dozen monsters hammering down
the corridor, a tidal wave of death bearing down. The two kids beside her sobbed, waiting for either death or salvation.

Anna removed the key card from the slot and reinserted it. Her
hands were shaking.

The card reader flashed red and buzzed again.

She removed the key card again, knowing there would only be
time for one more attempt. She took a deep breath and slid the
card into the slot carefully.

The reader flashed green. The door handle clicked.

The infected pounced.

Anna collapsed through the door along with the two kids. She
managed to kick out and close the door just in time. A second
later, the wood began to rattle on its hinges as dozens of infected
maniacs crashed against the other side.

"W-who the hell are you two?" Anna asked between heaving breaths.

The male of the pair stood up. He was shaking visibly and his
black dress-shirt was crumpled and sweat-stained. "We've been up

here for hours," he said. "We snuck away from the party last night to – well, you know – and then we heard everything going crazy downstairs. We stepped out and there were people being ripped apart. People I've worked with for months have gone completely Jack Torrence."

The girl stood up as well. Her blonde hair was a tangled mess and her cherry lipstick and black mascara were smudged. "We thought help was coming when we heard someone coming down the hall," she said. "We were sure you were it, but then we realised you were being chased. What is going on? Please, tell me?"

Anna went over and examined the room's door. It was weaker than the ones downstairs and wouldn't hold forever. Even now it bulged and rattled with every blow.

She put a finger to her lips to keep the young couple quiet. Then whispered to them. "If we keep quiet they should go away. They seem to operate on sight and sound."

"They?" asked Charlotte. "Who are they?"

"I don't exactly know. Something bad has happened to a lot of people. Pretty much your entire company came down with some kind of sickness last night. It's infected them with some kind of bloodlust."

"Paris Hilton's balls," the young man said. "This shit is crazy."

"Crazy," Anna agreed. "This is no joke. People are dead. Things are really screwed up."

"So what do we do?" Charlotte asked. She turned to the young man and grabbed his wrist. "Clark, I'm scared."

He hugged her close. "I know, baby. Everything's going to be okay, I promise."

"We need to get outside," Anna said. "There are people downstairs – uninfected people – that are relying on me. I came up here to lead the sick people away. Now that I have, we need to join back up with the group and get somewhere safe."

Clark nodded. "Okay. We're ready to get the hell out of here."

Anna went to the room's only window. Dawn sunlight flooded in and birds chirped outside as if all was ordinary. The ground outside beneath the window was grassy and likely soft, but the drop was significant.

"Strip the bed," Anna said.

Charlotte and Clark looked at her with confusion, but then did as they were told. In the meantime, Anna examined the room's window and located the catch, flicking it free. It was old-fashioned leaded glass window that opened outwards to one side. It wasn't the widest gap, but was big enough.

When the couple had finished stripping the bed, they watched the door anxiously.

"Concentrate," Anna said, snapping her fingers. "We'll be out of here before they get inside. Bring me the mattress."

Charlotte and Clark managed to drag the mattress over and, together, they propped it up against the window frame.

"It'll be a squeeze," Anna said, "but I think we can get this through the window. We can use it as a crash mat."

They worked the mattress onto the window ledge and started shoved it through. It was too wide to fit perfectly, but as they pushed, squeezed, and folded it, progress was made.

Crack!

The door splintered.

Crack!

"Oh, no," Charlotte cried. "They're going to get in."

"Just keep pushing. Focus on what we're doing, not on them."

They shoved as hard as they could, but the mattress started to feel heavier as muscles grew tired. Sweat began to bead on Anna's forehead.

The door rattled, loosened on its hinges.

Crack!

Anna shoved harder, gritting her teeth.

Suddenly there was movement and, all at once, the mattress tumbled over the ledge. It almost dragged Anna right out after it as it plummeted to the ground at speed.

"Charlotte, you go first. Quickly!"

Charlotte stared out the window and then looked back at Anna, shaking her head. "I can't just jump out the window."

"It's either that or stay here and get ripped apart."

"You go," she said, pointing at Clark. "Now, move!"

Clark didn't argue. He leaped up on the window frame and threw himself through. Anna watched him land face down on the mattress. He was disorientated for a moment, but was soon on his feet and waving up at them.

"Now you," Anna said to Charlotte. "You need to jump."

Crack!

Charlotte looked like a rabbit caught in headlights. She started hyperventilating.

A probing arm came through the door, clawing at the air with its bloody fingernails.

"Go!" Anna shouted. "Before it's too late."

Charlotte climbed onto the ledge tentatively, pausing to look down at the ground below. Anna placed a hand on the girl's back and shoved. She hit the mattress below and rebounded into the grass. She started sobbing but managed to give a thumbs-up.

Crack!

It was Anna's turn and she climbed up on the ledge. Her hamstrings were painfully tight from her desperate sprint through the hallway.

The door behind her continued to splinter as the infected threw themselves at it like battering rams.

Right, Anna told herself. I'll count to three.

One...

Two...

Thr—

She stopped herself when she realised she'd forgotten something.

Mike's wallet.

She didn't know why, but she couldn't leave without grabbing it first. She quickly hopped down off the window ledge and located the wallet in clear sight – right on the bedside table where Mike said it would be. She snatched it up quickly, surprised by how heavy it was.

The door burst open.

Anna raced back towards the window, but was cut off by a large man with a flap of skin hanging off his face. With a fresh surge of adrenaline, she was able to duck beneath his grasp and spring up onto the window frame in one fluid motion.

Clark and Charlotte waited for her below.

Before Anna managed to jump, arms grabbed her around the waist and tried to pull her back. Shoving all her weight forward, she managed to get her legs over the windowsill and let gravity take her. She fell. She fell fast and awkwardly, as a heavy weight bore down on her back. She hit the mattress like a rock and heard something snap. The fabric covered springs were less forgiving than she'd anticipated.

The next thing she knew, something was clawing at her back and trying to kill her.

CHAPTER 15

ANNA STRUGGLED. A flash of white-hot pain stabbed through her right hand, but she had no time to investigate the cause. If the infected man who had followed her out of the window managed to bite her, she was doomed.

Clark wrapped his arm around the infected man's throat and tried to pull him away. Charlotte grabbed a hold of Anna and yanked her to safety.

The pain in Anna's hand exploded once again, but she ignored it until she knew all danger had been dealt with. She kicked out at the infected man and sent him sprawling backwards. Clark followed up with a hard shove that sent their attacker to the ground.

"What do we do?" Charlotte asked, voice thick with fear.

Before Anna could answer, another body landed on the mattress and bounced off onto the grass.

Then another.

The infected continued to fall through the bedroom's open window. They jumped one after the other like lemmings. Four infected men and women now crawled up from the ground. One of them limped on a broken ankle.

Anna looked at Clark and Charlotte. "We need to get out of here now."

"No shit," Clark said.

They took off across the rear gardens of Ripley Manor, heading around the side and towards the front of the building. Hopefully Shawcross and the others would be there waiting for them.

The infected screeched and gave chase.

"They're coming after us," Charlotte cried.

"Just keep moving. The longer we're in sight, the more of those things will come through the window."

They rounded the corner of Ripley Hall and entered the front lawns. Now that dawn had arrived, the nearby buildings of the zoo and park were visible.

"This way," Anna said. "We need to meet up with the others."

Clark looked back over his shoulder. "They're gaining on us. How are they so fast?"

Anna looked back to confirm. Three of the four infected who had fallen through the window were now gaining ground on them. Something made them quick, like they were burning some kind of fuel inside.

Anna sprinted across the lawn, ducking between trees and hopping over bushes. She skipped over the body of the man who had attacked and bitten Bradley and noticed that the dead woman was gone.

Ripley Hall's front doors were hanging wide open, the foyer inside empty.

"Where are they?" Anna shouted. "Where the hell are they?"

"We should run back inside," Charlotte said.

"No, it's full of infected people. We need to find someplace safer. The others should be out here waiting for us. Where are they?"

The infected would be on them any second. There was no place to run that offered absolute safety, but staying and fighting would be suicide.

"Anna!"

She spun around to find Shawcross and the others. They were fifty yards away, shouting from the doorway of one the zoo's buildings.

"Come on," Anna said. "They're over there."

With safety in sight, Charlotte and Clark seemed to find additional strength. They picked up speed and managed to overtake Anna. The infected managed to pick up speed too. Their screeching was endless.

"Quickly," Shawcross shouted as he held the doorway open for them up ahead.

Charlotte and Clark sprinted the final thirty yards to the building. Shawcross ushered them inside to safety. He motioned urgently for Anna to hurry who was yet to make it.

She was going as fast as she could, but the infected almost had her. She could feel them right behind her. Her thighs burned and she just couldn't keep up the pace anymore. There were still ten yards left to run when she felt fingertips at her back.

Shawcross slammed the door shut.

She had no place to go.

The fingertips at her back turned into palms and progressed to grabbing hands. The infected grabbed her, yanked her to a halt.

She spun around, caught the nearest man in the jaw with her elbow, but was so exhausted that the momentum sent her sprawling onto her hands and knees. The three infected surrounded her, screeching and snarling.

The door to the building reopened and somebody emerged out of it.

Mike ran towards Anna with a length of broom handle raised above his head. He batted her attackers around the side of the head and tops of their skulls. Anna clambered back to her feet, desperately holding on to a glimmer of hope that she would find safety. Tremors wracked her knees, but she clenched her jaw and kept fighting.

Mike grabbed Anna by her lapels and yanked her behind him. He took another swing with the broom handle and hit the nearest attacker beneath the chin.

"Look out," Anna shouted. An overweight woman in a ripped blouse lunged at Mike, who managed to turn around in time to ram the broom handle like a spear right up into the woman's nose. He gritted his teeth as he forced the wooden shaft into her skull until the woman's entire body seized and went limp.

Mike let go of the broom handle and let the body slump to the ground. "Come on," Anna shouted. "Leave them. We have to go."

They galloped the last twenty yards towards the building and made it inside, panting and wheezing. Shawcross closed the door and stood anxiously beside.

Anna had a bone to pick with the man; but first she had to see why her hand hurt so badly.

CHAPTER 16

"**Y**OU WERE JUST going to leave me out there to die!" shouted Anna, clutching her injured hand against her chest. From a cursory examination, it looked like she had dislocated her finger. The building they were in was the zoo's reptile house.

"I have to look out for the group," Shawcross said. "I thought you were done for. They had you. You were never going to make it."

"And yet here I am, alive and well." She turned to Mike and nodded. "I owe you."

"Don't mention it," he said. "We never would've gotten out of that damned kitchen without you, so we'll call it even. Looks like you ran a little rescue mission, too." He motioned to Clark and Charlotte.

Anna nodded. "Yes, this is Ch—"

"Charlotte and Clark. Yeah, I know," Mike said. "We work together at the Tamworth branch."

"It's good to see you're okay, Mike," Charlotte muttered.

"Where did those infected come from?" Shawcross demanded. "And what is wrong with your hand?"

"We had to jump from an upstairs window. The infected followed us out. My hand is fine. Dislocated I think. I'm not bitten if that's what you're afraid of."

"Damn it!" Shawcross banged a fist against the corn snake's terrarium, making them hiss and flick their tongues. "We're trapped in here, no better off than we were in the kitchen."

"I wouldn't go that far," Mike said. "We have multiple exits and open space if we have to make a run for it. There didn't seem to be many out there – just a handful."

"What if they keep coming through the window?" Charlotte said. "There could be dozens more."

Anna shook her head. "I don't think they'll jump out the window unless they spot someone. As long as we lay low, everything should be..." her words trailed off.

"What?" Shawcross grunted. "What is it?"

"You left the front doors of the house wide open. There's nothing to stop the infected guests from spilling out into the grounds."

"Shit! You're right," Mike said. "We were in such a panic that we all just ran outside."

"We need to get those doors shut before they gather back in the foyer. We won't be safe otherwise. We don't know how long it'll be until help arrives. I'll have to go back outside."

"No way," Mike said. "You've already risked your neck enough. Look at you, you're exhausted."

"Then who? Is anybody else willing to volunteer?"

There was silence amongst the group.

Anna tutted. Their lack of courage didn't surprise her. People were selfish. Test them and they'd always look out for number one. Her ex-husband had taught her that lesson. "I'm going back out in five minutes," she said. "I just need to catch my breath first."

"Then, I'm coming with you," Mike said.

Anna shrugged, secretly surprised. "Fine. The more the merrier."

"I'll see if I can find something to defend yourselves with," Shawcross said, wandering off into the darkness of the reptile house. Anna had the feeling that he just wanted to be away from her and the guilt of what he had done. A reptile house was just the place for him.

Mike took Anna to one side. "I'm really sorry to ask, but did you—"

"Find your wallet? Yes, I have it. Almost died trying to get it, but I got it." She slid her hand into her jean pocket and hissed as a bolt of agony shot through her knuckles.

"What is it?"

Anna held her hand out in front of her. Her little finger was bent back at an unnatural angle.

Mike looked as though he might gag. "Christ. It looks broken."

She examined her twisted digit and shook her head. "I must have done it when I fell out the window."

"You fell out of a window? What do we do?"

She grabbed her little finger with her other hand and took a deep breath. "We don't do anything." Then she snapped the finger back into place, yelling out against the agony.

Then the pain was gone, replaced by a cold numbness.

Mike looked at her in astonishment. "That was pretty badass."

"No point being a vet if I can't even fix myself. Now, let's get the doors to Ripley Hall closed so we can finally sort this whole mess out. Here's your wallet."

Mike nodded and started to unbutton his bloodstained shirt, exposing a gleaming white vest beneath.

Anna put a hand out to stop him. "You sure that's the best thing, going out there in just a vest? What if one of those things bites you?"

Mike fastened the shirt back up. "Good point. I'm just starting to freak out about all this blood on me, you know?"

"Whose is it?" She could see it wasn't his, but from the pained expression that flashed across his face, she was sorry for asking so bluntly. "Sorry."

He waved his hand. "No, it's okay. It wasn't anyone I was close to, just a co-worker, Graeme. But he had a son and a wife, you know? He was a happy guy. Deserved better than to be ripped apart like..."

Anna placed a hand on his shoulder and rubbed. "We're going to get to bottom of this, okay? You're doing really great. You're my hero, in fact."

He smiled at her and straightened. "Thanks," he said, but then sighed deeply. He ran a hand through his messy black hair and seemed to prepare for whatever came next. "Let's do this," he said.

CHAPTER 17

ANNA DIDN'T GET going right away. She and Mike took Shawcross up on his offer of finding them weapons.

"Here, take this," Shawcross said, handing Anna a long metal pole with a kink at the end, normally used for dealing with the exhibit's many snakes. Mike found himself a shovel and weighted it up in his hands.

"So what's your plan? You know, eventually your luck's going to run out, taking all these risks."

Anna glared at Shawcross. He seemed perfectly happy to let her take all those risks when they benefited him. "If nobody does anything," she said, "then we're up shit creek with only half a paddle. I don't want to go out there, but somebody has to. If you're so worried, why don't you go close the doors?"

Shawcross gave her a thin-lipped smile. "I'm needed here. Guest welfare is still my responsibility."

"I don't think so," Mike said. "I think you're officially off-duty."

"I'm never off-duty. Ripley Hall is my building and you are my guests."

Anna looked at the gathering of shell-shocked survivors and saw there was less than a dozen in total.

"Fine," she said. "You carry on playing host while we risk our necks." She turned to Mike. "You ready?"

He nodded and they headed to the building's exit. "Should we try heading out through a different door?" he asked. "They could be right outside."

Anna thought about it. "I don't think we're going to be safe coming out of any door. At least we know what to expect behind this one."

Mike hefted the shovel up. "Okay, I'm ready when you are."

"Just remember," Anna told him, "don't let them bite you."

"I stopped getting hickeys at fifteen."

"Here goes," she said, easing the door open and peering outside. It looked all clear so she stepped through. Mike followed closely. "Wonder where they went."

"They'll be around here somewhere. Stay alert. We need to get to the house."

Anna took cover behind a concrete statue of a Chameleon and checked up ahead. Past the trees of the lawn, Ripley Hall was silent. Its doors remained open and its lights were still on, but all was quiet.

"Come on," she said, ushering Mike to follow.

They kept low and moved across the lawn, cutting a path through the sycamore trees. The man who had attacked Bradley was still lying in the grass. Once again she wondered where the woman was.

"What do you see?" Mike whispered to her.

"Nothing. I think it's safe. I'll go and close the doors."

"I'll watch your back."

Anna gripped her steel pole tightly and made her way over to the doors. She listened intently, ready for the first sign of danger, and as she got closer, the odour of blood wafted through the air. She was grateful she didn't have to go inside again.

The sound of infected milling about in the depths of the building was a chorus of moans and mad cackles, but the foyer itself was empty.

Anna stepped up to the door and grabbed the handle.

"Look out," Mike shouted.

Anna stumbled backwards as the dead woman lurched out of the foyer and collapsed on top of her. Another woman joined her: the maid, who had finally got free. The keyboard swung from her neck by its cord. Both women were slow and clumsy, their skin grey and mottled.

Anna staggered backwards and managed to slip free of the woman's grasp.

Mike ran up to help her but she shooed him away. "I got this," she said. She gripped the steel pole firmly with both hands and held it like a pike.

As the maid stumbled towards her, moaning and grasping at thin air, Anna shoved upwards. The tip entered over the dead maid's heart and sent her reeling backwards. Anna put her weight behind the pole and shoved harder. She cringed at the wet sucking sound it made, but was surprised by how easily the steel passed through flesh – dead flesh.

The woman didn't go down. She clawed and grasped at Anna, even with the steel pole through her chest. It was as if the eviscerating wound failed to even register. Her friend, the maid clattered towards her at a leisurely place

Anna yanked on the pole and tried to retrieve it, but it was stuck. The blood and leaking organs must have caused an airtight seal. Now she had no weapon to inflict an additional killing blow or defend herself against the maid. She did have control over the woman, though. She shoved the poled into the ground, still passing though the woman's chest cavity. It broke the surface of the mud and delved into the turgid soil beneath. The woman slid backwards on the pole like part of a shish kebab and with one last push, Anna forced the pole deep enough into the mud to anchor the woman permanently. Then she span around just in time to grab the approaching maid around the back of the head and shove her down on top of her friend. She slid onto the spike belly first and ended up face down against the other woman, both of them pin to the ground.

Mike stepped up to the two women and raised his shovel above his head, ready to deal with them for good.

"Don't," Anna said. "I've seen enough blood spilt for one day. Just leave them there. They aren't going anywhere."

Mike frowned at her, but slowly lowered the shovel and instead slammed it into the dirt where it stood erect on its own.

Anna headed back up the steps to Ripley Hall and carefully closed the front doors. The sound of the lock catching was like an audible victory.

"I don't see any more of them," Mike said.

As if to disagree, a beastly cry erupted from somewhere in the zoo. Anna recognised immediately that it was not the sound of the infected, but something else entirely.

CHAPTER 18

"**WHAT** IS THAT?" Mike asked her.

"It's coming from further away in the zoo."

"Should we check it out?"

Anna looked back at Ripley Hall. The doors were closed and the infected inside were oblivious. But if there were still infected people outside, wandering the grounds and park

With adrenaline still coursing through her veins, Anna made a decision. "We need to know what we're up against or we're going to end up trapped inside the reptile house, no better off than we were."

Mike seemed to be in a similar state of mind and nodded grimly. "Let's be quick about it then."

Anna honed in on the direction of the commotion – which was getting louder and more frenzied – and determined it was at the far side of the zoo.

"What do you think it is?" Mike asked. "That sound. It's horrible."

Anna had a suspicion but did not want to admit to it until she was sure. She recognised the noise, the calls. She quickly headed and made a beeline for where she suspected the sounds were coming from. The various animals in their exhibits were now awake, disturbed by the commotion. Pigs oinked and sheep yodelled anxiously.

Anna gasped when she eventually saw the carnage.

"Oh no," Mike said.

Half a dozen infected had managed to scale the walls of the orang-utan enclosure and were now attacking the primates inside. Anna watched in horror as Lily placed her baby in the elevated safety of the habitat's mangrove tree, before swiping and hissing at the infected closing in on her. The male orang-utan, Brick, was rushing back and forth, clubbing the invaders with his huge fists. He let out a vibrating bellow with each blow, his animalistic rage overcoming him. As Anna stared harder, she noticed that he held a fist-sized rock in his palm and was using it to bludgeon his attackers. One or two of them he had already turned into pulp.

Mike was shaking his head. "How do we help?"

It hurt Anna's heart to say so, but there was nothing they could do. "The drop over those walls is fifteen feet to the moat on the other side," she said. "We'll break our legs."

All of the infected in the enclosure sported broken legs, arms or ribs, depending on how they'd landed. Bones jutted from broken skin and blood leaked from a dozen places. Of course, the infected ignored their injuries – their ability to feel pain completely absent – and continued attacking regardless.

"Do you think that's all of them?" Mike asked. "If so then they've accidentally corralled themselves."

Anna frowned. "It's strange."

"What is?"

"They must've stumbled past a dozen animal enclosures on their way here, but they only chose this one to attack. They ignored the pigs, the birds, the horses."

"Maybe they only attack people," Mike suggested. "Maybe orang-utans are close enough to confuse them."

The battle inside the habitat continued. Lily swiped and clawed to protect herself, but for the most part, Brick was the one keeping the infected at bay. He stood tall in front of his mate and bludgeoned the skull of any infected that came within range. A couple already laid dead, their brains spilling out onto the grass in glistening pools.

Brick was coming off badly, though. A jagged wound had opened beneath the fur of his left shoulder, torn open by vicious teeth. Anna held her breath as an infected girl in a torn cocktail dress and broken stilettos leapt onto Brick's back and chomped on his neck.

Brick wailed. He managed to drag the infected woman off his back and slam her to the ground where her dress rode up and exposed her lack of underwear. Brick brought his bloody rock down so hard that it spilt the woman's face in two.

There were only three infected people left now; the most injured ones. One sported a broken femur, which stuck out like a branch. Another infected had two snapped arms hanging limply at his sides. Brick wasted no time in engaging them both.

Once the enclosure was once again secure, Brick fell to the ground, wheezing. Lily began to sob as her mate languished in her arms. Now that the fight was over, his body had finally given in. His mighty chest heaved in great gasps of air and then stopped. The last spark of life drifting away. Brick had protected Lily and her infant bravely, like any human father would. Now that he was gone, Lily held him in her arms like a loving partner. Her pained wails made her grief plain to see that tragedy wasn't exclusive to the human race.

Lily hooted at her infant still in the mangrove tree and it climbed down to join her.

Anna noticed the danger before Lily did and shouted out a warning. "Look out!"

But it was too late.

One of the infected was still crawling along on its belly. It snatched at the infant as it passed by and caught it by the leg. By the time the baby orang-utan realised the danger it was already to late to escape. The infected man sank his teeth into the infant's belly. It squealed in agony.

Lily let go of Brick and leapt into the air, clearing the distance between herself and her baby in one movement. She twisted the infected man's head right around, breaking the neck with a vicious flick. Then she picked up her bleeding infant in her arms and rocked it desperately, patted its head, sniffed its face, and swung it to and fro.

But her baby was dead.

Lily's wails filled the dawn.

CHAPTER 19

ANNA KNOCKED ON the door to the reptile house and said her name. A few seconds later, Shawcross opened it. Inside, everyone was now armed with various rudimentary weapons.

"Is it safe?" Shawcross asked her. "Are the doors of the house closed? What was all the noise?"

"Ripley Hall is secure," Anna reported. "As long as we all stay back from the grounds, the infected people should stay inside."

Shawcross seemed satisfied. "What about the zoo, the park?"

"I think it's safe. There were some infected people wandering around outside, but they're dead now – dead dead."

"You killed them?"

"Not exactly, but they've been dealt with, trust me."

"Then we should leave," he said. "Find help, someone who can clear this whole mess up."

"If that's what everybody wants to do, fine."

"We don't know that it's any safer elsewhere," Mike said. "Back in the kitchen nobody could get a call through on their mobiles. And you," he nodded at Shawcross, "put a call through on the land-line when things first went bad. Nobody has come."

Shawcross rubbed at his temples and then stared at Mike. "So what are you saying? That we're doomed? That nowhere is safe?"

"I'm just saying that I don't think we should take safety for granted. If we are okay here then we should stay here."

Anna put her hands on her hips and weighed things up in her mind. "You really think we should stay put?"

Mike nodded. "We're five-hundred feet above the ground, surrounded by woodland. If this thing – whatever it is – has spread, I feel much safer up here then going off to find help that might not even exist."

Shawcross tutted. "Nonsense. We need to report all this to the police."

"Not if it means dying," Mike said. "

Shawcross folded his arms. "We're leaving."

Anna raised a hand. "Hold on a minute. You don't speak for everyone. Maybe we should try to find out what the situation is down below first, before we get in our cars and set off into the unknown."

Shawcross growled. Anna noticed then that his slick, ginger hair was now neatly back in place, re-styled and orderly. Had he gone off somewhere to sort out his appearance? Was that what mattered to him right now?

Someone else in the group spoke up to fill the tense silence. "I'm not going anywhere unless I know it's safe."

"Me either," said another.

"I want to go home," someone else disagreed.

"It seems we're not sure amongst ourselves," Anna noted.

"We should try to get some news first," Mike said. "Find a television or some place with internet."

Anna nodded. "Good idea. There's a small office block and a warehouse at the rear of the zoo, I've been there before. There are computers. We may be able to get something to eat there as well. I think there are snack machines."

"Sounds good to me," Mike said. "I doubt we'll be getting any sleep, so a bit of grub sounds like a good compromise."

There were murmurings of agreement at the mention of food. The thought of fulfilling a basic need was enough to re-motivate people and they all needed the energy boost.

"Then if we're all decided," Shawcross said. "I'll lead the way." He brandished a thick branch that he'd probably taken out of a reptile exhibit and held it like a staff in front of him like he was Moses.

"It's your rodeo," Anna said, not really caring. "Just try not to leave anybody else to die."

Shawcross shot her a scathing look, but quickly readjusted it to a warm smile. "Of course not, Anna. It's important that we all stick together."

He headed for the door and stood beneath the fire exit sign, where he then looked over the group to make sure they were all ready. Then they set out.

Outside, the day had become bright and clear, the air crisp and invigorating.

"The offices are over there," Shawcross said.

Everyone kept to a tight formation, glancing around nervously, ready to run at the first sign of danger.

Anna craned her neck to take in the eastern side of the zoo. She tried to make out what was happening inside the orang-utan's exhibit, but it was too far away now to see. Her heart still ached for Lily.

The group passed by the various animal enclosures before Shawcross stopped. "Okay," he said, "these are the offices, just over there."

Anna had only been inside the cement office block a handful of times whenever she had needed to fill out paperwork for the zoo's indemnities. As the head vet she had been required to make official reports on the welfare, conditions, and health of each animal.

Shawcross pulled on the front doors but they were locked. "We're going to have to break in." He sighed. "I suspected as much."

Anna raised an eyebrow. "Break in? How do you propose we do that?"

"I'm sure we can manage to break a window," he scoffed.

Anna looked around. The windows of the rectangular building were all thick, double-glazed, and not easy to smash through.

"What you reckon?" Mike asked her.

"Don't know. We need to get inside, but I worry about making noise. What if there's an alarm."

"There's no alarm," Shawcross said. "The park employs security guards. As long as we put the window out in with a single blow, it shouldn't make any racket at all. We just need to find something suitable."

"How about that?" Clark pointed to a nearby vehicle.

Anna recognised the large flatbed truck as being Bradley's. It was parked next to a small warehouse, but the truck wasn't what Clark was pointing at. It was what was in the flatbed that was important.

Shawcross clicked his fingers. "Perfect. It's going to be heavy, so could I have a volunteer to help me, please?"

Mike volunteered.

The stack of breezeblocks on the flatbed were perfect for breaking windows. Shawcross dragged one of the blocks to the edge of the truck and then he and Mike shuffled with it over to the building.

"We could use a third pair of hands for this," Shawcross said, growing red in the face.

Anna hurriedly placed her hands underneath the breezeblock and helped the two men.

"After three," Shawcross said. "One...two...

"Three!"

They heaved the block into the air and watched it tumble towards the window. The glass cracked and gave way immediately, its pane splitting into several large shards and leaving the frame safe to climb through.

"Come on," Mike said. "Let's get inside."

It was a typical office space, with cluttered desks and coffee-stained keyboards. Anna picked up a photo frame from the nearest desk and examined it. There was a woman with two young boys. Anna wondered if they were okay.

"Hey, I just had a thought," Clark said. "If everything is alright elsewhere then people should start arriving for work soon. It's gone eight."

Mike shrugged. "I really hope so. I'll give a kiss to the first person I see, but..."

Anna nodded. "It's a pretty big hope."

"There's no way this thing isn't happening elsewhere," Mike said.

"We should find a television," Anna suggested. "Then we'll know."

Shawcross led them into the building's main corridor and raised a hand to keep everyone back while he checked the coast was clear.

The hallway was empty. Whenever Anna had visited in the past it had been filled with people. It was eerie to see it now.

"This is the staffroom," Shawcross stopped beside a door then opened it and walked in.

The room gave Anna a strange feeling of normality. The pool table in the centre was still littered with balls and cues where a game had been abandoned mid-session. An empty crisp packet adorned a cabinet. A forgotten coat hung from a wall peg. The room's plush sofa felt inviting. Somebody had left a paperback on one of its cushions. The room had a lived-in feel and spoke not of the horrors that had occurred so close by.

"Thank my giddy aunt," Mike cried excitedly as he ran across the room to a pair of vending machines. He pulled some change out of his pocket and shoved it into the slot.

"Is there a phone in here?" Charlotte asked. "I want to call my mom."

"There's no phone," Shawcross said, "but there's a TV." He plucked the TV remote from the sofa and pointed it at the modest flatscreen fixed to the wall near a corner.

The news came on, loud and blaring. They hadn't even needed to change the channel and search.

Banners at both the bottom and top of the screen read: NATIONAL CRISIS IN PROGRESS.

The anchorman providing the report looked mortified, not at all like the usual unflappable journalists of the BBC.

"We are getting word from France that Paris has been declared a quarantine zone, joining other European capitals, Athens, Berlin, Brussels, Prague, Madrid, Rome, and of course London. Armed forces are forming a perimeter around Paris and there are suggestions from local sources that the UK Government is preparing similar measures for London and other major cities."

Shawcross shook his head. "This cannot be."

"We take you now to scenes outside Westminster," the anchorman continued, "where an emergency government assembly is holding crisis meetings. Prime Minister Ferry, as previously reported, died in the early hours of this morning."

There was total silence in the staffroom as they all realised just how much trouble they were in.

The news switched to a camera feed from a helicopter above the Thames. The lens was focused on the spiny architecture of the Houses of Parliament. Big Ben was dented and scorched as if some airborne vehicle – perhaps another helicopter – had collided with the Elizabeth tower.

Gathered in the thousands, laying siege to the parliament buildings in force, were ranks and ranks of infected people, their affliction obvious from their animal-like movement and relentless screeching. The infected covered the streets of Westminster like the legions of Hell.

The camera-feed cut back to the studio where the anchorman continued to report.

"Acting Prime Minister Glade is currently under siege, but has assured us, through sporadic communication, that the Government is working hard on a solution. Armed forces have been deployed nationwide and all military personnel stationed abroad have been recalled with immediate effect. However, with allied nations also under attack, it remains to be seen whether or not our servicemen will make it home safely. It is currently unknown if the situation has spread to America, but current indications are that it is likely."

Shawcross collapsed onto the sofa. Anna went and rubbed the back of his neck and told him to take deep breaths.

The news continued. "Again, these scenes are real and are happening live. This devastating attack on our shores seems to have emanated from the Southern coastline after travelling throughout mainland Europe overnight. We have seen our loved ones, our neighbours, our teachers, our doctors, and even our police officers succumb to this madness and death. However, if there are people out there still unaware of the crisis, particularly in the North where the virus is still partially contained, we urge you to remain indoors. Construct whatever barricades you can to keep your property secure and defend yourselves in whatever way you can. Armed forces are working urgently to regain control of the nation's cities, but the death toll is already in the hundreds of thousands and the number of infected has become unaccountable. Great Britain, and perhaps the entire world, is under siege by the greatest threat it has ever faced. It is what some religious groups are calling 'The End of Days'. We ask you to pray for one another and to remain strong in the way that the people of this great nation always have. Ration your food, defend yourselves, and wait for help to arrive. In the meantime..." the reporter stared into the camera with tears brimming. "God be with us all."

The program switched to more scenes of devastation. The Eiffel tower burned as thousands of writhing bodies moved down the Champs Elysees. German forces flattened the streets of Munich with their mighty tanks. Pictures from the Italian countryside showed roving bands of militia fighting outside the walls of Rome. All of the images made one thing clear: the battle was being lost. The infected's relentless pursuit of survivors was unstoppable. Mankind was being exterminated.

Charlotte began to freak out. "I need to find a phone," she shouted. "I need to call my parents. They'll be worrying about me. What if they're in danger? I need to go home."

"Calm down, honey," Clark told her, but Charlotte wasn't listening. She ran towards the door they'd come through and yanked it open. "I need to get out of here. I need... I need—"

The bald and bearded man was on Charlotte immediately. Before she even had a chance to cry out, he was tearing apart her face with his teeth.

"It's Tom," Shawcross yelled. "The night watchman."

Tom threw Charlotte's limp and bleeding body to the ground and snarled at the rest of them. Clark leapt behind the pool table, causing Tom to go after Shawcross, who was nearest.

"Get back," shouted Shawcross as he swung the thick branch he had kept since leaving the reptile house. He struck Tom on the head and kept him at bay.

But Tom would not be deterred. Blood dripping down his chin and staining his greying beard, he snarled at Shawcross and kept on coming.

Anna could see that Shawcross's feeble attacks with the branch weren't going to work, so she looked around for something better, quickly grabbing a pool cue. She held it upside down so that the thick end was pointing at Tom. Then she took her shot.

The pool cue snapped as it struck Tom's skull with an audible crack! The blow would have put a normal human in the hospital, but all it did to Tom was disorientate him. Anna had expected the pool cue to break and so she readjusted her grip and wielded it like a makeshift dagger, ramming the broken end right into Tom's temple.

Tom fell to the floor with the broken pool cue jutting out the side of his head. Anna wiped his blood from the back of her hand onto her shirt and grimaced. It was cold, not like human blood should be.

"Charlotte!" Clark ran across the room and sprawled beside his already-dead girlfriend. "Oh, shit, Charlotte. Don't worry, babe, we'll get help."

"She's dead," Mike said. "I'm sorry."

Clark shook his head and wept.

Anna took him by the hand and led him over to the sofa. "Just take a seat," she told him, then nodded to Mike. "Fetch him a drink."

Shawcross was busying himself by dragging Tom's body back out into the corridor.

"Is there likely to be anybody else hiding in this building?" Anna shouted over to him.

"I don't know," he said. "I would suppose not. Tom was the night guard, but as far as I know he's the only one that works during the AM. And Bradley, of course, when needed."

Anna sighed. Both were now dead.

Mike handed a bottle of water to Clark, who took it with trembling hands and said, "This is so messed up. Charlotte can't be dead. None of this can be real."

Anna rubbed his back. "We're all in this together. It's not your fault."

"We should be safe now," Shawcross said. "Forgetting about Tom was a lapse in my judgement, but there should be no one else. We're safe, I'm sure of it."

Anna nodded and then looked around at what was left of their group. "Okay, well in that case, I think it's about time I finally got to know everybody."

"This is Michelle from HR," Mike said, pointing to a pretty little blonde. Then he indicated to a skinny man in a tailored short-sleeved shirt, "and this is Greg from Sales."

Anna nodded to the two of them as a middle-aged man with a greying moustache introduced himself. "My name is Alan, from

Logistics, but might I just bring something to the group's attention before we get too relaxed?"

Anna shrugged. "What?"

"Well, it's more of a question, really. What I want to ask," he pointed to Charlotte's dead body, "is what we're going to do about her?"

"What do you mean?"

Mike's eyes suddenly went wide. "He means she's going to come back."

Anna realised it was true. Based on what they'd seen, Charlotte was going to come back as a slow, stumbling, yet very very lethal, zombie.

And then she'd try to eat them.

CHAPTER 20

"HOW SHOULD WE do it?" Mike asked as he stared down at Charlotte's body. Her neck had stopped bleeding and her flesh was turning pale.

"Why do we have to do anything to her?" Clark muttered, staring at the floor.

"We have to deal with her Clark," Mike said softly. "She'll get back up as one of them. We've all seen it."

"I haven't. I was with Charlotte," he wiped a tear from his face, "and now she's dead."

"Let's just break another pool cue and stab her in the skull," Shawcross said. "Seemed to do the trick with Tom."

"It's not about doing the trick," Anna spat. "It's about being humane."

"There's nothing humane about any of this," Mike admitted. "Maybe Shawcross is right. The pool cue was effective on Tom."

Anna sighed, too tired to argue. "Fine. Should I do it?"

Mike shrugged. "Do you want me to?"

Clark leapt up from the sofa. "Listen to you all. You sound like you're haggling over the last beer in the fridge. You're about to crack somebody's skull open. That somebody was my friend."

"None of this is your fault, Clark," Anna reiterated. "Lots of people are dead and none of us are to blame. We didn't do this."

Clark picked up the remaining pool cue and rolled the length of wood in his hands, examining it intently.

Mike frowned. "What are you doing?"

Clark smashed the cue over the edge of the table and made everyone flinch. The thick end went hurtling across the room and left a dent in the wall.

"Let me do it," Clark said. "She was my friend."

"I don't think it's a good idea," Anna said. "You shouldn't have to do it."

"No offence," Clark said, "but fuck you. You didn't even know her."

Anna believed Clark performing the act would only make his emotional condition worse, but she stepped aside and let him do what he wanted. There was a chance, she supposed, that it might bring him closure. You never could tell. People's minds fractured and fixed in different ways.

Clark knelt beside Charlotte and placed the jagged cue against her forehead.

"Turn her head to the side," Anna instructed. "The temple is softer. It'll be...cleaner."

Clark turned Charlotte's head sideways, causing the wound on her neck to open up wider. A fine spray of blood released and stained Clark's shirt. He didn't seem to notice and raised the broken cue above his head.

Everyone in the room but Anna turned away. She made herself watch, not wanting to ignore the things that were happening. She needed to retain her humanity and the best way to do that was to face things head on with her eyes open.

The cue in Clark's hands trembled for a moment, but he kept his courage and went through with it. He brought the cue down forcefully and pierced Charlotte's skull. Anna was glad he didn't have to give it a second go.

Clark's body trembled as sobs took over him. His girlfriend's blood covered him.

After a while, they all decided to leave Clark alone with his grief. The remainder of the group gathered over by the television.

"So what's our next move?" Alan asked grimly, twiddling his moustache nervously.

Anna shook her head. "I have no clue. Does anybody have a suggestion?"

Faces were blank, shoulders shrugged.

"Then I suggest we just hide out here for a while. Once we've rested up, maybe things will become a little clearer. We can find a phone and keep the TV on. I'm sure we'll know more soon."

To her surprise, even Shawcross was nodding in agreement. It was clear that everyone was exhausted, and that none of them had slept for ages. Right now, all anybody really cared about was getting off their feet and maybe catching some shuteye.

Alan cleared his throat. "I would like to make sure that this place is really safe, before we all settle in for the long haul. We should check out the rest of the building."

"I agree," Mike said. "We also need to move Tom and Charlotte somewhere else. We can't have them so close by."

Anna nodded. "You're right, it's a health hazard."

"I'll organise everybody." Shawcross ran a hand through his slick ginger hair. "We'll split into groups for efficiency."

Anna said, "Fair enough. I'll help Clark with Charlotte's body. We should be able to move Tom as well. We'll place them both in the office we came in through. It's the least safe room for us to be in so it makes sense to use it as storage."

"You mean as a morgue," Alan said.

"Call it what you will, but it's something that has to be done."

"Just be careful," Mike said. "I don't want to have to put your body in there."

Anna smiled. His concern was unexpected.

A buzzing sound from the television caused them all to look up. The anchorman was back on and looked in a worse state than before.

He began, "While it has long been suspected, reports from the World Health Organization have now confirmed that the dead are indeed coming back to life. While the initial infection causes high fever and uncontrollable rage, it is not until the infected are rendered deceased that the true horror makes itself known. When an infected person dies, against all the rules of nature, they come back. The reason some of the infected are slower and less ambulatory than others is because they are no longer living. The only way to prevent an infected person from coming back, it appears, is to inflict massive head trauma. Damaging the brain is the only confirmed way to dispatch an infected person permanently."

The reporter stopped for a few seconds, taking a sip of water. Weariness hung densely over him.

"As I report to you, it may all seem like some kind of sick joke, but the reports are real. This is happening. If you have loved ones with you, enjoy them while you can. If you have a safe place to go, go. This very well might be the end of life as we know it. Do whatever you have to do to survive." The reporter placed a finger to his ear, as if getting a message from an earpiece. "I'm about to be cut off, folks, for saying things that I shouldn't have. It doesn't really matter, because we're about to go off air with immediate effect anyway. An emergency message will be left to play, but there will be nobody here broadcasting. Reports have come in that small enclaves of military, police and civilian resistance are gaining footholds in certain areas north of Sheffield and that rescue might still be a possibility for some of you, but for the most part rescue will not be forthcoming. I hope that some of us make it through this terrible tribulation. My name is Ben Hutchinson and this is—"

The feed went dead, replaced with a beeping tone. The words on the screen simply read: STATE OF EMERGENCY. FURTHER NEWS TO FOLLOW. STAY TUNED.

Anna stared at the television and held her breath for almost a minute. Then she said something she couldn't believe she was actually saying. "I think this might be the end of the world."

CHAPTER 21

I T TOOK MORE than twenty minutes for Anna to help Clark carry Charlotte's body into the office. What made it more difficult was that blood spilled from her body whenever they tilted her even slightly. Anna wondered whether the blood was infected.

Now they were in the middle of disposing of Tom's body, and the plump security guard was more much heavier than Charlotte.

"Did you know him?" Clark asked.

Anna shook her head. "Never met him. I wonder what happened to him. How did he get infected all on his own?"

"Maybe he came to work already infected."

Anna reaffirmed her grip on Tom's legs as she felt him slipping. They were almost back at the office now. "I don't know how it's even possible for a virus to infect the entire world overnight."

"Maybe whoever is to blame coordinated several outbreaks of the virus at once. Maybe a bunch of terrorists synchronised their watches before tipping the biological motherlode into the local water supplies."

She and Clark set Tom's body down beside a large, freestanding photocopier. "You know, that sounds pretty plausible," she said. "If this was terrorists then it would make sense to release it in multiple locations. I just can't believe that anyone would be so insane. Surely no one is that much of a monster."

Clark huffed. "The only difference between Adolf Hitler and the lowlifes on the street is power. When people get the power to destroy their enemies and further their own agendas, that's exactly what they do. If any terrorists had the ability to wipe out the western world, I bet all of them would do it in a heartbeat."

"Wow, you're pretty jaded for such a young man. Anyway, we don't know that this is exclusive to the western world."

"No, we don't, but time will tell. Somebody is behind this, and they'll probably be eager to come forward and claim their victory."

Anna told him, "You're quite the theorist."

"I'm doing a part-time History Degree, not that I expect to go to classes again now. People aren't that different today than they've ever been. Same nature, same behaviour; it's just the technology that changes."

"I wouldn't know," Anna said. "I've always been more of an animal person than a people person."

"Then you're in luck, because it looks like the human race has been turned into a bunch of animals."

Anna watched Clark carefully. He seemed to have snapped out of his shocked daze but now seemed angry. "How are you doing, Clark?" she asked him.

"How do you think?"

"I know, I know. We're all doing shit, but do you need anything? Are you going to be okay?"

He turned away and leant over one of the desks. "I really loved her. She didn't know that, but I did. She was way too beautiful for me. I felt lucky when we were together."

"You're going to get through this, Clark. We're all going to stick together and come through the other side, okay?"

"I'll be alright. I think I just need to be on my own for a while. Would you mind? I want to say goodbye to her in private."

Anna looked down at Charlotte's body. "Okay. I'll leave you to it. Just stay back from the window in case there're any infected people outside."

"Will do. And thanks again, Anna. Charlotte and I would still be cooped up in that hotel room if you hadn't rescued us."

Anna smiled at the boy and then stepped out of the office to give him peace, closing the door behind her.

She found Mike in the corridor.

"Hey," he said. "I was just coming to find you. Everything okay?"

"As well as can be expected. I've left Clark to himself for a while. He's not doing well, but I think he'll be okay."

"Not surprised. He's what, twenty, maybe? That's pretty young to be stuck in a situation like this. Losing Charlotte must be devastating. What can you do, though?"

Anna sighed. "Nothing. We're all lucky just to be alive. I suppose we should find the positive in that."

Mike held open the door to the staffroom for her. The pool table was now home to a modest collection of snack food and bottled drinks.

"I've been checking around for rations," Alan explained. "Found some odds and ends in people's desks upstairs, but this is pretty much it. We've got the vending machines in here to go through as well, so we should be good for a day or two."

Shawcross entered the room carrying a fan heater. "I found this in one of the offices upstairs. I'm thinking it might get pretty cold during the night."

"Good idea," Anna said, "but I figure it isn't long before the power goes out. We all saw how bad things are on the news."

"Shit, I never thought of that," Mike said. "How long do we have, you think?"

"There's a backup generator," Shawcross said. "They built it to keep the heated exhibits functioning even during a power cut. I don't know how much juice they keep in the batteries, but I think we'll get at least a couple extra days once the grid fails."

Anna frowned. "How do you know about that? I didn't think you had anything to do with the zoo."

"I was here when they installed it. It's buried in the woods where guests can't see it. Thing makes a terrible racket, but thankfully it's only been put to use once before. It will come in handy, though if everywhere loses power."

"Or we'll be lit up like a beacon," Anna said. "The only place with power for miles."

"A beacon?" Shawcross queried.

"Yes, a beacon. You don't think they'll be other people out there looking for safety. If we light up in the dark, then any survivors nearby will come running our way. I think our biggest asset right now is anonymity."

"I think so too," Michelle said meekly.

Shawcross shook his head. "I think the opposite. The news said there are still rescue operations taking place. Tomorrow we should light a signal fire to let people know we're here. Smoke from all the way up here would be seen for miles. We have a better chance than anybody at being rescued."

"I think that would be totally dumb. We have something that everybody in the world will be looking for: a defensible position. The last thing we want to do is advertise what we have to a desperate population."

"She's right," Mike said. "What if we light a fire and a hundred people turn up on this hill? The food we have left would be gone in an hour. And what if some of them are bitten and don't know what that means yet? We could be crawling with infected before the day is through."

Shawcross thought about things for a moment, then shook his head adamantly. "If we still had access to Ripley Hall, I might be inclined to lay low, but we're all doomed if we try to stay here indefinitely. We're too exposed. Rescue is our only priority, and tomorrow that is what we must work towards."

Anna went to argue, but stopped herself. She didn't have the energy. "Fine...whatever you say. I'm going to get some rest. If the world stops ending, you have permission to wake me."

Without waiting for a reply, she ambled over to the sofa and collapsed face-first on it. The slumberous feeling that immediately washed over her was heavenly. Her muscles turned to jelly and within seconds sleep snatched her away.

CHAPTER 22

EVERY TIME ANNA went to sleep sober, she dreamt about her baby. She dreamt about the baby she never knew, the little boy that never was. She dreamt about Baby.

She saw her son's face, his closed eyes and tiny nose – eyes that would never see and a nose that would never breathe. She only got to hold her baby boy once, and he had been dead.

Every time she thought about him she wondered what he would've looked like now if he'd lived to be four-years-old. She wondered if Baby would've looked like his father. She wondered if Baby's father would still be around.

Then she would wake up in tears, every night the same.

Until she found alcohol.

Then the dreams stopped, but the headaches and nausea began.

Tonight, though, she couldn't escape her dreams. They kept hold of her and tore at her soul. Tonight she dreamt of Baby as a ghoul, back from the dead to drag her to Hell. Baby had died in childbirth, murdered by his mother who was too weak, too inhospitable to bring him to term. He was denied the most basic gift of life, while his wicked mother lived on. Now Baby was back. His tiny teeth were bloody and coming for Anna's flesh. They would tear her apart; chew her up slowly, until there was nothing left but her disembodied, screaming mouth.

And as she screamed so too did Baby. Baby screeched like the infected people. It hurt her ears and she begged for it to stop.

Stop, she cried. Please, Baby, stop.

I'm sorry. I'm sorry.

I wish it were me who had died.

I wish you were alive and I was dead.

Please, Baby, stop screaming. I'm begging you to stop.

Anna shot bolt upright in the dark and clawed at her neck, trying to get free of whatever clung to her.

It was a coat. Someone must have covered her with it.

She remembered falling asleep on the sofa in the staffroom. She remembered, with oily sickness in her belly, all of the other things that had happened too. All of the death came flooding back to her in a horrific slideshow of mental images.

Bradley.

Kimberly

Charlotte.

Anna could hear people snoring. She also heard something else. She heard wailing.

The muffled sound of someone – or something – in torment floated into the staffroom like a ghostly visitation. The melancholy sound seemed to echo off the walls.

Anna left the sofa and went to the nearest window, ducking her head beneath the curtains and looking out at the moonlit night. There was nothing outside but the narrow silhouettes of trees.

The wailing continued. It was a weak, pining, and eventually, Anna figured out where the sound was coming from.

It was Lily.

The thought of such a noble creature, alone and in such pain was more than Anna could bear. Pain bloomed in her own chest. It was a pain she only ever felt when she thought about Baby.

She fiddled with the bottom of the window and eased it open, letting in the cold night air before climbing outside. She was grateful for the noisy whir of Shawcross's fan heater and the audible cover it provided her.

She rounded the corner of the building and headed for the orang-utan habitat, keeping her eyes peeled for any danger. What she was doing was mad, but with all that had happened, she felt unable to feel any more fear.

It was disorienting to walk around the park in the dark. Bradley had always been there to guide her in the past. She missed her colleague, wished she'd had the chance to take him up on his offer of having a meal together. There were many things she would regret now.

Up ahead, the ghostly visage of a mangrove tree came slowly into view. Anna found Lily sitting at the base of the tree, weeping loudly like any other childless woman. The body of Brick and the infant were lying in the centre of the enclosure, placed together, father and son. Lily was not looking at them. Perhaps it was too painful.

"You poor, poor thing." Anna spoke softly as she observed the heartbroken creature, but in the silence of night, and with keen animal hearing, Lily heard the voice. The orang-utan slowly raised her head.

"I'm sorry," Anna said, not feeling silly at all for talking to an ape. "I didn't mean to creep up on you. I didn't mean to invade your privacy."

Lily stared at Anna for what seemed like forever, but during that time her weeping stopped. Then the orang-utan raised one of her arms and waved at her. It was a sad wave, a weak wave, but the fact that she'd ceased whimpering made it clear that she did not want to be alone. She was glad Anna had appeared. Lily was glad not to be on her own.

Anna had an extremely stupid idea, but it was something she needed to do, something the broken soul inside this enclosure needed. She approached the entrance to the enclosure, which was opened via a magnetic key-lock for which she knew the code. She keyed it in now and let herself into the keeper's bungalow.

Inside, lay a cement prep area and a small office cubicle. There was also a wire mesh cage that housed an indoor sleeping area for the orang-utans. It led to the enclosure via a tunnel.

To Anna's dismay, the mesh cage was padlocked. Instead she tried the office door and was happy to find it unlocked.

The office was cramped and dingy, but the glow from a computer monitor gave enough light to make out a few details. Her attention immediately fell on a small metal closet mounted on the wall. She fumbled with its edges and found a small catch to open it. Inside was a collection of keys, all clearly labelled.

She snatched up the key labelled CAGES and headed out of the office. The brass key fit perfectly in the padlock to the mesh cages, but she took a deep breath before unlocking them.

Was she really about to do this?

Yes.

With her mind made up, Anna entered the cages and crawled through the tunnel into the enclosure.

The odour of death hung heavy, but so did the natural musk of the orang-utans. Lily was sitting in the same place as she had been, and when Anna got closer, she turned and snorted a warning sound. For a second the whole idea seemed insane. The last time humans had been in this enclosure there had been bloodshed. Anna wondered if Lily could distinguish between the infected and the uninfected. Did she know Anna was no threat?

Despite her fears, Anna kept moving forwards.

Lily eyeballed her suspiciously.

"Hey, there." Anna kept her voice calm, unthreatening. "I'm not here to hurt you. I just want to make sure you're okay."

She was now within a few feet of the orang-utan and all seemed stable. The atmosphere was tense, but the primate seemed to tolerate her proximity.

"There you go." She reached out a hand. "It's okay, Lily."

Unbelievably, Anna found herself within a single foot of the great animal and was even able to sit herself down next to it.

Letting out another billowing snort, Lily extended one of her own long arms. Her huge fist struck Anna and made her cry out, but she quickly realised that the orang-utan was not trying to hurt her, just being curious. Lily's fingers caressed the fabric of Anna's shirt.

"I'm usually a little cleaner than this," she explained.

Lily hooted. It was a curious sound, not aggressive in the least.

Is this actually happening? Anna asked herself. Amidst all the horror and bloodshed, there was still joy to be found in life. There were still connections to be made between kindred spirits. Nature was beautiful, even if man had become so terribly ugly. In that moment, Anna remembered why she'd become a vet in the first place: to help innocent creatures like this.

Lily's hand moved further up Anna's shirt and began probing at her face and fondling her hair. The gentleness of the gesture made Anna close her eyes, and it wasn't long before she felt sleepy.

Before she fell asleep on the ground beside Lily, Anna thought she heard an alarm going off. It was faint, somewhere in the distance. She felt too tired, and too safe to worry.

CHAPTER 23

NNA WOKE WITH an aching jaw and it quickly became apparent why. She was lying facedown on the ground, shivering, yet cosy beneath a soft woollen blanket. Despite its softness, the blanket smelt musky and foul. Anna threw it aside and looked around. The sun was rising. A new day. The terrors of the night seeming more nightmare now than reality.

Anna leapt to her feet.

A mound in the centre of the enclosure was covered with the same kind of blanket that had been covering her. Brick and Lily's infant lay beneath it.

Anna looked around for the female orang-utan but couldn't find her. The mangrove tree was undisturbed and the enclosure was still. Perhaps Lily had gone inside the cages where it was warmer. But when Anna headed through the tunnel and back into the bungalow, Lily wasn't there either.

The wire mesh door to the cage hung wide open.

Anna put both hands to her face as she realised what she'd done. She'd let a wild animal loose. It was reckless and irresponsible, but the more she thought about it, the less she cared. With things the way they were, there was no one left to take care of Lily anyway. It was better that she was free. At least that way the animal wouldn't die in captivity.

Anna exited the bungalow and headed back to the office block to join the others. They'd probably be wondering where she was. She rubbed at her shoulders and shivered against the cold. A spiky sheen of frost covered everything.

"Anna!" Up ahead, Shawcross was standing outside the office block and looking around nervously. "For heaven's sake," he said. "What are you doing outside?"

"I went for a walk last night. Trying to clear my head."

"A walk? How do we have a hope of getting through this if people start doing their own thing? It's dangerous out here."

"Sorry, I just needed some fresh air." She didn't want to tell him about where she'd slept last night, or that an orang-utan was now loose somewhere.

"There is a lot to be done, Anna, so get back inside. Tell Clark the same thing. I assume he went with you."

"Wait, what? Clark's gone?"

"Yes, I thought he was with you. I don't know how long he's been gone. Everyone pretty much fell asleep once things were settled."

"How did you get out of the building?" Anna asked. "Did you climb through the broken window in the office?"

"No, Alan and Greg managed to get the front entrance open last night. We can come and go as we please now, so we'll probably get that broken window boarded up today."

Anna had a bad feeling. Something wasn't right. She pushed Shawcross aside and over to the broken window they had originally entered the building by.

"What's wrong?" Shawcross said, but she didn't answer him. She didn't want to voice what she was thinking, not without being sure.

She pulled herself up and through the broken window and dumped herself down on the other side. The stench of death overwhelmed Anna immediately, scraping at the inside of her nostrils and making her want to gag. Tom and Charlotte lay in the centre of the room, already starting to decay.

Clark's body was fresher and had not yet begun to rot.

"Oh no," Shawcross said, climbing into the office behind her. "What did that silly boy do?"

Clark hung from the light fixtures by what looked like a length of grey telephone cord. He'd probably hanged himself shortly after she'd left him alone.

"I could have prevented this," Anna said, wishing she could blink or turn away. "I left him alone in here. I should never have left him."

Shawcross sighed heavily. "Suicide is a selfish act, Anna. There's no one to blame but Clark. We can't let it distract us from what needs to be done."

Anna stared at him and almost hissed like a snake at him. "Are you really this much an asshole or do you have to try really hard?"

"I'm not willing to waste time worrying about things that can't be changed. I would rather turn my attention to the living and what can be done. I suggest you do the same. This wasn't your fault, Anna, so put it out of your mind. You barely knew the boy."

With that, Shawcross left Anna alone. She didn't know if she wanted to thump the man or thank him for his absolving words. He had a way of dividing her opinion like a hot knife through butter.

Mike entered the room five minutes later and immediately placed a hand on her back. She flinched at first but then enjoyed the warmth of his contact. "I just passed Shawcross in the hall," he said, staring at Clark's swinging body. "I can't believe it."

"I know. It's not right."

"Should we cut him down?"

"What's the point?" she asked. "There's death everywhere. It would just be a waste of time for us to clean up after it."

Mike rubbed at her back again and pulled her closer. "Don't give up. You're the only one of us with their head on straight. We'd all be lost without you."

Anna huffed. "Bullshit! All I've done is get people killed. Bradley, Kimberly, Charlotte, and now Clark. You'd all have been better off in the kitchen where I found you."

Mike fixed his dark brown eyes on her. "Hey, if we were still in that kitchen, we'd all just be waiting to die. I'd rather earn my death."

"Wouldn't you rather just give up?"

He scratched at his chin thoughtfully. "You're a vet, right?"

"Yeah, so?"

"You know a lot about animals, so answer me this: what do animals do when humans invade their habitats?"

"They die out, or end up in zoos like this one."

"Okay, I'll give you that some do. What about all the other animals that don't die out or end up in zoos?"

"I'm not following," she said. Mike's gaze was bewildering her. She felt her cheeks throb and wondered when he was going to look away from her. Not that she wanted him to.

As if sensing her discomfort, Mike moved away and sat in a chair. "I'm talking about the animals like rats, birds, cats, rabbits, even bears. They live around people, don't they? You can't go anywhere in the city without a pigeon eyeing you up for food, and in America, bears and racoons come right out into the streets and raid people's bins; so do foxes in this country."

"What's your point, Mike?"

"My point is that animals adapt. When things change for them, they don't feel sorry for themselves or crawl up and die, they deal with it."

"So you're saying that we need to, what, just deal with it? Like rabbits?"

"Exactly. Are we so arrogant that when our cushy way of life is threatened, we'd rather just give up than have to adapt and survive? Every other species on earth has had to do it because of us, so why can't we do it now?

"Look," he continued. "I don't know what lies ahead. I'm guessing it's not going to be a day at Disneyland, but I'm not about to give up without a fight. Whatever has happened is bad – really bad – but it's only the end of the world as we know it. People have died, yes, but as long as there are some of us left, we owe it to the human race to survive. The world has changed, but at this moment we are still very much a part of it."

Anna chuckled. "You're not going to shout FREEDOM at me, are you?"

Mike spun around on his swivel chair and leapt out as he came full circle. "I haven't gone all Braveheart just yet, but that's the mentality we need. That film just proves my point that when people are up against it, they fight, whatever the odds. Maybe this thing isn't as big as we fear, but we need to prepare ourselves in case it is. We have to earn our place in this new world."

"Maybe you're right," she said. "Can we just get out of here for now, though? I kind of want to go hide someplace and forget the world for a while."

"Fair enough. Come on, everyone's in the staffroom. We're going to start planning."

Indeed everyone was in the staffroom, gathered around the pool table and trying to thrash things out. From the way Shawcross was gesticulating, the man thought he was Winston Churchill.

"The phones still aren't working," he told Anna as she walked into the room. "All of the computers in this office are security protected and nobody knows the passwords. Ripley Hall is off limits and we have no idea what it's like in nearby towns. To say our current situation is perilous is an understatement. Our only hope at this point is to secure rescue."

"How?" Greg asked, twiddling at his greying moustache, as he was wont to do. Michelle stood beside him, staring into space blankly.

"We start a signal fire," Shawcross said, echoing his previous statements.

"Bad idea," Anna said. "I already told you. What if the fire attracts the infected, or people who want to take what we have?"

"You may be correct," he admitted, "but what other choice do we have, really? We have no food beyond what lies on this table and I'm sure it's only a matter of time before we lose power and perhaps even water. If you don't agree with a signal fire, we could head for the staff car park behind the manor house, or even head down the hill via the cable cars. We can cut through the woods into the nearest town."

"The towns won't be safe," she said.

"Neither is here. We have to leave."

"Wait a minute," Alan said. "Isn't this a theme park?"

"What?"

"This place is a theme park and zoo, right?"

Shawcross shrugged. "What's your point?"

"My point is that there must be a burger bar or restaurant with supplies to last us a little while longer."

Anna nodded. "There's a burger place in the zoo and a pub and eatery in the theme park. We should explore what we have now before we start looking elsewhere."

Shawcross raised his hand. "Regardless of how many supplies we have, we will at some point run out. We need rescue. Sooner rather than later."

"What if we don't run out of supplies?" Anna asked.

Everyone looked at her curiously. Shawcross most of all. "What do you mean?" he asked.

"I mean that the zoo is partly self-sustaining. Bradley was telling me about how they produce much of the animal's feed in a big greenhouse in the woods, and that there's also a small plot of vegetable gardens. If we can find those, we might be able to grow our own food."

"And we can eat the animals," Greg said.

Anna didn't like the thought of that, but she knew it made sense. "If things get that desperate, then yes, I suppose so. Even better, the petting zoo has chickens and a pair of cows. We can get eggs and milk."

"This is absurd," Shawcross said. "We need rescue, not a bloody community project."

Anna stomped her foot in frustration. "Yes, we do need rescue. But we won't get it by throwing our lives away. We can keep a look out for help – we're five hundred feet in the air – but if help is a far way off then we need to make preparations. We need to prepare for the worst not wish for a miracle."

Shawcross shook his head. "You're wrong. I think—"

Anna cut him off. "Maybe I am wrong, but maybe so are you. You're not in charge here, Shawcross. These people can make their own decisions."

Shawcross grew red in the face and his upper lip curled into a snarl, but then he smoothed out his shirt and gave her a bright smile. "Of course they can make their own decisions. We're just talking here, Anna. No need to get upset. I'm sure we'll all come up with whatever is the best solution."

Anna rolled her eyes. The patronising son of a bitch. "I'm not upset," she said. "So don't worry yourself about that. As for coming up with a plan, I think the best option would be to vote."

"Well, I'm not sure that—"

"I'm happy to vote," Mike quickly said.

Alan shrugged. "Me too."

Greg and Michelle also agreed to a vote.

"There we have it." Anna smirked at Shawcross. "Our first vote is to vote. The second is whether we light a signal fire, or whether we find ways to try and survive here."

"I vote we stay and prepare," Mike said.

Anna glanced around the room. "All those in favour?"

Everyone's hands went up except for Shawcross's.

This'll teach him. "Motion carried."

Shawcross stomped across the room. "You all just made a very bad decision, but it was yours to make. Just remember that I was against it." He slammed the staffroom door and was gone.

"He going to be alright, you think?" Mike asked.

Anna shrugged. " He just needs to get used to the fact that he's not the manager of anything anymore. Like you said, we all need to adapt."

Mike put his fist in the air. "FREEDOM!"

She laughed and punched him on the arm.

Then they all heard something that made their blood freeze: the frenzied screeching of the infected. It sounded like a hundred of them.

And they were close.

CHAPTER 24

NNA AND THE others spread out into the courtyard. The screeching of the infected wasn't coming from the park, but from somewhere else nearby.

"Come on," she said, rushing towards the cable car station that led to the Rainforest Café at the bottom of the hill. "I think it's coming from to lower car park."

"Then we should probably keep a low profile," Greg said.

"We need to know if we're in danger. We need to check it out."

Nobody seemed to like the idea, but nobody argued either. If they had to make a run for it, their chances would be better knowing what they were running from.

"It's coming from down the hill," Shawcross said, stating the obvious.

Reaching the cable car station, Anna looked down the hill and gasped. Five hundred feet below were hundreds of screeching infected. They were everywhere, like ants around an ice cream cone. They seemed to be focused on something.

"There're uninfected people down there," she cried. "Look, there's a man standing on top of the café...and there, look, another, sneaking around the back."

The man in a long black coat crept around the back of the café with an old lady in tow. The large man on the roof seemed to be running some kind of distraction for them, screaming, shouting, and waving his arms like a maniac.

"They're screwed," Greg said. "There's no way they'll be able to escape all of those infected."

She waved a hand dismissively. "Just wait," she said. "They're running some kind of plan. The man on the roof has them all corralled at the front of the building, while the other two are running into the woods."

"Well, how are they going to get the man down off the roof?" Greg said. "There's no way."

Anna had no idea either, but Greg's pessimism was beginning to get on her nerves. The only thing clear was that the strangers down below were working together to survive.

"Maybe we can run a distraction of our own," Mike suggested. "Try to draw the infected away from them."

"We'll do no such thing." Shawcross objected. "You want to get us all killed."

Mike looked to Anna for her opinion, but unfortunately, she had to agree with Shawcross this time. "We can't risk it," she said. "We'll just bring the infected up here to us."

Mike didn't argue, just sighed. "Man...that sucks."

Anna watched the stranger in the long black coat enter the woods with the old woman and then reappear a moment later without her. He seemed to exchange a few words with the man on the roof, then climbed through a window at the side of the building. The man on the roof continued keeping the infected corralled at the front.

Time went by and nothing happened. Anna stood silently, her skin tightening, her heart beating fast.

"The infected people are heading into the café," she said suddenly. "Look!"

The infected were shuffling into the café, clambering through the windows at the front. After a while, the man on the roof was able to head to the back of the building without any of the infected noticing him. Anna watched in amazement as the other man, the one in the black coat, exited the building from a side window and then raced to join his colleague round back as he leapt down from the roof. Within seconds, both men had disappeared into the treeline safely.

"They did it," Mike said with a big grin.

"But where are they heading next?" Shawcross mumbled.

"Hopefully, they'll make it up here," Alan said. "They'll be safe with us."

"If they don't end up leading all of those infected up the hill with them," Anna said. "We discussed this and I'm not sure having people join us is a good idea. I'm glad they're safe, but we can do without them."

There was silence in the group as they digested the possibilities. The truth was that none of them knew what the other group of survivors were like, whether they were good or bad. They could be dangerous; insane or infected. One thing was certain, though: if the other survivors tried to make it up the hill, no one could stop them.

"You know what this means?" Greg said.

"What?"

"It means that we're surrounded. There're infected people down there in the hundreds. There's another few dozen trapped inside Ripley Hall. It's pretty clear that there's no rescue to be had. If there was, why are those people down there running for their lives? We have infected all around us."

It was a grim realisation, made even grimmer when Anna spotted another group of survivors running out of the woods and onto the car park. This new group contained the two men and the old lady from the café, but this time they were all being chased by a pair of infected who had come from the direction of the woods. The horde from inside the café spotted the group running across the car park and let out a screech. The group of survivors had nowhere to run. They had no hope.

Then the group below altered their direction and headed for the base of the hill. Anna panicked for a moment, assuming they were going to try and run up the hill. But the desperate group were headed for the cable cars. They managed to make it, but had to leave the old woman behind. As they filtered inside the two cable cars, the old woman fell beneath the tide of infected people and disappeared.

"Jesus!" Mike said. "Poor dear."

Anna shook her head in horror as she watched the horde of infected surround the two cable cars and begin rocking them violently.

"They're going to get ripped apart," Greg said. "Those cable cars won't hold them out for long."

Anna wanted to see the plucky group prove Greg wrong, but she could see no way how. She glanced around, not sure what she was looking for until she found it. The control booth was a small shed sporting a long glass window. Without telling the others what she was doing, Anna ran over to it. Mike was the only one who followed. Everyone else continued staring down the hill intently.

"What are you doing?" Mike asked her as he entered the cable car station behind her. A small console sat atop a steel podium at the far side of the platform and that was where she headed.

"The park still has power," she said. "If we switch on the cable cars, those people will rise to the top of the hill."

"To safety," Mike said enthusiastically.

"Exactly." Anna eyed a small silver key that was already inserted into the console. Next to it was a green, circular button that said START.

Mike raised an eyebrow as he watched her. "You said it would be a bad idea to let people up here."

Anna nodded. "I did say that, didn't I?"

She turned the key and the motors came to life, rattling the cable cars on their moorings.

"You sure about this?" Mike asked her. "These people could be dangerous. They could bring the monsters up here with them."

Anna looked Mike in the eyes. "If we leave them down there to die, we become the monsters."

She punched the START button.

CHAPTER 25

NICK CRANED HIS neck, trying to get a good look at the top of the hill. Ominously, the silhouetted stranger stood rooted to the spot, staring down at them as if in judgement. Their saviour or executioner.

"What do you see, brother?" Jan asked him.

"Not sure. There's someone waiting at the top for us, but I can't make them out."

"I hope they're friendly," Cassie said, staring at her feet.

"Me too, but given what we've been through, they can't be any less friendly than we're used to. They saved us by turning on the cable cars."

The car continued to climb. The one with Dave and the others inside was following right behind. If the people on the hill meant them harm, there was nothing they could do to escape now. They were being reeled in a hundred feet above the treetops.

"We're almost there." Jan was wrenching his large hands nervously. "I don't like this."

Nick didn't say anything. In the world that existed only days ago, meeting a stranger was no big deal, but now it was monumental.

The cable car levelled out at the top of the hill and entered the upper station. There was a man and woman standing on the platform, anticipating their approach. They seemed cautious.

When both cars were in the station, the motors stopped abruptly. "Stay where you are," said the woman on the platform. She was rugged, yet attractive, probably in her thirties. She wore a thick shirt and wellington boots and was appraising them from behind some sort of control column.

He put his hands in the air and stood in the open doorway of the cable car. "We're not dangerous."

"Nor are we," said the man with the woman. "Unless we have to be."

The door to the other cable car opened further back on the platform and Dave stepped out to join the reception.

"Hey," the woman on the platform shouted. "Stay where you are."

Dave ignored her and kept advancing. He waved a hand and laughed heartily. "Don't be afraid, my dear. We're grateful for the rescue. My name is Dave and—"

"I said stay where you are!"

Dave suddenly halted. "Alright, luv, keep your hair on."

The woman placed her hands on her hips and sneered. "I'm nobody's luv. And you haven't been rescued, yet. That'll be decided in the next thirty seconds."

Dave is going to ruin this for us all, Nick thought as he watched the woman bristle and take offence.

Several other strangers appeared and Nick counted that their hosts numbered at least six. All of the strangers carried makeshift weapons and looked like they were in no mood to be nice.

A ginger-haired man approached the woman in wellington boots and seemed to be furious with her. "What the hell have you done, Anna?" he whispered in a voice that was somehow also a shout. "We have no idea who these people are."

"We're not dangerous," Nick assured them.

"Be quiet!" the man snapped.

"There's no need to be rude," Dave said.

The man stepped forward, getting up close to Dave where a brief stare-off ensued. "I don't think you're in any position to discuss etiquette with me, sir. You've arrived on my property and I will decide how things proceed from here."

"You own this place?" Dave asked.

"I am Mr Shawcross, the manager of Ripley Hall."

Dave huffed. "You're just an employee. You don't own this place any more than I do."

Jan leaned close to Nick. "What is he doing? He's going to get us all kicked right back down the hill. These people look ready to snap."

Nick approached the strangers cautiously. "Look," he said, "my companion is being a little rude, but I promise you that we will respect whatever you say. We just want to find somewhere safe. Things have gotten really bad down below. Everywhere is chaos."

The woman in wellingtons stared at him. "You've seen the towns? Is there any order left at all?"

"None. People are infected with some disease and there's nothing but death everywhere. That's not the worst of it, though. The dead—"

"Are walking," the woman finished. "We know. We've had our share of encounters."

Nick deflated. "So it's not safe here, either?"

The woman shrugged. "It's...secure, for now."

"Great," Dave said, rubbing his hands together. "Then we're lucky to have found you."

Anna glowered at Dave and took a few measured breaths. "You seem to have a problem controlling your mouth. I want you to take a good hard look at what you're facing. My people have weapons; yours have none. My people are in charge of this place; you are guests. I'm going to give you one last chance to make a good impression, before we decide whether or not to beat you bloody and send you back down the hill."

Dave went to speak but Nick cut him off. "We apologise. My name is Nick Adams. A few days ago, I had a wife and a son. Now, all I have are these people. They are good people, but desperate and afraid. I promise you that you will like us. Even Dave here, once you get to know him."

Anna studied Dave and then took a long, appraising look at Nick. Eventually she said, "My name is Anna. You can stay."

"What are you doing?" the one called Shawcross shouted.

"Making the best of a bad situation," she replied. "They're here now. We can't exactly send them back down the hill, can we?"

"Thank you," Nick said. "You've saved us."

"Just don't make me regret it," she said. "I don't make a habit of trusting people."

"Me either, but I'm glad you made an exception. Is it okay if we all come out now?"

She nodded.

The rest of the group got out of the cable cars and huddled up on the platform.

"Those two are convicts!" Shawcross shouted, pointing to Jan and Rene.

"Easy there, brother," Jan said. "We're cool."

"Like hell you are. You need to leave."

"Where exactly do you expect us to go, brother?"

"I don't care, but you're not staying here."

Nick moved to the front of his group. "Jan and Rene are good people. They were sprung loose when things got crazy and they've more than proven their courage since they joined up with us. In fact, Jan has already risked his life for other people and saved my life personally."

"None of that means anything to us," Shawcross said. "Criminals are not to be trusted."

"I'm sorry," Anna said, much to Nick's surprise. "No one will feel safe with criminals amongst us."

"I understand," Nick said, having once felt the same way. "But what do you suggest?"

"Lock us up," Jan said.

Anna frowned. "What do you mean, lock you up?"

"I mean that if you feel criminals should be locked up, then lock us up somewhere secure. We'll behave as long as you feed us, but please don't turn everyone away because of mistakes I made years ago."

"Okay. We'll find some place to put you, but if you try anything, we'll put you down like dogs."

Jan raised an eyebrow. "Damn, lady. You sure you've never spent some time inside yourself?"

"No. I'm just a pissed-off vet. And you don't want to piss off a woman that puts her hands up backsides for a living.

"I think we understand one another," Nick said.

"This is a bad idea," Shawcross said. "They could all be criminals for all we know."

"Perhaps," Anna admitted, "but right now, we're all trying to stay alive against the same threat. I think it's in our best interest to trust one another."

"The enemy of my enemy is my friend," Jan said.

Anna nodded. "But sometimes friends can become enemies, so don't cross us."

"Well, then," Dave said. "Are you going to show us around now that it's been decided we're all staying?"

Shawcross let out a sigh. "Fine. I'll give you the tour and find somewhere for your illicit companions to stay."

Anna glanced apologetically towards Nick. "I wish I could say he gets nicer."

Nick glanced at Dave and chuckled. "It's okay, I'm starting to get quite tolerant of assholes, long as they aren't infected."

"Not many of us left," she said.

"No, not many at all."

Shawcross headed to the front of the new combined group and raised his hands in the air. "Welcome to Ripley Heights," he said with pride.

CHAPTER 26

"I CAN'T BELIEVE I'M here again," Eve said excitedly. "God, the memories..." She pointed at a nearby carousel that had dragons instead of horses. "That's the Magic Circle. My sister and I used to go on that all the time. And look, there," she pointed at a roller coaster at the edge of the park. "I think that's the Hood."

"It is indeed," Shawcross said. "They repainted it recently, but it's the same old ride. I take it you visited here a lot as a child?"

"Lots!" Eve gushed. Nick liked her excitement. It was the first positive emotion any of them had felt for days and it was infectious, even if it was destined to only be temporary.

"We need to be careful," Anna said. "We're pretty sure the zoo is safe, but we haven't explored the amusement park yet."

"Thank you again for helping us," Nick said. His heart still battered against his ribs. He couldn't believe he had survived.

"I just hope you haven't brought all those infected up the hill with you," she said.

"They seem to lose interest when they can't see you. I don't think any of them followed."

Anna nodded. "You noticed that too, huh? How did you survive out there?"

"Dave picked us up in his bus. We drove around for a while and then ran out of petrol in the nearby woods. I think luck has more to do with it than anything else."

"Dave is the guy who doesn't know when to shut his mouth?"

Nick nodded. "That's him. He was pretty much our saviour to begin with, but I've been changing my mind about him since."

Anna stopped. "He's not going to be a problem, is he?"

"No, no, of course not. At least...I don't think so."

She shook her head and started walking again. "Great, what have I let myself in for?"

"I promise he'll behave," Nick said, but wondered if he could even control such a thing.

"I'll just have to trust you then, Nick."

The group came to a stop in the centre of a midway games area. There were several prize huts and one of those laser-target shooting galleries with animated props. It felt strange being somewhere where fun was supposed to be had.

"Right!" Shawcross clapped his hands. "The Big Dog restaurant and pub is just ahead. We need to start stockpiling supplies. I'd say that with the soft furnishings inside Big Dog, and the fact that it has cooking facilities, it would make an ideal place for us to situate ourselves while we ride this thing out. I believe there is also a cellar where we can accommodate our...less desirable guests."

Jan grimaced. "Guess I should be used to being in a cell by now."

"Is that absolutely necessary?" Nick pleaded. "Jan and Rene really aren't any danger."

"We had a deal," Anna said firmly.

Jan cleared his throat. "Don't sweat it, brother. I agreed to the terms. I'm not backing out."

"It may only be temporary, anyway," Anna said. "Just while we get used to one another."

"Or we may keep you locked up until the police arrive," Shawcross added.

"Come on," Anna said. "Let's go inside where we can all introduce ourselves properly."

The group headed over to Big Dog restaurant and climbed a short flight of steps. The door was locked but it seemed like something the original group were used to. Shawcross put through the window with a metal pole and cleared away the jagged shards.

"Hope nobody minds climbing," he said. "Doors aren't getting as much use these days."

Everyone hopped up on the window ledge and funnelled through into the restaurant. It was very similar to the Rainforest Café, but better maintained.

"Now, I haven't been here for a while," Shawcross said. "The amusement park and zoo are separate to the manor house of which I am in charge but, if memory serves me, there should be a soda fountain that we can use while there's still power. We should also gather as much water from the kitchen as we can."

"Now that you mention it," Nick said, "how come you guys still have power? It went off down below."

"A generator," Anna explained. "It must have kicked in without us knowing it. Shawcross said it can power the park for a couple of days if the grid goes off. Tell you the truth, we didn't even know the power had gone out everywhere else."

Nick shrugged. "It set the alarms off down below a couple hours ago, but I'm not sure about the surrounding area."

Anna huffed. "So that's what that noise was. I thought I heard an alarm just before I fell to sleep."

Shawcross leant against the restaurant's bar. "Shall we get the introductions out of the way? Then we can get on to more important matters."

"Okay," Nick said. "I've already introduced myself, but this big guy here is Jan who, like I said, has already saved my life once. He also helped me save our friend, Margaret...but she never made it. Neither did Jake, Mark, or Carl. Jan's companion is Rene, but he doesn't talk – don't ask me why. This here is Pauline..." Nick continued to point around the group. "Cassie, Eve, and—"

"Dave," he answered for himself. "I'm the one who got us all together in the first place."

"Well done," Shawcross said. "I am responsible for our own little group. You already know Anna and myself, but may I also introduce Mike, Michelle, Greg, and Alan. There were more of us at one point but...well, I'm sure you know."

Everybody greeted one another.

"Should we be asking if anybody has any skills?" Eve asked. "That's what they do in the movies, right?"

Shawcross scratched his chin. "I suppose so. Anna would be our medic, for want of a better word."

"I'm a vet," she corrected, "but I know my way around human tackle too, more or less."

"I'm a builder," Alan said. "Retired."

"I'm an accountant," Michelle said. "So none of you need to worry about your tax returns."

Everyone chuckled.

"Anybody else do anything useful?" Shawcross asked.

There was silence.

"Well, it doesn't seem that we're in a great position to restart civilisation, so let's just hope things improve."

Some hope, Nick thought as he took in his new surroundings. He wondered how long this dingy restaurant would end up being his new home. He yearned for his old one, and the family he had shared it with.

Shawcross headed over to Jan and Rene. "The cellar is this way, gentlemen. Are you ready to settle in?"

Jan shrugged. "After you, Warden."

Nick knew it was wrong as he watched Jan and Rene head for their imprisonment, but he understood where the other group was coming from. He'd felt the same way about the prisoners not long ago, and in Dash's case his concerns had proven correct. But when it came to Jan, he felt like he owed the men.

"I think that's the drinks machine over there." Cassie pointed across the room and, sure enough, there was a long vending machine with a line of draught taps.

"Okay, great," Anna said. "Cassie, is it? Do you want to start filling up all the cups with soft drinks and water?"

Cassie headed off, probably glad for something to do.

"I'll help her," Pauline said, heading after her.

"And what are we going to be doing?" Dave asked, somewhat irritably. He probably wanted to be the one giving orders.

Anna sighed. "I don't know, Dave. What would you like to do?"

"Nick and I can go take a butchers at the kitchen? See what food we can rustle up."

She stared at him blankly. "So go do it then."

Nick and Dave headed through a door at the back of the restaurant and entered the kitchen. They found it in woeful condition, grime on the floor and grease on the walls.

"Glad I never ate here," Nick said.

"Nothing wrong with it," Dave argued. "Dirtier the kitchen, better it is. Bit of grease never hurt anyone."

"Think we'll have to disagree there."

Dave laughed and grabbed a long bread knife from a wall hook and let out a whistle. "Think I just found my weapon of choice. You should grab something too, Nick."

"I'm more interested in settling in with the new group right now. I don't think arming ourselves to the teeth is going to put them at ease."

"Arming ourselves is exactly what we need to do. That ginger tosser and the mouthy vet are going to be on our balls about every little thing if we let them. This place doesn't belong to them, so why are they acting as if it does?"

"Because they were here first and we would be dead if they hadn't brought us up. They seem like nice people."

"Yeah, maybe. I just don't fancy being defenceless if they decide to lock us up with the convicts. What the hell happened to Dash, by the way? I saw him fall out the goddamn cable car. Can't say I was sad to see him go."

"It's a long story," was all Nick was willing to say about it. "Now's not the time."

"Well, like I said, I want to be ready if these new people start trying to strong-arm us. We're outnumbered now they've locked up Jan and Rene."

"They're just being sensible until they know us better."

Dave huffed. "You sure about that? It's every man for himself now and I see a return to tribalism."

"Tribalism?"

"Yeah. People are going to start looking out for their own. The strong will take what the weak have."

"I think we should all just stick together. It's only been a couple days and you're already trying to go Lord of the Flies. If we don't help one another we may as well feed ourselves to the people at the bottom of the hill."

"Those monsters are the reason I'm right about us turning on each other. What are we going to do if there's a falling out or a disagreement, or frustration when we all begin to starve? Nobody can go anywhere, so the only option left is to fight for your point of view. We're all going to be stuck on this hill together and there's no longer the option for civil disagreement."

Nick sighed. "You don't have a lot of faith in people, do you?"

"When you've been a bus driver for twenty years, the one thing you start to know well is people."

"Let's just play things by ear for now, okay?"

"Of course. I'm just being prepared. Now, how about we take a look in those fridges?"

"Sounds good."

Inside the pit of his stomach, Nick felt more than just hunger.

CHAPTER 27

ANNA DIDN'T KNOW what to make of the newcomers. Two of them were criminals and one of them was a complete arsehole. Nick, at least, seemed to be on the level and the women in his group seemed to trust him.

She hadn't objected to Nick and Dave heading into the kitchen alone, but now she wondered if it had been such a good idea. She decided it would probably be wise if she joined them.

Before heading off, she glanced at Eve, Michelle, Greg, and Alan. They were all standing around aimlessly and needed something to do. Anna didn't know how she had fallen into the role of order-giver but they seemed like they needed her permission to act.

"Maybe you lot can gather up the furniture and make some sort of living space. It might be worth us having a barricade as well, just in case."

The four of them nodded and got to work. Anna headed behind the bar and entered through the kitchen door. Nick and Dave were at the far end with their heads in the fridges.

"Found anything?" she asked them.

Both of them spun around.

Nick answered, "Most of the food here is frozen, which suits our needs well."

Anna headed deeper into the kitchen and pulled open a metal door against the far wall. She thought about the last time she'd opened a freezer unit, and shuddered.

Inside was plenty of food to keep them going: mostly burger patties and fries.

"It's not Michelin star," she said, "but it'll do. Best leave it where it is for now. We'll have to make a list of it all and plan out rations."

"I agree," Dave said. "You're a clever girl, you. I can tell."

"Thanks," she muttered. "Must have been all those years at university."

"So, what's next on the to-do list?" Nick asked her.

"We'll have to check with Shawcross. No doubt he'll have an opinion on what to do next, but to be honest there's not a lot we can do other than sit tight. When everyone is feeling up to it, we should start making a perimeter around the park, in case any infected people arrive."

Nick nodded. "Yeah, I like the sound of having fences between us and them. We should maybe look around for stuff to keep us warm as well. If the power goes off, it's going to get cold."

"Good point. I'm not sure we're going to come across any blankets, though."

The three of them exited the kitchen and re-entered the restaurant. Michelle, Alan, Greg, and Eve were busy moving tables and chairs up against the windows and doors. They'd already turned some tables on their sides, creating private berths for people to lie down between. All in all, it was a job well done.

Over at the far side of the room, Cassie and Pauline were diligently filling up plastic cups with soft drinks and placing them on the floor in rows. With a bit of luck, the machine would keep spitting out liquids for a while. People seemed a lot less tense when they were busy.

"Our guests are secure and comfortable downstairs," Shawcross said, marching towards them with Mike by his side. "You'll also be glad to know that there are several barrels of soft drinks and beer down there. We will need to bring those up, of course. Can't leave them with the prisoners, lest they have themselves a party."

"Jan and Rene aren't like that," Nick protested.

Anna was glad the prisoners were secure, but she did wish that Shawcross would show a little more tactfulness in how he spoke about them. They were obviously well respected by Nick and the man bristled every time his companion's morals were called in to question.

"We were planning to check out the perimeter," Anna told Shawcross. "See if we can reinforce our position."

Mike laughed. "We sound like soldiers."

"Sooner we accept that we are, the better," Dave said. "I'm ready to go and check things out now. Anybody want to join me?"

Anna didn't want the new man to wander off alone, but she didn't want to be stuck with him either. "Mike," she said. "Could you get Greg and Michelle and go with him? I think more heads would be better."

"Sure thing. I'll get them now."

"I'll start making an inventory of what we have," Shawcross said.

"Excellent," Anna said. It was a job she was hoping he would volunteer for. It would keep him busy and out of the way for a while. She turned to Nick. "Should you and I go look for bedding material?"

"Sounds good to me," he said. "Let me just check in with Eve and the others, so they know what's happening."

Anna waited while Nick checked in with his companions. He seemed to take responsibility for their welfare and she had a feeling it was to mask a deeper concern. Clearly something was eating away at Nick, but he was dealing with it by concentrating on looking after his group. Perhaps that was what she too was doing. Usually she didn't care about other people, yet had somehow found her way into a position where they were relying on her.

After a few moments, Nick returned. He was holding a pint of coke and took a sip from it. Then he offered the glass to her. "Hope you don't mind, but with all the excitement it feels like I might faint if I don't take a drink."

She waved a hand. "Hey, you're very welcome. We need to be tight with our supplies from now on, but you folks are more than entitled to a drink."

He motioned toward the window. "Shall we?"

Anna nodded and they both headed for the broken window.

"So," Nick said. "What's the deal here? Do all of you work here?"

"No, actually. Just Shawcross. I'm a vet that was on-call here. Everyone else was staying in Ripley Hall for a company function."

"Really? Wow. Do you think you'd be alive if you hadn't been called out here?"

"I doubt it. Being here is probably the only reason I'm alive, if the news is anything to go by."

Nick's eyes went wide. "You've seen the news? What did it say?"

"Not a lot. It went off soon after, but it was pretty clear that this is happening everywhere."

They made it through the window and headed out into the park. "This is the goddamn apocalypse, isn't it?"

Anna tittered. It was crazy to use the word in a literal sense, but it was the most apt. "The news said there was military in some places, but didn't say where other than up north. Maybe if we hold out long enough, things will change."

"Let's hope so."

There was a brief silence as they walked and Anna took the opportunity to probe her new companion. "I guess for some of us, it already feels like the world has ended."

Nick nodded. "Pretty much."

"You said you had a wife and child?"

Nick looked away from her. "Yeah. Deana and James. They were both infected. I left Deana alive, but James..."

"I get it. You don't have to say. I can't imagine what you went through." She did, however, have some idea. She'd had a son once, too.

"The people in your group seem pretty glad to have you around. Most people are infected or gone, so I guess we should try to count ourselves lucky that we're even still here. Least that's what I keep telling myself. Only thing that's keeping me from going crazy."

Nick glanced at her. "Did you lose anybody?"

"Yeah, I lost someone, but not because of all this. Guess I'm lucky that none of this horror has directly affected me like it has other people."

"I don't think anybody's lucky anymore. I'm sorry for your loss, whenever it might have been."

Anna smiled glumly. "Thank you."

They were back to the midway games area and Nick came up with a suggestion. "We could use the plush toy prizes as pillows – some of them are pretty big and they look soft."

Following the same train of thought, Anna had an additional suggestion. "I think they sell wet weather ponchos in the gift shop. They could be good for bedding."

"Looks like we're on our way, then. Let's get started."

Nick vaulted the basketball midway game and begun pulling stuffed dinosaurs off the shelves. Anna entered through the back of the Arabian Derby and started grabbing the biggest plush toys she could find. There would be more than enough to use as pillows and cushions.

"We're going to need a bag or something to carry this stuff back," he said. "Any ideas?"

"The gift shop might have tote bags."

Nick vaulted back out of the basketball game and joined Anna on the pavement, where they then headed over to the gift shop.

Nick picked up a rock from a nearby flowerbed and let fly with it. The window shattered.

"That's how you guys do it, right?"

Anna laughed. "Nowadays we do. Got to tell you, though, I really miss using doors."

They climbed through the broken window of the gift shop and made it inside. Anna went straight to a hanger full of souvenir hoodies. "These should keep us all warm."

"And here are the ponchos," Nick said, thumbing through a folded-up pile of plastic sheets. "They've got souvenir towels over there as well."

"Here are the tote bags."

Nick laughed. "Well, that was easy. Makes me wonder when something's going to go wrong."

Right then, there was an explosion. It shook the floor beneath them but came from far away.

Nick looked at her and went pale. "What the hell is that?"

Anna chewed at the side of her cheek. "I don't know."

She hopped back through the window and told Nick to hurry after her. There were still aftershocks coming from whatever had exploded and several mini-explosions made it quite easy to pinpoint the direction.

"What are you going to do?" Nick shouted over the noise. "It's not like we can go down the hill to investigate."

Anna skidded on her heels as she headed around the park's Magic Carpet carousel and arrived at the cable car station. From there she had an unobstructed view from the top of the hill to the area below. In the distance, past the woods and forests that surrounded Ripley Heights, was a nearby village. It was in flames. The fires blazed from a hundred different sources and, as she scanned the horizon, she saw other distant villages ablaze also. The earth was burning.

"It's all over," Nick said. "Totally over."

Anna couldn't argue. Civilisation was aflame and for all she knew they were the last human beings alive, stranded up there on that hill.

Shock would not allow her to speak.

"What if the fire makes it over here?" Nick asked

Anna finally found her voice. "It'll be the end of the last safe place on Earth."

CHAPTER 28

LOOKING OUT AT the blazing remains of civilisation was a surreal experience. Common sense suggested that Nick should be on his knees, crying out in desperation, but all he could do was stare. The level of horror was so high that his brain desensitised him to it in order to cope.

Anna stood next to him and was staring with the same numb expression. Suddenly, she pointed. "Look! They're moving away."

Nick stared down at the car park and saw. Like a herd of grazing buffalo, the massive horde of infected began to turn toward the flaming village on the horizon. A factory in the distance ignited.

"It's the explosions," Nick said. "It's leading them toward the village."

"That makes sense. They operate off sight and sound. They're heading for all the noise. We might actually be about to catch a break here."

Nick took one last look at the infected, funnelling away into the distance, and then turned to look at Anna. "Let's get what we need and tell the others."

"Okay, let's head back to the gift shop and load up the tote bags."

"Ready when you are."

They headed back to the gift shop and got to work. They loaded up the tote bags with the plastic ponchos and hoodies. The last thing they gathered were the plush toys from the midway games.

"This should be more than enough," Nick said, peering over the top of his load.

Anna agreed and they started to make their way back towards the restaurant. With tote bags wrapped around both of his arms and a pile of plush toys balanced in front of him, Nick was having a tough time seeing. It reminded him of how Deana used to make fun of him for determinedly getting all of the shopping bags from the boot to the house in a single trip.

There was rustling up ahead, as if Anna was heading into the hedges. He was just about to ask her what she was doing when he heard her cry out.

Nick dropped the bags and looked around frantically. As he did so, he ended up treading on a stuffed dolphin. His ankle twisted and he cried out in pain, hopping onto his other foot.

Anna was struggling with an infected woman on top of her. There was a second infected person coming out of the bushes too, a Chinese man with broken spectacles.

Nick knew instantly that he'd have to take the Chinese man down first. Anna was incapacitated by the woman on top of her, which would make her easy prey.

He lolloped towards the Chinese man, determined to reach him before he got to Anna, and leapt into the air. He placed an awkward kick into the man's chest and sent him stumbling backwards into the bushes. Then he landed down on his bad ankle and hissed in agony.

Anna had the infected woman around the throat, struggling on the floor.

Nick went to her aid, grabbing the infected woman around the waist and throwing her backwards. At the same time, Anna kicked out her legs and struck the woman's abdomen. The extra momentum sent Nick reeling backwards to the ground with his arms still wrapped around the woman's waist. He held on tightly as Anna hurried to her feet to help him.

"Keep her there," she shouted.

"Yeah, no problem," Nick said, sarcastically.

Anna disappeared for a moment, making Nick panic, but then she reappeared and dove at the infected woman on top of him. She held a jagged rock in her hand and smashed it into the infected woman's skull until it was dripping with blood.

Nick limped over to her. "Are you okay?"

Anna's eyes went wide.

The infected Chinese man tackled Nick from behind. He fell to the ground and struck his head on the pavement, going still. His vision dimmed. His head buzzed.

Nick was hardly aware of what happened next as he lay on the ground impotently. Sounds of a desperate struggle ensued, but he was unable to do anything but stare up at the sky.

There was a wet sound. Then silence.

Nick was still dazed when the struggling stopped. He wanted to roll onto his back to see what was happening, but every time he tried to move, a wave of nausea flooded over him and his head clanged like a kettledrum.

"Anna?" he moaned. "Anna, are you there?"

A hand clamped down on his wrist and squeezed hard.

"I handled it," Anna told him, leaning over him.

Nick took many deep breaths before he was able to place his palms on the pavement and push himself up. Anna helped him to his knees and then, slowly, to his feet. His ankle throbbed.

"You took a pretty big bang on the head," Anna told him. "I can already see the swelling. Do you feel okay?"

"No, I don't feel right, I..." His words trailed off as he saw the blood pouring from Anna's neck. He reached out a hand, but then stopped himself. Her blood might be infected.

Anna frowned at him. She followed his gaze until she was looking down at her own shoulder. When she saw the blood there, her mouth dropped open. "Oh, no," she said. "No, no, no."

Nick stepped forward and put his hands on both of her shoulders. Suddenly his headache was gone, removed by trepidation and fear. "Are you bit?" he asked her, but she didn't seem to hear. "I said, are you bitten?"

"I...I don't know."

Nick shook his head. "Damn it!"

Anna unclasped the buttons of her shirt and tugged the material away from her neck and shoulder. Nick leant forward to examine her.

There was a lot of blood, bright red and already clotting. It wasn't from a deep wound, but that wouldn't matter if it came from a bite. He followed the bleeding to its source, until it became clear what they were dealing with.

He stepped away and let out a sigh, shook his head.

"What?" Anna pleaded. "Am I bitten?"

He didn't answer her. Instead he reached a hand around her neck and plucked the thing he had discovered embedded into her shoulder.

Anna flinched. "Ouch! What was that?"

Nick held the sharp twig out in front of her and watched the relief take over her. He couldn't help but laugh. "It was sticking right out of you. It was in pretty deep, but there's no bite. Must have been when you fell."

Anna put a hand to her forehead and rubbed. She obviously couldn't fight the tears that escaped her. "Thank you, thank you, thank you. Thank God! Thank everything. Jeez, that was close."

"What were they doing up here?" he asked her. "I thought they were all heading away."

"They must have followed you up in the cable car," she said. "Climbed up the hill after you and where already in the park when the explosions began. We need to be more careful."

Nick looked around anxiously, eyeing the treeline that surrounded the park. "You think there are more?"

"I bet there are more in the trees, but if we get out of sight they should all head back down towards the village with the others. These two must have been nearby when the explosions happened. They probably already had us in their sights."

Nick looked down at the scattered items they'd been carrying and quickly gathered them all up again. "I think that once we get all this stuff back, our main priority should be getting this place secure. The infected may be heading away for now, but I'm sure they'll be back eventually."

Anna nodded, staring at the ground as she thought about how close she had come to death. "We need to make this place a fortress."

"And we need to do it fast," Nick said. "Or else we're all dead."

CHAPTER 29

LMOST THREE WEEKS had passed since everybody had settled on top of Ripley Heights' monolithic hill. Nick was grateful for stumbling upon the survivors there, for he knew he would be dead if he hadn't.

Several more infected people had found their way into the park grounds during the days that followed and Greg had been lost to them early on. He'd been checking the woods when an infected man took him to the ground and bit him. He was dead before anybody could get to him.

The group had mourned his loss for a day or two, sharing regret that nobody had known him well. It made everyone feel luckier to still be alive, and more eager to know one another.

Nick had hunted down most of the infected in the nearby woods after that by himself. He went out with only a handful of knives strapped to his belt and came back every night covered in blood. There were things inside his head that he was trying to deal with and somehow violence was the only thing that made him feel in control of himself. It worried him.

It had now been more than four days since any infected had been spotted inside the park. The makeshift walls, fences, and barriers added to their feeling of security, but it was still far from ideal living. The power had finally failed and the water pressure was getting lower each day. They no longer used any of the park's toilets and had taken to finding individual spots in the woods. It was a degrading devolution of their once civil habits, but it was necessary. Human superiority had been reduced to nothing and they were no longer anything more than animals in the way they lived.

With time to rest, a dark mood had fallen over the group as each of them mourned the losses of their previous lives. Many times someone would wander off alone to cry.

The group had formed their camp around the Big Dog restaurant where they'd erected a waist-high wire fence around a large portion of the surrounding ground. It wasn't high enough to stop any infected from entering, but it would at least slow them down.

As things went, they were in as good a position as they could hope to be. The burning villages in the distance made clear that any remnant or morsel of safety was a privilege. To still be alive after all that had happened was a lottery win.

"Hey man, you're never going to believe this," Mike said to Nick.

"Believe what?" Nick muttered.

"Just come with me."

Nick followed him into the zoo. The group hadn't spent much time amongst the animals, but Anna had been making sure they were all fed and watered. They had already started to get milk from the three cows and eggs from the various chickens. Nobody said it, but they all knew the animals would probably end up as food themselves eventually. No one wanted to get too attached for that reason.

Mike led Nick past the pig sties and up to a large enclosure with a big fat tree in its centre. He looked at Nick like things should be obvious.

Nick shrugged. "What am I supposed to be seeing?"

"You blind or something? Look!"

Nick's mouth dropped open. "Wow! Is that real?"

"Course it's real."

Nick stared up at the orang-utan perched in the trees and could barely believe it. Why wasn't it in an enclosure?

"Is it...dangerous?" he asked nervously.

"Beats me. Alan's run off to get Anna. She'll know what to do."

Nick sat down on a patch of grass and propped his head in his hands, gazing at the magnificent creature in the treetops. The orang-utan seemed completely at home and seemed satisfied to have such freedom after likely being enclosed for what may have been its entire life.

For some reason, seeing an animal so wild and free lifted Nick's spirits. It brought him back slightly from the deep melancholy in which he'd been drowning. When Anna finally arrived at the scene, he'd not taken his eyes off the animal once.

"Lily!" Anna put a hand to her mouth.

Nick stood back up, patting the dirt off his coat. "Lily? Is that the monkey's name?"

"She's not a monkey, she's an ape."

"Okay. So where did Lily come from?"

"The enclosure you're standing right in front of. This was her habitat."

"How'd she get out?"

"I let her out," Anna said. "Sort of."

"Is she dangerous?"

Anna chewed at her lower lip and said, "Could she be dangerous if she wanted to be? Sure. She could crush our skulls with a single swipe, but do I think we need to be worried? No. From what I know about her, she's very intelligent and sensitive. She's lost her family just like the rest of us."

Nick glanced at her. "What do you mean?"

"There was a mate in the pen with her, and an infant. You can see them, there, under the blankets. When the first infected people appeared they flooded into the enclosure and attacked Lily and her family. She was the only one who made it."

"So, the infected attack animals as well?" Nick said.

Anna shook her head. "They walked right past the other animals. I'm guessing that a primate is enough like a human to pass for a target. They must get confused."

"Should we feed her?" Nick asked.

"I don't think Shawcross would like that," Mike said. "He and Dave are already kicking up a fuss about the daily rations being too high."

"Screw them," Anna said. "We feed her what we can. Lily's a part of this group, too. A survivor. Anybody has a problem with that, they can talk to me."

"Fine by me," Nick said. "I think we're better off with her around. She might make a good look out from up there."

Anna smiled. "How's your head?"

Nick felt the faint bump on his forehead from when he had fallen days before. "It's better. I still feel a bit sick when I first wake up, but the headaches have stopped."

"I think you probably had a mild concussion."

"I'm just lucky to have such a small brain. Otherwise I could really have been hurt." He laughed.

"Let me know if it gets worse. You and Mike are the only people I can talk any sense to. You're both just the right amount of insane."

Nick laughed again. "So, where are Shawcross and Dave?"

Both men had been in a constant battle for authority since meeting. The pathetic thing was that neither man had noticed how little the rest of the group cared who was in charge. It was a thankless job that no one else wanted.

"They're both back at the restaurant with Pauline and Eve," Anna said. "They're working on a map of the park and marking it with emergency food stashes, weapons, and stuff. Dave doesn't think it's a good idea to have all our supplies in one place. Shawcross agreed with him for once."

"Probably a good idea," Mike said. "At the moment, we're screwed if we lose the restaurant."

"So what are Alan and Michelle doing?" Nick said.

"They were rooting through the warehouse next to the office building last I checked," Mike told them. "Alan said they found a bunch of fireworks."

"Don't think there's going to be much chance for a display," Nick said.

"No, but they'd be a perfect signal for help if it ever arrives in the villages below."

Nick didn't think it was a possibility, but it couldn't hurt to be prepared. "Anything else in there?"

"Some gardening equipment. Alan suggested digging some pits around the edge of the park, like booby traps, you know?"

Nick nodded. "Over time we could probably dig quite a few."

"So what are you going to do for the rest of the day?" Anna asked him.

Nick shrugged and looked up at Lily in the trees. "I guess I'll fill in where I'm needed. First thing I'm going to do, though, is tell Eve about the newest member of our group. She's been pretty low the last few days – we all have – so maybe it'll cheer her up."

"Okay," Anna said. She and Mike waved Nick off as he headed back for Big Dog restaurant.

The restaurant was near the centre of the park and was now fronted by a minefield of plates, pans, and cutlery. The windows had also been boarded up permanently with tabletops and chairs, with only a single window left clear to act as an entrance.

Heading up the few steps to the building, Nick could already hear Dave and Shawcross bickering. They were discussing Jan and Rene, who were still imprisoned in the cellar. Nick had been visiting them a couple times a day, bringing food and beers. Their good nature about the situation was beginning to sour and Jan now expressed a growing desire to be let out.

"They can help with the jobs around here," Dave said. "They're two strong men."

"They could kill us all in our sleep," Shawcross argued.

"They're not murderers."

"You have no way of knowing what they were in prison for. The big one looks like a sodding serial killer."

Nick hopped through the window and joined the conversation. "His name is Jan, and he's a reformed bank robber. He told me how much he regrets his past and I believe him."

"Of course he said that." Shawcross folded his arms and sighed. "He probably had it rehearsed from all of his failed probation hearings."

Nick rolled his eyes and decided not to say anything more. There was no point getting caught up in their ceaseless bickering. Dave probably didn't even care if Jan and Rene were released, he just liked undermining Shawcross.

Eve and Pauline were sitting at a table nearby, sharing a cup of lemonade. Eve smiled as Nick approached. "We were supposed to be working out our defences," she said, "but then they started arguing."

"It's been twenty minutes so far," Pauline added.

"Best to just let them get on with it." Nick took a seat and started telling them all about Lily.

"So, she's just sitting there in the trees?" Eve confirmed.

"Go see for yourself. She seems friendly, even waved to Anna."

"No shit? Soon as I'm done here, I'm heading straight to the zoo."

"What's this supply map I've been hearing about?" Nick asked.

"Dave's idea," Pauline told him. "We're going to choose a few places around the park to drop off food and weapons. They're just trying to work out whether or not to let Jan and Rene help. I think Shawcross has taken it far enough now. We should let them out. Cassie told us about what they did to save you and what Jan did to try and help Margaret."

Nick nodded. "I'd be dead if not for Jan. Where is Cassie, by the way?"

The two women shrugged. "I haven't seen her since this morning," Pauline said.

"Me either," Eve said.

Nick had a bad feeling. "I think we should go find her."

The three of them made to head out. "We're going to find Cassie," Nick shouted over to Shawcross and Dave, but both men were so busy arguing that they didn't even hear.

"You don't think she'd try to hurt herself do you?" Eve asked as they headed away from the restaurant.

"I don't know," Nick admitted. "I'm sure she's fine."

They were quiet for a while. The tense silence made it clear what they were all thinking. Cassie was the most delicate of all the survivors and she was usually the last person to want to go off alone.

The office building lay ahead. Anna had explained that there were bodies inside one of the rooms that had become the unofficial morgue of the park; not somewhere to visit for any other reason. Beside the office block was an open warehouse with a large truck parked outside. Alan and Michelle were both milling about inside.

"Hey," Nick said as he entered the warehouse. He spotted several cans of petrol, which seemed a little unsafe to be stored next to commercial fireworks.

Alan noticed Nick staring at the fireworks and grinned. "Quite the collection, isn't it? With all this petrol we might be able to get the generator juiced back up."

"What were all these fireworks meant for?" Eve asked.

"Shawcross said the park used to hold fireworks displays at Halloween, New Years, et cetera. I guess they bought in bulk."

"Makes sense," Nick said. "I hear there's been talk of using them as a signal if rescue arrives?"

Alan nodded. "Michelle and I are going to set up a crate of rockets at the edge of the hill so we can set them off if we spot help. We'll cover them with some tarps to keep them dry."

"Sounds good," Nick said, then remembered what he was there for. "Have you two seen Cassie? Nobody's seen her for a while."

"No, I haven't seen her," Michelle said.

"Wish I could help you," Alan said, "but I haven't seen her all day."

"Okay, then we'll leave you to it."

On their way out of the warehouse, Pauline said, "Maybe we're overreacting. She might just need some alone time, Nick."

"I don't think she'd wander off without telling anybody."

"I don't think she'd hurt herself though," Eve said.

Nick stopped walking. "Really? What makes you so sure?"

"The way she's been talking the last few days, I guess. She told me how glad she was that we were all safe and that she hoped rescue would arrive soon. She was looking forward, you know?"

"Then where is she?"

They carried on exploring. For the zoo's animals, life was normal. They carried on unaffected. Life was no more complicated for them than it ever had been. Nick envied them. Their food came to them each day and all they had to worry about was when to sleep. An easy life.

They were coming back around to the orang-utan enclosure so Nick glanced up at the treeline to see Lily. He was disappointed, too, when she wasn't there.

"This is where the orang-utan was," he said. "Hopefully she'll come back."

"That sucks," Eve said, pouting. "I really wanted to see her."

Pauline sighed. "Isn't Cassie our main concern right now?"

Mike came speeding around the corner.

Nick immediately assumed the worst. "You've found Cassie, haven't you?" he said

Mike nodded. "Yeah, she's at the restaurant."

"At the restaurant?" Pauline frowned. "We just came from there."

"She was in the cellar," Mike explained.

Nick suddenly felt weak. "What's happened to her?"

Mike frowned. "Nothing. She's fine."

"Then why have you come to get us?"

"Because she's broken Jan and Rene out. Your prisoner friends have escaped."

CHAPTER 30

"CASSIE, WHAT'RE YOU doing?" Nick demanded.

She was standing with Rene and Jan, all three of them brandishing knives. Standing opposite, also armed, was Dave and Shawcross.

Cassie stared at Nick determinedly. "We can't keep Jan and Rene locked up like animals anymore. Jan saved me. He saved you too, Nick. I'd feel safer with them free."

Nick nodded. "I never thought they needed to be locked up in the first place."

"Well, it's not your decision," Shawcross said. "You made a deal when we let you stay."

"Bullshit," Jan grunted. "We showed you good faith. We could have forced you to take us in, but we trusted in you being good guys. Enough is enough. Rene and I aren't staying locked up a moment longer. It's been weeks and we haven't even been let out to see the sky. This is worse than prison."

Shawcross shrugged. "Then you'll have to leave."

Jan shook his head and Rene stood unwaveringly beside him, yet silently. "Leave? Are you crazy? There is no leaving here. We're all stuck."

"You're not a part of this group," Shawcross said.

"Yes, they are," Cassie shouted. Her entire body trembled. It must have taken an awful lot for her to make such a stand.

"Just put the knives down, Jan," Dave said. "This isn't how we do things."

"Really?" Jan said. "Is that what you were thinking when you tried to bash Kathryn's skull in? Seemed like you were pretty willing to use force then."

"If you'd let me, Carl would probably still be alive."

Nick stepped closer, his hands out in front of him. "Come on, everyone. Let's just calm down. We can discuss this like adults."

Shawcross shook his head. "We discussed it already. The prisoners stay locked up or they leave."

"I think the jury is still out on that one," Dave said. "You know I think we should let them out."

"Who cares what you think?"

Dave turned now, pointing his knife at Shawcross. "You know something? I've had enough of your attitude, you pompous sod. I don't know why I'm even arguing with you." Dave turned back to Jan and Rene. "You two are free to join the rest of us. Lower your knives, relax. We're done taking orders from this dickhead."

Shawcross's face went bright red before twisting into a furious scowl. He pointed at Dave's smug face with a long, bony finger. "How dare you! I am in charge here. I am the manager of Ripley Hall."

Dave turned his back on Shawcross and walked away, laughing. "You ain't shite. Just a no mark who thinks he's important."

"Do not speak to me that way. You have no right. No right!"

Nick watched in detached bewilderment as Shawcross rushed at Dave with his knife. Dave had his back turned and didn't see the danger.

"Look out," Nick shouted.

Dave acknowledged the warning just in time. He half-turned and managed to sidestep the attack by a hair's breadth.

Shawcross slashed at the air but quickly readjusted and raised the knife again, preparing for a second attempt. This time Nick managed to intervene. He leapt forward and caught Shawcross across the jaw with a punch. The man pirouetted to the floor, his elbow bumping a table on the way down. He was out for the count, the first man that Nick had ever hit.

Dave grinned at Nick and patted him on the back. "Way to go, slugger. I owe you one."

"I didn't do it because I'm on your side. He was going to stab you. This is all a huge mess. We have to live together. We can't go around stabbing and punching each other. I already have enough wounds, thank you."

Dave looked persecuted. "Hey, don't tell me. It was that bloody muppet who tried to get all stabby."

"You provoked him, though."

"What the hell is going on in here?" Anna was climbing through the window and as soon as her eyes fell upon Shawcross, she lit up. "What the hell are they doing out? What happened to Shawcross?"

"It's okay," Nick said.

"Like hell it is. What's going on?"

"I punched him," Nick said, not knowing quite how to qualify it.

Anna stared hard at him and, eventually, she said, "It's about time somebody did, but you better have a damn good reason for doing it."

"Look, I know this looks bad. There was a standoff over whether or not to let Jan and Rene free..."

"I know," Anna said. "Mike filled me in." She glared at Cassie. "Wasn't very diplomatic the way you went about things, darlin'. We can do without troublemakers."

Cassie stared at the floor.

"She was just doing what she thought was right," Jan said. "I made a promise to protect her the day all this started. She probably feels she owes me."

Anna sighed. "I'm sure she thought she was doing what was right. The problem with that, though, is that people have differing opinions of what's right and what's wrong."

"We tried to talk it out," Dave said, "but that loon came at me with a knife."

Anna looked to Nick for verification. He nodded. "It's true. Shawcross was the one who got violent."

"Well," she said. "I doubt he would have done so unprovoked, but what's done is done."

"So what do you want to do?" Nick said. "Can we let Jan and Rene out?"

"Looks like the decision's already been made. I don't trust either of them, I'm not going to lie, but I trust you, Nick. If you think they should be free, so be it. Just don't make me regret it."

"You won't," Jan said. "I promise."

Anna looked at Jan and rolled her eyes. Then, without saying anything else, she exited the building through the window.

Shawcross stirred on the floor, moaning.

"What should we do with him?" Cassie said.

"Lock him in the cellar," Dave growled.

"No," Jan said. "Nobody else is being locked up. I think it's time for a fresh start. An equal one. No more prisoners."

"But he tried to stab me," Dave shouted.

"And he got his clock cleaned for it. He's probably learned his lesson. If not, then he only gets this one chance."

Dave huffed. "Fine, you just keep him the hell away from me, Jan."

"I'll personally guarantee it. I appreciate you going to bat for me, brother."

"You're welcome. Just be sure to make yourself useful, and remember your loyalties."

Right then, Eve climbed through the window. She placed a hand on Nick's arm. "Anna just told me things were all sorted in here. What happened?"

Nick sniffed. "My hand's swollen from punching Shawcross for trying to murder Dave, but other than that everything's hunky dory."

Shawcross continued moaning and started to drag himself up against the bar.

Eve looked down at Nick's injured hand and winced. "Wow, you must really have hit him hard."

"Yeah, I suppose so. It's fine, I'm sure, just bruised. Hopefully Shawcross will be okay too."

Eve grinned at him like he was misbehaving. "Come on, let's go back to the kitchen and bathe it in cold water."

Nick felt the fuss unnecessary, but he went with Eve anyway. The kitchen was now filled with pots and pans full of water in anticipation of the day where the water stopped coming through the taps. There had been a lot of discussion recently about using some of the water to wash with, but Shawcross and Dave hadn't been able to agree on anything.

"Over here," Eve said. She stopped next to one of the kitchen sinks. "It's not ice-cold, but it should be cool enough to stop some of the swelling."

"You're quite the nurse," he said.

"I used to look after my little brother sometimes. He was always getting into scrapes."

Nick saw the sadness that appeared briefly in Eve's eyes. The less they all thought about their old lives, the better.

He dipped his swollen fist beneath the water and used his other hand to pull Eve into a hug. He gave her a quick squeeze and kissed the top of her head. "I'm sorry," he said. "I haven't checked in with you much the last few days. Are you doing okay?"

Eve hugged him back. "I think we're all doing about the same. Personally, I'm feeling a little shell-shocked, like this is all just a dream or something. I can't really be stuck with a bunch of strangers while monsters devour the earth, can I? That's not real, is it?"

"I guess the difference between nightmares and reality has become pretty thin recently."

"You're telling me. I keep expecting to wake up."

"Me too. Every morning I wake up wishing that my wife was beside me. Then I remember everything that's happened and I realise that I'll never see her again. It takes everything I have just to face another day."

"I know what you mean. I don't know if I can keep doing it anymore."

"Get up every morning and just get on with it," Nick said. He clenched his fist in the water and winced at the pain. "We're all survivors. We're all strong in our own way. We just have to concentrate on doing what we can with whatever the day brings us. I don't know if I would've made it this far without you. If you ever find that things are getting to be too much, come find me, because I owe you my life."

Eve moved closer to him and looked into his eyes. "Things are getting too much for me," she whispered. "I need you to be here for me now." She went to place her lips against his.

Nick backed away. "Eve, I'm married."

"You were married."

It hurt Nick, even if it was technically true. To him, marriage wasn't something that ended a few weeks after your spouse's death. James and Deana were still in his heart. He was still committed to them.

Tears appeared in Eve's eyes and she looked away. "I'm sorry," she whispered. "That was a really shitty thing to say."

Nick shook it off. "It's okay. No harm done."

Eve made herself look at him again. "It's just...I'm so frightened and I feel...I feel so alone."

Nick held her close again. "You're not alone, Eve."

"I don't want to lose you, Nick. You're the only person that makes me feel safe. I just want to hold onto that, because it's the only thing that makes me feel like I still have anything human in my life."

"I understand, but you don't have to be with me in that way just to keep me close. We started this thing together. We're friends and I care about you more than anyone here. I'll always have your back."

Eve started sobbing.

"I'll keep you safe," he said. "Don't be afraid anymore, okay? Things are going to be alright, I promise."

"You can't promise that," she said.

"Maybe not, but I'd rather live in a world where we can still make promises, than one where we're all too afraid to. I promise to keep you safe no matter how impossible the odds, okay?"

"Okay."

Setting himself a mission and giving himself a responsibility made Nick feel stronger. It gave him back the purpose he'd lost when he stopped being a father and a husband. It was the part of him that had been missing. The protector.

He kissed the top of Eve's head. "Come on. I think it's about time we all had a little fun."

CHAPTER 31

ANNA KNEW THINGS were going to get tense. When she'd entered the restaurant and found Shawcross half-conscious and the two prisoners holding knives, she'd known she had to stay calm and not take sides. If she had, she wasn't even sure which side she would pick. Her two closest friends were Mike and Nick.

As it stood, she'd decided to trust Nick's judgement. She knew his inclination was towards peace rather than confrontation. Loud-mouthed Dave, on the other hand, was a small man with large ambitions, just like Shawcross. In Anna's experience, men like Dave and Shawcross were trouble – abusers of power.

Mike caught up with Anna just as she was entering the zoo. The animals were due for a feeding.

"I heard Shawcross went at Dave with a knife," he said.

"I wasn't there. I wouldn't put it past him, though. He's a petty man with a bad temper."

"You're not a fan then?"

Anna shrugged. "I've seen Shawcross treat his staff like dirt in the past, enough times to know that he views other people as commodities. He won't like not being in charge."

"You think there'll be more trouble?"

"I'd bet on it. The only thing more dangerous than the infected people at the bottom of the hill are the healthy people at the top."

"You included?"

Anna nodded. "I suppose."

"Glad I came prepared then." Mike lifted his shirt to show her a crude vest of armour. "Made it out of some magazines I found in one of the offices. I don't want to be the next one to get stabbed."

She laughed.

"What's so funny?"

Anna shrugged. "It's just that before all this happened, I hated my life. I spent every night trying to drink myself to death. I suppose I was committing slow suicide, not brave enough to do it the quick way. It took the end of the world to make me realise how much I actually like living."

Mike stared at her. "You wanted to die?"

She nodded. It felt good to admit such weakness to him. "I was just done with things. Tired, you know?"

"Why?"

"Because one day I was pregnant and married, living in a three bed semi, and the next I was giving birth to a stillborn baby, divorced, and alone in a cramped flat."

Mike was silent and his shoulders scrunched together like somebody had pinched his neck.

"Sorry," she said, sensing his discomfort. "I doubt you're very interested in my life story, especially when it's so depressing."

Mike remained silent and plucked something from his back pocket. It was the wallet she'd retrieved for him weeks ago in the hotel room. Amongst the useless money and credit cards was a photograph. Anna studied the picture with interest. It was obvious that the girl in the photo had Down's syndrome.

"Who is she?"

"My daughter, Lucy. Dead now, I suppose."

"That's why you wanted your wallet."

Mike returned the wallet to his pocket and lowered his head. "I guess I sensed early on that things were pretty bad. I didn't want to not ever see her face again. This is the only picture I have of her."

Anna looked at Mike and realised, for the first time, how much sadness the man carried with him. He wore it around his neck like a lead-weight. "You've been so brave," she said. "I never would have guessed you had a daughter."

Mike cleared his throat and looked away. "Not talking about her doesn't mean I'm not thinking about her. It's just the way I deal with things, I guess. The best way to cope with her condition was to always be positive. It's a habit that stayed with me."

Anna grabbed Mike's hand, which was clammy. "It's a good habit to have. You're very courageous."

"So are you, Anna. What you went through..." He sighed. "At least I got to know my daughter, if only for a little while."

Anna didn't know which was worse, her having never known her child, or losing a child after raising her for years.

"What about Lucy's mother?" she asked. "Do you know what happened to her?"

Mike shook his head. "We separated a long time ago. All I know is that they would've been together at the end. I hold on to that." It seemed, for a moment, that he might cry. Instead, he said, "Thank you for giving her back to me. The photo, I mean."

She patted him on the back. "My pleasure. She was beautiful."

Suddenly, Mike leant down and kissed her. To her surprise, she let him. They broke apart after several seconds and Anna felt her cheeks growing red.

She cleared her throat. "What was that for?"

Mike stroked her face with the back of his hand. "Life has become unpredictable; no point spending all of it just trying to survive. We've got to actually live sometime."

Anna couldn't help but laugh. "I'm sure there was a big philosophical point in there somewhere."

Mike smiled and kissed her again. Anna's stomach fluttered and she held on tightly as they embraced.

When they finally broke a second time, they heard someone laughing.

Mike looked around in confusion. "Do you hear that?"

Anna nodded. "Sounds like people having fun. Almost forgot what that sounded like."

"Let's go check it out."

"Okay, but then I need to feed the animals." She found herself blushing as she asked the question, "Would you like to come along?"

Mike squeezed her around the waist. "Where you go, I go."

Anna wrapped her arm around him and they headed towards the laughter. It was strange how much a single kiss could change a relationship, but it had.

After walking hand-in-hand for a few minutes, they found Nick, Eve, Pauline, Cassie, Alan, and Michelle gathered in the midway. Earlier events had apparently been forgotten and they all wore gleeful smiles.

"What are you all up to?" Anna asked.

Nick tossed her a basketball. She flinched but caught it, then held it up confusedly.

"Well, don't just stand there," he said. "Throw it in."

Anna looked up at the row of nets inside one of the booths. She didn't see the harm so reared back and thrust the ball up into the air. The basketball hit the backboard and bounced away. Eve leant over the shelf and retrieved it. "Good try," she said.

Anna grinned, feeling good. "What's this all about?"

"It's about fun," Nick said. "I think we all need a break from supplies and defences and rations. It's time to kick back for an afternoon and try to remember what life is all about."

Mike motioned to receive the ball. "I've just been saying the exact same thing. How 'bout we get into teams?"

"Sounds good to me," Nick said.

Everyone else agreed.

Anna and Mike joined up with Alan and Michelle. They took turns making baskets, but it wasn't long before Nick's team was several points ahead.

"Were you a professional basketball player in your old life?" Anna asked Nick. "You never miss a basket."

"I used to play a lot as a teenager," he said. "It's like riding a bike."

Mike wiped sweat from his forehead. "Well, I think we should remix the teams. You lot are whipping our arses."

"What is going on here?" Dave was marching towards them with Jan and Rene close behind.

"Nothing," Nick said. "We're just having a bit of fun."

"Fun? Fun? We have things to do. We all need to be working."

Eve picked up the ball and stood defiantly. "Says who?"

"Says me!"

She rolled her eyes. "And who the hell are you?"

Dave bristled. "Apparently, I am the only one looking out for this group."

"Look, you're not in charge of everyone, Dave, and neither was Shawcross," Nick said. "You had your little coup d'état in the restaurant, but the rest of us are going to do what we want to do, not what you tell us to."

"We'll end up dead with that kind of attitude. There is danger all around us and you're playing...basketball!"

Anna sighed. She knew Dave had a point, but Nick was right as well. They all needed to let off steam or they were going to end up having nervous breakdowns and killing each other. "We're just taking a break," she said. "We'll be back to work soon."

"Now," Dave said. "You all need to do the jobs assigned to you now."

Everyone stared at Dave. Anna couldn't believe the gall of the man. What made him think he had any right to order them around?

After a while, when he saw no one was going to budge, Dave shook his head and spat at the ground with rage. "Nick, are you going to back me up here? You know, since I picked you all up, I've only had this group's interests at heart."

Nick sighed. "You know what, Dave? I don't know what your motivation is, but I do know that we're all getting pretty sick and tired of you assuming that you have any right over the rest of us."

"Nick, you need to understand—"

"We're playing basketball, Dave. Either join us or go away."

Dave's eyes narrowed and he glared at Nick as though he was trying to burn a hole through his forehead. Then he spun in a huff and marched away.

Anna took a deep breath. "I think you just made an enemy there," she said.

Nick grabbed the basketball and bounced it. "I'm a big boy," he said. "I can handle it."

He threw the ball and made another perfect basket. Nobody picked it up again, though. Suddenly the fun was over.

CHAPTER 32

THE EVENING WAS tense, particularly between Dave and Nick. Nick had felt Dave's angry gaze fall upon him several times throughout the night and he was getting sick of it.

The whole group was now in the restaurant eating dinner. The food was horrible, but satiated everybody's hunger. Seeing how much food they'd consumed for just one meal made it dauntingly obvious that their supplies wouldn't last much longer.

Shawcross sat alone, eating his meal with his head down. He was a broken man, obviously unused to violence, and the ease of which it had stripped him of his self-respect. Nick felt guilty for having been the one to punch him, but the man had brought it on himself.

After they'd finished playing basketball, everyone got back to work. Nick returned to the restaurant to clear the air with Shawcross, but the man had been nowhere in sight. He'd only reappeared less than an hour ago and told no one where he had been for the three or four hours in between.

To Nick's great surprise, Jan and Rene had chosen to sit with Dave during dinner. They even shared a few beers together. Perhaps they appreciated his lobbying to get them out of the cellar.

Nick finished the last of his lukewarm burger and stood up. He felt a headache coming on and the growing darkness in the restaurant was diminishing his mood.

"Where are you going?" Eve asked him, a concerned look on her face.

"I just fancy a walk and some air."

"You want me to come with?"

Nick shook his head. As much as he enjoyed Eve's company, he just wanted to be alone. "I won't be long," he said.

Eve seemed unsettled that he was leaving on his own, but she didn't say anything more.

Nick headed outside into the shadows of the park. The moon was full and everything seemed to glow. The park's rollercoaster, the Hood, towered in the distance but Nick headed the other way towards the zoo. The animals had a calming effect on him lately. Their calmness rubbed off on him.

However, whenever his eyes caught sight of the smouldering fires in distant villages, reality always came crashing back.

Coming up on his left was the empty orang-utan enclosure. It was a serene landscape of shadows and dark angles. He leant up against the enclosure's barrier and let his head drop tiredly. Beneath him were the rotting bodies of the infected that Anna said had attacked Lily and her family. It spoiled the peacefulness somewhat, so he looked for somewhere else to settle.

The bungalow at the edge of the habitat was sloped, low on the side that faced the footpaths and taller on the side that faced the enclosure. A drainage pipe ran up one side of the building, almost seeming to invite someone to climb it.

Nick didn't know why, but the thought of getting up on the roof was appealing. Five-hundred-feet above the ground and still he wanted to go higher. Maybe it was his inner child, wanting to make believe that being up high gave safety and security. It was certainly true in the case of the hill they all lived on.

He hopped up and grabbed the drainpipe, making it easily to the top. From up high, Nick had a better view of Ripley Heights as a whole. Ripley Hall rose in the shadows at the back of the park, its rooms full of shrieking horrors that could be released at any moment. He shuddered as he thought about what would happen if the doors were ever opened. He chose instead to look over the amusement park, but even that had taken on a sinister façade. Its unused carousel, its abandoned pirate ship, and its dormant big wheel had all taken on an ethereal quality under the moonlight. The whole place was haunted, echoing its past of children giggling and parents kissing, all things the park would never see again.

Thud!

Something hit the roof behind Nick and made him cry out in fright. He twisted around and almost lost his balance, but grabbed the edge of the roof and managed to steady himself.

"Jesus Christ!" he said when he realised what was behind him. His first instinct was to flee, but the orang-utan made no attempt to hurt him in any way.

Lily examined Nick curiously and raised an arm towards him. Gradually he raised his own hand to meet hers. Lily's rough fingertips slid over the cold flesh on the back of Nick's hand and she let out a soft hoot.

"I heard we have something in common," he said softly. "I lost my family too. At least your man did his job and protected you, though. I let my family down."

Lily's breath was audible as it escaped through her deep nostrils. Her smell was unpleasant, yet comforting. It was a reminder of what man really was deep down: an ape – egotistical and self-involved, but really nothing more than an ape.

"I'm sorry for your loss, Lily," he said.

At the sound of her name, Lily hooted again. Then she took off into the night as quickly as she'd arrived. Nick missed her as soon as she was gone, disappearing into the trees. Now that he was alone again, his thoughts would resume their torment of him. His memories had talons and they were poised to rip him apart.

He was almost glad when he heard someone cry out. The scream had been male, short and abrupt.

Nick slid from the top of the roof, hung, and landed back on the pavement. He winced as a shooting pain went from his ankles to his knees, but managed to walk it off quickly.

His first thought was that an infected person had found their way past the fences, but when he saw the knife jutting out of Dave's chest as he lay in the middle of the path, he knew he was wrong.

Anna came running. "We heard screaming," she said and skidded to a stop when she saw Dave lying there.

"Where's Shawcross," Nick said, shaking his head and clenching his fists in anger. If this was murder, there was only one man responsible.

Anna shook her head. The rest of the group appeared behind her, Shawcross included. "Shawcross is with us," she said. "He didn't do this."

Nick shook his head confused. "Then who. I heard him scream. The blood's still coming out of him."

"He was on his way to see you," Jan said. "He said he didn't want to hold grudges and that we all needed to work together."

Rene nodded, confirming Jan's statement.

"It's true," Eve said. "Dave asked me if I knew where you'd gone so he could make peace."

Nick shook his head. "That doesn't sound like Dave."

"No shit," Eve said. "Surprised me too, but I guess we don't know each other well enough to make judgments. He seemed pretty genuine."

"He was glaring at me all night. Didn't seem regretful at all."

Eve shrugged.

"It's a tragedy that you took his approach as a threat rather than the apology it was meant to be," Shawcross said, sounding smug. "Seems as though you may have gotten the wrong end of the stick."

"What? I didn't do this."

"Nobody else could have," Anna said. "Every one of us was in the restaurant. You left and then five minutes later Dave followed. We all came when we heard the scream."

Nick looked to Eve for help, but she just looked confused.

"I didn't do this," he shouted at them.

"We need to lock him up," Shawcross said. "Until we decide what to do with him."

To Nick's utter disbelief, Mike and Alan grabbed hold of him. He shoved them away, swinging his fists and kicking his legs. "Get the fuck away from me. I didn't do this."

He managed to land a punch on Alan's cheek, but was too late to react when Shawcross came and took a swing at him, clubbing him under the chin in an exact reverse of what had happened earlier in the day.

The force of the blow was too fierce for Shawcross not to be holding something in his fist. By the time Nick fell to the ground, he was already unconscious.

CHAPTER 33

NICK HAD TO flutter his eyes for a few seconds before he could see properly. His head and jaw hurt badly. He tried to open his mouth but couldn't.

"I'd try not to speak if I were you," Jan said. He was sitting in a wooden chair against the wall. Rene was right beside him. Candles lit the corners of the room.

Nick realised he was in the restaurant's cellar. The prison. It was musky and damp. "What am I...?" Nick winced as the pain exploded in his jaw, but fought past it. "What am I doing here?"

"I think you know," Jan said. "You did a stupid thing, brother."

Nick rubbed at his jaw and cleared a wad of phlegm from his throat. "Dave...? I had nothing to do with that."

Jan shrugged. "We were all together in the restaurant, everyone except Dave and you. Things are tense, people need someone to blame."

Nick sighed and let his head drop. "I can't explain it, but it's true. I didn't touch Dave."

"Can't say I don't believe you. You've always been a straight up guy. But if you did kill Dave, you're in a lot of trouble. Shawcross is campaigning to have you sent down the hill. Can't say I blame him if you're a murderer."

Nick spat on the floor and laughed. He was already tired of being accused of something he didn't do. "This is his doing. Somehow. And how dare you judge me, Jan. You're a bank robber."

Jan smiled. "Attempted bank robber. I was never any good at it. It's a whole lot different than murder, anyway, brother."

Nick hissed. "Just fuck off, Jan. I'm innocent."

Jan stood, his tall frame stretching almost to the ceiling. "Like I said, I can't say I don't believe you, brother. Hopefully time will clear things up. Just keep strong. Try not to think. Time goes slower when you do. Especially if they're guilty thoughts."

"I'll be ready and waiting for your apology," Nick said. "I was big enough to give you one when I judged you wrongly."

Jan nodded but didn't say anything in reply. At the stairs, he turned and looked at Rene. "You coming, brother?"

Rene shook his head.

Jan shrugged. "Fair enough. Come find me when you're done."

Jan left the cellar.

"So, what the hell do you want?" Nick demanded of Rene. "It's not like you're here for conversation, you don't even talk."

"Don't talk is not the same as can't talk, my friend."

Nick almost flew back in his chair. "Y-you can speak. What...why?"

"People take speech for granted, Nick. It is what separates us from the animals, and yet we treat our words with disinterest. We ignore their power."

Hearing Rene talk was surreal. He had a softly spoken Nigerian accent, but what he was saying was hard to follow. "I don't get it. You've been able to talk all along but you haven't. Why?"

"Because more can be learned from listening, my friend. God told this to me."

"God did?"

"Yes. I was once a bad man, Nick. A charlatan, a trickster. I would use my words to fool people into giving me their money. I took people's savings. I took people's lives. Then I went to prison and my life changed."

"You found God?"

"No, Nick. God found me."

Nick grunted. Religion wasn't his thing, but he played along, not wanting to offend Rene. "How did God find you?" he asked.

"An old lady came to visit me in prison. I had taken her life's savings by pretending to be from the gas board. I convinced her that her boiler was dangerous and she needed a new one immediately. She handed over her chequebook and I emptied her account the next day.

"When she came to see me, this woman, she asked me why I did it. I said I did not know why I did the things that I did other than wanting the money, but she disagreed. She told me I was afraid. I was afraid of how hard life could be, which is why I took the easy ways like cheating and stealing. She told me that deep down, I felt worthless and she was sorry for me. Then she told me that she forgave me and she was a friend if I needed one."

Nick sighed. "More fool her."

Rene carried on, undeterred. "I asked how she could forgive such a wicked man. Her reply was that God had given me great weakness so that I might one day find great strength. She told me to seek him out, and so I did as the old lady asked. I sought out the Lord. I learned of his ways, read his teachings. Soon I realised that words were precious and that I must use them no longer if I was to make my penance – if I was to find my great strength I would have to give up my greatest asset. I was a conman with no voice."

"So you really just stopped speaking?"

Rene smiled. "Yes, for many reasons, my friend. So that I could listen, learn, but mostly as penance, you understand? I decided that the next time I spoke it must be with purpose and a desire to do good. Only then could I hope to redeem myself."

"You sound crazy," Nick said.

"Perhaps, but this is a crazy world we are living in, no? Is it not crazier to be sane with all that we have seen?"

"I suppose so. Why are you talking to me now? What good can you do me?"

"To do good. I believe you did not kill Dave."

Nick sighed. It was actually a relief to hear that someone, at least, believed him, even if it was a strange bird like Rene.

"Deep down, I do not believe that Jan condemns you either, but he is afraid. He values his place here and does not want to lose it. He will go along with the group consensus...up to a point."

"Why not you?" Nick asked.

"Because my mind is clear. I have observed for many days. While the rest of you have bickered, I have watched silently. I see a man's intentions better than most, and yours are not of murder."

"No, they're not, but then who is responsible? Everyone was together when Dave was murdered."

Rene shook his head and then got up. "I do not know. Whoever it is, they are benefitting from you being blamed, and by Dave being dead. He may even have killed himself and this is all one big misunderstanding, though I doubt it. Dave did not have a coward's heart and his scream was not one of pain, but fright. I heard it well."

Nick closed his eyes to think, but came up blank. "There's nothing to gain from Dave being dead. We're all in the same messed up situation no matter what."

Rene smiled at Nick. "You are naïve, my friend. There is always power to be gained and there are always men who wish to take it. The world is not so different."

Nick's eyes widened. "You think Shawcross was behind it, don't you? But how?"

Rene rolled the wedding band on his finger that Nick had never noticed the man even wore. "Shawcross is a weak man with selfish intentions," he said. "I have seen this with my own eyes. Now that Dave is gone and his closest male ally is locked in this cellar, he will be able to assume authority easily. You were the only other who could oppose him so this fits his plans perfectly."

"Me? I'm no threat to anyone."

"People respect you, Nick. You have a level head, no? The thought of you committing murder has damaged the group badly, made them feel lost and insecure. This is the time to establish a permanent hierarchy – while the populace is desperate and weak."

"I don't see the point. What is there to be in control of? We have nothing."

Rene smiled knowingly. "At the moment, nothing. Later, however, there will be life at stake. To be the man who controls who gets food is an envious position. To decide who lives and dies is to be God. The one true Lord does not look kindly on such ambitions. That is why he has told me to help you."

"Help me?"

"Yes. I will remain here with you. Whoever killed Dave will likely prefer you permanently out of the way. I will make sure that does not happen."

Nick thought the whole thing ridiculous, but Rene seemed deeply serious. With all that had happened, it was better to be overly cautious than foolhardy.

"Okay," Nick said finally. "Thank you."

"You are a good man, Nick. I hope that is proven."

"Me too, but what if it's not? Shawcross couldn't have stabbed Dave himself, so what the hell happened."

Rene tilted his head. "Only the Lord knows."

The door at the top of the stairs opened and Eve came down holding a plastic tray. "I brought you some food," she said indifferently.

Nick got up and walked over to her. "I didn't do it, Eve. You know me."

She handed him the tray. There was a pint of coke and browning leaves of a salad. "Do I? I thought I did."

Nick put the tray on the floor and looked her dead in the eyes. "Yes, you do, Eve. You know me better than anybody else left on Earth. I didn't do this."

Eve stared at him and sighed. "I don't know what to think right now. Dave was a pig, but he didn't deserve to die. There was no one else who could have done it."

Nick nodded. "I agree, he didn't deserve to die."

Eve started back up the stairs.

"Eve," he shouted after her, but she ignored him and disappeared. The lock clanked behind her.

Nick sat back down and looked over at Rene. "I guess you really are all I have."

Rene nodded solemnly. "Things change, my friend. You just need to be patient. God will shine his light of truth on those who are guilty."

Nick stared down at the wilting salad on the floor and wrinkled his nose. "I just hope the truth comes out before I starve to death."

CHAPTER 34

IT HAD BEEN almost a week since Dave's death. Anna had dragged the man to the morgue herself to join the bodies of Clark, Charlotte, Tom, and Greg. She couldn't get over the fact that Nick had committed murder. In fact, there was a part of her that didn't even believe it all. She was a person of logic, though, and the only logic available said that Nick had murdered Dave. Everyone else had been accounted for.

"You okay, Anna?" Mike asked her as they fed the Clydesdale horses. The foal she had delivered two weeks ago was doing well.

"I'm just thinking," she said. "Not about anything important, so never mind."

"I'm out of food. Do we have any more nearby?"

Anna nodded. "There's one of Shawcross' emergency stashes over there. I've been using it for feed and veterinary drugs. It won't be long until we have to go out in the woods to find that greenhouse. What we have won't last forever."

Mike nodded. "I'll go see what we have."

"The stash is inside the green bin." She pointed to a large, round receptacle. She'd helped Shawcross empty it herself before storing additional supplies in it. There were dozens of similar stashes all over Ripley Heights.

Mike pulled the lid off the bin. "Um, Anna?"

"What?"

"You sure this is the stash?"

"Positive. I used it yesterday. It was full."

"Not anymore. Come look."

Anna hurriedly glanced inside the bin and frowned. There was nothing left other than a few discarded medical supplies, bandages, and a spare feeding bottle for the foal.

"What the? This was chock-a-block with stuff yesterday. There were weapons and water bottles and medicines."

"So, what then? Did somebody move it?"

Anna thought about it. "No, somebody stole it."

"Who would be that much of an arsehole?"

Anna stared at the empty space where the supplies should have been. "I'm not about to start accusing people just yet. Let's just go tell the others."

Mike sighed. "Shawcross is going to flip his lid."

"I know. Can't say I'd blame him, if it turns out that we have a thief."

Mike took Anna by the hand. "Well, the only person I trust for sure is you."

Anna laughed. "You don't know it wasn't me. I could be the thief. Mere weeks you've known me, you fool."

Mike shook his head. "You care too much about what people think, you know that?"

"Me? I don't care. People do nothing but disappoint me."

"Yet you never stop trying to help them. That's why I know it wasn't you. That's why I'm falling in love with you like a teenager."

Anna choked. "You love me? Don't be so silly."

"I'm not being silly. Anyway, I said I'm falling in love with you, so don't get ahead of yourself. This last week you and I have barely been apart. I've gotten to know you more than I think I've ever known anyone. There's no point hiding how I feel about you. Life's too short – especially now."

"You don't know me. None of us even know ourselves with all that's happened."

"I think the opposite. I think it takes a situation like this to show who people truly are. All of our bullshit – the vanity, the ego

– gets stripped away. The only thing left is who we really are. And who you are is beautiful."

Anna stared at Mike for a while, trying to find the right words. "Mike, I…"

"Can't say you love me back. That's okay. I have time. Not much, maybe, but I can wait as long as I have."

Anna shook her head and grinned. "Wow, you're always so dramatic, do you know that? Come on, let's go find Shawcross and give him the bad news."

They headed out of the zoo and found Shawcross by the cable car station. He was staring down at the car park below.

"What're you doing?" Mike asked him.

Shawcross spun around with a grave expression on his face. "They're back," he said grimly. "Look."

Anna peered down the side of the hill and saw that a few dozen infected people had found their way back to the car park surrounding the Rainforest Café. More were wandering in from the distance.

Mike cringed. "Oh, shit."

Shawcross put a finger to his lips and shushed him. "I'm sure if we keep a low profile we'll be quite safe. We're prepared to deal with the odd one or two that find their way up here, but we have to make sure we don't attract them in large groups. Being quiet is key."

Anna looked further into the distance. The fires that had been burning in the nearby villages had finally died out. It somehow made things feel even more final, like the candle of civilisation had finally blown out.

"They must have wandered back from the towns," Anna said. "Look some of them are burnt."

"There's obviously nothing left to keep them there," Shawcross said, "so they've dispersed, probably in every direction. A depressing thought indeed."

"They're all dead," Mike said.

Anna turned to him. "What?"

"Look, they're all slow and clumsy. Not a single one of the fast ones amongst them."

"Perhaps the virus has burned through all of the infected and killed them," Anna said. "Now they're all dead."

"It certainly smells like it," Mike said, wrinkling his nose. "If there are only the dead ones left, maybe they'll die-off too eventually. Won't they just keep on rotting until there's nothing left?"

"Perhaps," Anna said, "but we still need to be careful. The dead are slower than the infected, but they don't give up."

Shawcross nodded. "I'd like to think that we can liberate Ripley Hall at some point, but I think it'd be best that we continue to lay low for now. No unnecessary risks. No commotion. If we're smart, we may just make it through."

Eve came running up from the amusement park, panting.

Shawcross ran a hand through his slick, ginger hair. "Eve, sweetheart. Whatever is the matter?"

"The supplies," she said. "I've checked half-a-dozen places and they're all gone."

"Gone?"

Anna exchanged a knowing glance with Mike.

"You must be mistaken," Shawcross told Eve.

Eve shook her head. "We have no food."

"Actually," Anna said, "the reason Mike and I have just come from the zoo is that we've discovered supplies missing from there, too. I think we might have a thief."

Shawcross' eyes narrowed and his lips went thin. "Get everyone together," he ordered. "Now!"

* * *

It took less than ten minutes to get everybody together, excluding Rene and Nick.

"We have one very serious problem here, people," Shawcross said, standing in the midway that was now being used to store supplies.

The group stared at one another blankly.

"There is a thief amongst us." Shawcross almost shouted the word thief. "A dirty scoundrel. Who is it? Speak now, or God help you later."

"Don't look at me," Alan said.

Michelle folded her arms. "Me, either."

Shawcross snarled. "Well, somebody is responsible."

"Maybe it's the monkey," Cassie muttered.

Shawcross cocked his head. "What?"

"The monkey," she said. "Maybe it's been raiding our supplies at night, trying to survive."

Anna objected. "Lily isn't taking our supplies."

"How can you be so sure?" said Shawcross.

"An orang-utan would have no need for the weapons and medicines that we stashed along with the food and blankets. She could potentially take things she could eat, but I don't see her taking lengths of pipe and rope, do you? But that's not even the main reason I know it's not Lily."

Shawcross raised an eyebrow. "Oh?"

"I know, because I've been leaving food out for her at night and by morning it's all gone. She's living somewhere in the woods nearby and she's well fed."

Shawcross went bright red. "You've been giving our supplies away to a goddamn monkey?"

"No," Anna said calmly. "I've been giving a few supplies to an intelligent primate. One of very few left alive – even before the world went to shit. She has as much right to survive as the rest of us."

"Nonsense! You're a thief."

"Hey!" Mike said. "Let's take it down a notch with the witch hunt, yeah? Anna is a vet and took an oath to help animals in need."

"Actually, vets don't take an oath," Anna whispered, "but thank you."

Mike carried on speaking. "Anna is the only person who can help any of us if we get sick or injured, so I'd say we best be nice to her."

Shawcross folded his arms. "So we should just let her do whatever the hell she likes, regardless of the rest of us?"

"Hell yes. We were all stuck in a kitchen when she found us. Without her we might still be stuck there or, most likely, dead. She risked her life for us on more than one occasion, so how dare you attack her like this?"

"I don't mind feeding the monkey," Cassie said.

Mike shrugged. "Me either. I couldn't watch it suffer and starve."

"She's an ape," Anna said, "but I'm glad you don't mind feeding her because I'm doing it regardless."

"What if we end up starving?" Michelle said. "It's just an animal. We're people."

"Exactly," Shawcross said. "We'll be using animals for meat soon enough, so what's the point in feeding them?"

Anna shook her head. If they were happy letting a rare species die, why bother wasting the breath to argue? If that was how they felt, the world would eventually become a very bleak and meaningless landscape, devoid of beauty. Anna would rather die than live in a world like that. She turned away from the group, not wishing to discuss it further.

"Where the hell do you think you're going?" Shawcross shouted after her.

"To find your thief," she said. "Then maybe you'll stop blaming an innocent animal."

"If I find out that you're behind this, Anna..."

"You'll what?" Mike said, before hurrying after Anna. The feeling of having someone on her side, ready to fight for her, was unfamiliar. It'd been a long time since somebody had supported her like that.

"You're really sure that Lily didn't take the supplies?" he asked her.

"Yes. She's been taking the scraps I've been leaving and can probably live off some of the local vegetation too. There's no way she could have carried off all the supplies we left. Whoever is responsible for the missing supplies is much more calculating than an orang-utan."

"You're right. Whoever's taking the extra food is making a conscious decision to screw the rest of us over."

Anna took a seat on one of the park benches. In front of them was the cable car station and behind it open sky. The sun had begun to dip beneath the horizon and evening would arrive soon.

"You know what's crazy, Mike?"

He put his hand on her knee. "What?"

"That people scare me more than the infected do. The undead don't keep me up at night. Shawcross does."

"The undead? Are we calling them that now?"

"May as well call a spade a spade."

"I can't believe Dave was murdered and now someone's stealing from the group. You'd think that with all that's happened, people would finally want to stick together."

"Looks like the opposite is happening. Life is about survival of the fittest – everyone out for themselves."

Mike asked the question: "Who do you think took the supplies?"

Anna chewed her lip and thought about it. "Do you really think that Nick killed Dave?" she asked instead of answering the question posed to her.

"Couldn't have been anybody else. Trust the evidence. Didn't they used to say that on some TV show?"

"I don't know. I've forgotten what watching television was like." She leant back on the bench and stared up at the sky. "So, you think Nick did it, then?"

"I don't know," Mike admitted. "Wouldn't have pegged him as the killing kind before it happened, but I suppose none of us are in any position to trust one another."

"Don't you trust me?" Anna asked him, surprised that she was hurt by his words.

Mike blushed, his angular cheeks blooming with colour. "Of course I trust you. You're the exception."

Anna smiled at him. "Good, because one of the only things keeping me sane right is knowing that I have you on my side."

"Always." He leaned in for a kiss and when they broke apart a minute later, the world had gone dark. It took a couple of seconds before Anna realised that the darkness was coming from a shadow cast over them. Before she could see who was standing over her, something heavy struck her head and things got darker still.

CHAPTER 35

T WAS NIGHTTIME when Anna opened her eyes again and she
quickly realised she was sitting inside a greenhouse. She lifted her
head, and winced as a lump throbbed at the back of her skull. She
was tied up, bound to a chair by her wrists and ankles. Mike was beside her, unconscious.

"Mike," she whispered. "Mike, wake up."

Mike didn't move.

"I think he may be asleep a little while longer," said a famil-
iar voice. Shawcross emerged from the shadows at the back of
the greenhouse and eyed her like a hungry vulture. "Mike received
quite a blow to the back of the head. Might not wake up at all, I
fear to tell you."

Anna spat. Just seeing the man made her skin crawl. Knowing
he was the one behind this current indignity made her furious;
that he felt he had any right to tie her up...

"Shawcross, you fucking weasel. Get me out of this chair right now."

"Now, now," he purred. "There's no need for such hostility. I've
let you in on my little secret. You should be honoured."

Anna looked at him with disgust. "What secret?"

Shawcross stretched his arms wide and gestured to his surroundings. "What do you think? I found the greenhouse. There are
enough plants in here and crops outside to sustain a small group
of us indefinitely. A small group."

"When did you find it?"

"After you all turned on me and put that brute Dave in charge. I
was going to leave, but on my trek through the woods I found this

place. Besides, I couldn't leave Ripley Hall to you peasants. I need to be nearby for when it's reopened someday. I am its manager, after all."

Anna looked around at the greenhouse interior. There were long shelves; three tiers high, brimming with tomato plants, cucumbers, and a whole host of other fruits and vegetables. Stacked up in the corner of the building were all of the group's missing supplies.

"You took the supplies," she said. "All the shit you gave me, and it was you!"

Shawcross laughed. "Not exactly, but close enough. Like I said, there's enough here for a small group to survive indefinitely. Our current group, however, is slightly too large."

Anna's stomach rolled as she absorbed what she was being told. "What are you playing at, Shawcross?" she demanded, rocking back and forth. "Untie me from this goddamn chair."

"I'm afraid I cannot do that, Anna. I'm sorry that things have ended up like this, because I have always respected you, even if I have never particularly liked you."

"I always thought you were a wanker. Looks like I was right"

Shawcross growled at her and pointed his finger in her face. "You're in no position to sling insults. I thank you for making this easier for me."

"You can't seriously be planning to kill me."

Shawcross slapped a palm against his forehead. "Have you been listening to a word I've said? That's exactly what I plan on doing. The group of us won't make it through with the food we have. We'll eat ourselves to death in a matter of months. However, with a few less mouths to feed, we'll be just fine. Nick is locked up with that retard, Rene, and you and Mike are here with me, about to be disposed of. To my knowledge, that's all of the troublemakers dealt with."

"Troublemakers?"

Shawcross nodded. "Yes. You and Mike have been quite outspoken in your defiance of me. Today it became unfortunately clear that neither of you are going to respect my authority."

"That's because you have none."

Shawcross scowled. "Don't I? Just look at the position you're in. Look at what happened to Nick after he attacked me. Look what happened to Dave for going up against me." Shawcross put a hand over his mouth. "Oops! Whatever have I said?"

"You killed Dave."

"Of course I didn't. I was with you the whole time."

"Then how?"

"Not for you to worry about, Anna. You know, it really is such a pity that you couldn't see my way of thinking. If civilisation is over as we know it, then you and I would have made a great match for a repopulation effort."

Anna felt revulsion. "I'd rather fuck a pig."

Shawcross exploded, the look on his face inhuman; so full of hate and malice, twisted insecurities. "Maybe I'll have you fuck every animal in the zoo before I kill you, or maybe I'll show pity and just teach you a lesson myself. You think I'm not man enough for you? You'd rather choose an ambitionless moron like Mike – a man with zero ambition, zero intelligence, zero—"

Mike flew out of his chair, ropes hanging loose around his wrists. He tumbled into Shawcross and tackled him to the ground.

"I'm intelligent enough to get the drop on you, you greasy-haired motherfucker." He held Shawcross down and let fly with his fists.

While this was going on, Anna started struggling frantically with her own bonds. The ropes were thick, but the chair wasn't. As she yanked and twisted, she felt the joints of the old wooden chair begin to loosen. The armrests began to rattle.

Mike was still pummelling Shawcross on the floor. Anna shouted out to him. "Mike! Help me."

He saw her struggling to get free and ran over to help her. "One sec," he said, grabbing at the ropes around her wrists.

The ropes slipped away and she was free. With a hiss, she rubbed at her stinging flesh of her wrists. Layers of skin had been grazed away, leaving two sore, red rings.

"Come on," Mike said, grabbing her. "Let's get out of here. We need to tell the others about what this piece of shit has done. Then we can all decide what to do with him. I vote for lynching."

Anna jumped up from the chair and glared down at Shawcross on the floor. He'd rolled onto his side and was looking up at her with hazy eyes, slowly regaining their focus.

"You son of a bitch." Anna kicked Shawcross the ribs and the wind exploded out of him in a pained gasp. Then she kicked him again.

When she was done, she turned back to Mike and the two of them headed for the exit at the rear of the greenhouse. She had no idea where the hell they were other than in the woods some place.

As they hurried, Anna had a sudden, random thought. How did Shawcross have time to drag both her and Mike out to the woods before anyone noticed? How did he kill Dave while he was with everyone else? He couldn't have done it alone.

"I can't believe this," Mike said. "Was he always this much of an arsehole or was he—"

He stopped mid-sentence, stumbling back against a rack of root vegetables. He placed his hands to his stomach, a long knife sticking out.

A stranger emerged from the shadows. A man Anna did not recognise.

Despite his wound, Mike threw himself at the stranger. "Run!" he shouted at Anna. "Run!"

CHAPTER 36

ANNA FOUND HERSELF in an open field; deep woods surrounded her on all sides. Behind her, she heard Mike's struggles as he fought with his attacker. Someone had stabbed him. Mike was badly injured and she was running away. But if she could find the others, she could come back and help him.

Battling with the urge to stay, Anna shot off across the field as fast as her legs would carry her. Roots and unearthed vegetables tripped her several times but she kept on going. She entered the treeline and left the open field behind. Shadows enveloped her as the moon failed to penetrate the leafy canopy with any except a few thin shafts of light. It was like running with her eyes closed, dodging trees at the last minute whenever she was about to crash into them.

"Here pussy, pussy, pussy."

The voice was far off, but still near enough to stoke Anna's panic anew. She didn't recognise the voice, hadn't recognised the man it belonged to back at the greenhouse. She prayed to God that Mike was okay, but knew that he must have lost the battle if his attacker was now chasing after her.

She ducked off in a random direction, hoping it would lead her back to the park.

"Just stop running, girl. I'll be gentle, I promise."

Anna jinked around a bush full of nettles and headed for a tight cropping of trees, hoping they would provide cover.

"Bitch, you winding me up now. Give it up and come here."

Fuck you! Anna almost shouted, but managed to stop herself. The last thing she wanted to do was give away her position.

She was surrounded by apple trees. Their spoiled fruit littered the grass and crushed underfoot as she ran. She found a long straight rut and moved into it, the hard, clear ground allowing her to sprint more surely. The pair of parallel dips suggested the regular use of vehicles in that area, which was encouraging as it might mean she could follow it back to the park, if it led there.

"Bitch, I gunna find you. Then I gunna party hard wid you."

The voice was getting closer. She might have only seconds before he found the clearing and spotted her. He was faster than her, not as beat up as her.

Anna felt as if her knees were turning to jelly as she thudded across the hard mud. A thicker treeline up ahead was tantalisingly close, yet she just couldn't seem to make it. It always seemed close.

"Come out, come out, wherever you are!"

Anna burst through the treeline just as she heard her pursuer's voice echo through the clearing behind her. She'd made it into fresh cover just in time.

She might still be able to get away.

Then something moved ahead of her and she screamed.

"I hear you, bitch. Now you in big trouble," came the voice behind.

But it was in front of her that mattered. Anna looked up at the branches overhead and was shocked to see Lily. The orang-utan stared down at her and hooted.

The stitch in Anna's side was enough to drop an elephant, but she had to keep going. She had to keep going until there wasn't a single drop left in the tank.

Lily swung ahead, keeping to the branches. Eventually she stopped and hooted.

"What?" Anna said. "What do you want?"

Lily leapt to a new branch and hooted again.

"You want me to follow?"

Lily swung to the next tree, hooted again.

Anna followed Lily.

The orang-utan swung from branch to branch, tree-to-tree, altering direction slightly every now and then. Anna used the last of her reserves to keep up with the leaping animal.

"I see you, bitch," the stranger shouted close behind her. "Time to give it up for Daddy."

Anna screamed. "Help."

The gap between the trees widened and the moonlight got brighter. Anna threw herself out of the woods and then her legs finally gave out. She fell face-first onto the ground. Pavement. She had fallen onto a path.

"Now you screwed, sweetheart."

Anna flipped onto her back, but didn't have the energy to get up. She was done.

The stranger stood over her.

She tried to crawl away, but could only flap her arms uselessly. She screamed out for help.

"Anna, what's wrong?"

Alan raced down the path and then stopped to look at her quizzically.

"Alan," she cried out. "You have to help me."

"Nobody be helping you, darling," said her attacker. She saw now that it was a young black man. His left eye was bloody and gouged, but seemed to be a few weeks healed. His clothing was torn and muddy, a grey tracksuit just like the ones Jan and Rene had worn upon their arrival.

Anna managed to climb up and threw herself into Alan's arms, clinging to him desperately. "He's trying to kill me, Alan. He stabbed Mike. Shawcross... Shawcross"

"Where is Shawcross?" Alan asked calmly.

"He's in a greenhouse. He found the zoo's agriculture plot."

"Yes, I know," he said.

Anna looked up at his face. "Y-you know?"

Alan nodded. "Yes. Shawcross showed a handful of us yesterday. Explained the food situation."

"What situation?"

"That too many greedy mouths to feed is going to mean big problems." The young black man had moved closer to them without any kind of urgency or fear.

"Alan," she said slowly. "Do you know this man?"

Alan smiled then shrugged. "Calls himself Dash. Shawcross bumped into him a few days back. He's been staying at the greenhouse. He's been helping us get set up."

Anna pushed Alan away. "He stabbed Mike."

Alan sighed. "Hey, I liked Mike, but there's not enough food for all of us. Tough decisions have to be made."

"Decisions made by who?"

"By me." Shawcross emerged from the treeline, his face matted with blood and one of his eyes was swollen shut. Mike had really done a number on him before taking a knife to the belly.

"You're a psychopath," she shouted at Shawcross. "What gives you the right?"

"Taking it, gives me the right. Some of us recognise what the world has become. If the human race is going to survive, some of us need to be pragmatic. Until things are more stable, we can support only the core group."

Anna took a step back as he approached her. "Core group? What are you talking about?"

Shawcross grinned. "You could say the people who respect my way of thinking are the core group. The rest of you are...disposable."

Anna tried to run, but Alan grabbed hold of her. "I'm sorry," he said. "I really am." He seemed to genuinely mean it, for there was no pleasure in his eyes at all. She still wanted to kill him, though.

"Let me go, Alan."

"I can't do that."

She tried to shrug off his grasp, but he was too strong, so she opted to knee him in the groin.

Alan doubled over in pain, but managed to keep hold of her as he went down, still keeping her from getting away.

Dash planted a right hook on her cheek and sent her vision spinning as the ground came up to meet her.

"You right, Shawcross. She a feisty bitch."

"Just take her into the woods and deal with her."

"My pleasure."

Anna blinked, trying to steady here vision. She couldn't get her feet to move as Dash moved to grab her.

Something descended from the trees. It landed behind Dash and then all of a sudden he was rocketing forward. He landed on his face beside Anna, unconscious.

Alan screamed. Shawcross backed away.

Someone had come to Anna's rescue.

Lily stood over her protectively, making a guttural huffing sound as a warning to anybody stupid enough to come close.

Anna lay on her side in shock, unable to move, until one of Lily's hands grasped at her shirt and tugged. Get up, the ape was trying to communicate to her. Get up now.

Anna pushed herself onto her feet and started backing away. Shawcross made a move towards her, but Lily hooted aggressively, and he changed his mind.

Anna looked around and realised she was in the zoo, not far from the cable car station. From there, she could make it to Big Dog restaurant and find the others. She had no option but to find them and hope that they would help her.

"You'll regret this," Shawcross shouted as she ran away. "You and your goddamn monkey."

Anna gritted her teeth. She's an ape, you idiot. For the last time, she's an ape! And she just saved my life.

CHAPTER 37

U P AHEAD, THE Big Dog restaurant came into view.

With nobody pursuing her, Anna allowed herself to slow down. If she didn't she was going to collapse again.

She hobbled up the steps to the restaurant and approached the open window. Peering through the gap, she saw the glare of a half-dozen candles. Out of energy and almost out of fight, she climbed through the window.

"Anna? What the bloody hell's happened to you?" It was Eve. "Are you okay?"

Anna shoved Eve away from her. "Are you with them? Are you with Shawcross?"

"W-what do you mean?"

"Shawcross, Alan, and...and some other guy. They killed Mike. They're trying to kill me. Are you with them?" Eve stood awkwardly, staring at her like she was mad. But Anna was not mad. She lashed out and grabbed Eve by the throat, surprised by her own ferocity. "Are. You. Fucking. With. Them?"

Eve shook her head eagerly "No, no. Hell, no. I don't even know what you're talking about, Anna. Let me go. We'll sort this out."

Anna let the girl go. "I...I'm sorry."

"You're safe now," Eve said. "Okay?"

Anna said nothing. She slumped against the wall and slid down to the floor. Eve disappeared into the shadows, but returned with Cassie and Pauline. Cassie held out a drink for Anna, which she took greedily.

She swigged the lemonade down in one gulp and let out a gasp. "T-thanks. I needed that."

"What the flipping hell is going on?" Pauline asked her.

"Shawcross is a fucking psychopath, that's what. He kidnapped me and Mike. Now Mike is dead, at least I think he is. I don't see how he's not." The thought of losing Mike was enough to send her into an endless flood of tears, but for now she just used it to fuel her anger.

Pauline put a hand to her mouth. "You can't be serious."

Anna got back to her feet. "I'm serious. Shawcross will be coming here any minute. I need to find out who's on his side and who's still fucking sane."

"I had nothing to do with it." Eve quickly said. "I swear."

"Me either," Pauline said.

They all looked at Cassie, the only one yet to speak.

"What?" she said. "I didn't know, either. I promise."

"Okay," Anna said. "So the only people I don't know about are Michelle and Jan. Where are they?"

Blank faces.

"I don't know," Eve said. "Michelle was with Alan earlier."

"I think it's safe to say that Michelle will be on whichever side Alan is," Pauline said. "They've been stuck together like glue for weeks. He's become a bit like a father to her."

Anna sighed. "Great. That makes us outnumbered, especially if Jan is with them."

"I reckon he is," Eve said. "He's been pretty close to Shawcross the last few days – think he sees him as the boss. He's an ex-prisoner, probably likes having a regime to follow."

Anna slumped against the wall. "Great. Last thing we need is having to go up against a hardened criminal the size of the Hulk." She suddenly thought of something. "That reminds me. This new guy with Shawcross, he was wearing prison clothing. Spoke like a wannabe gangster."

Cassie whimpered. "W-was he black?"

"Yeah, do you know him?"

Cassie nodded and became ghostly pale. "It can't be."

"No way," Eve said. "It can't be Dash...can it?"

"Who the hell is Dash?"

"A degenerate we picked up along with Jan and Rene. We thought...well, we thought he was out of the picture."

"Well, now he's back in the picture and he seems pretty dangerous."

Cassie whimpered again.

Anna stared at the girl. "You okay?"

"Dash tried to hurt me once. He...he frightens me."

Eve and Pauline both placed an arm around her. Anna didn't have time to join them. "We need to arm up," she said. "Let's get whatever we can, right now."

"We can't fight them off," Cassie said. "There are more of them than us, and they're men."

"No. Mike was a man. These are little boys trying to have all the toys as well as the whole nursery. They may have the advantages, but that doesn't mean I'm going to lie down and get fucked."

"I'll go get some things to defend ourselves with," Eve said.

"Okay, make sure mine is something long and sharp. I need something to shove up Shawcross's arse."

Pauline looked Anna dead in the eye. "You really think we have any chance of holding them off on our own?"

Anna thought for a second and then smiled. An idea had just occurred to her. "We're not going to be doing it on our own. We have reinforcements."

"What do you mean?"

"Nick didn't kill Dave. It was Shawcross. He admitted it to me. He must have had Dash do it."

"I knew it," Pauline said. "I knew Nick wouldn't do something like that. Let's get him out of that damn cellar."

Anna nodded and marched across the restaurant. There was a door at the back of the bar, which opened to the cellar staircase. She grabbed the brass handle and twisted.

It was stuck. Locked.

"Does anybody know how to get this door open?"

"Shawcross has the key," Cassie said.

Anna booted the door in its centre and then again next to its hinges. There were no weak points. It wouldn't give.

"We'll never get it open in time," Pauline said. "They'll be here."

Anna shoved up against the door once more but then gave up and sighed. If they had any chance at all of fighting Shawcross's coupe, they needed Nick. The other three women trusted him and would crumble without him.

Anna banged her fists against the door. "Nick! We need to get you out of there."

CHAPTER 38

NICK OPENED HIS eyes and sat up. He was hot and threw his itchy, woollen blanket to one side. Rene, who hardly ever seemed to sleep, was already up and was standing over Nick patiently, as if he'd been waiting patiently for him to awake.

"W-what's going on?" Nick asked.

Rene motioned silently to the cellar door. He had stopped talking again after their very brief conversation.

"Nick, can you hear me?" Anna was shouting from the other side.

"Anna, is that you? What is it? What's wrong?"

"It's Shawcross. He's lost the plot. Mike's dead and there's some thug called Dash running around doing Shawcross's dirty work. They set you up over Dave's murder."

Nick wondered if he'd just heard her correctly. "Did you say Dash?"

"Yes, Dash. As in the third prisoner you picked up with Jan and Rene."

Nick looked at Rene who stared right back at him with wide eyes. There was no way Dash could be alive, not after the fall.

Nick climbed the stairs. "Open up."

"Shawcross has the key."

Nick grunted and punched his fist against the concrete wall. "Damn it!"

Rene placed a gentle hand on his shoulder. "Shawcross does not have the only key, my friend." From within the pocket of his tracksuit, Rene pulled out a long brass key that was attached to several others via a Ripley Heights key ring. "Perhaps he should have checked beneath the bar too, no?"

Nick stared at Rene with disbelief. "You mean you could have let me out of here at any time?"

Rene tilted his head, a sagely expression. "Escaping your cell would not have restored the other's trust in you. I had this key only for emergencies..."

Nick was just glad to have a way out. He took the key from Rene and slotted it into the lock, giving it a solid twist. The lock clicked and the handle released.

Anna wore a puzzled expression when he opened the door. "What? How did you—"

"It's not important." He moved past her and spotted Eve, and immediately headed towards her.

"Eve," he said. "I've missed you."

To his surprise, she wrapped both arms around him and squeezed him tightly. "I'm so sorry," she said. "I should have believed you. Shawcross is responsible for Dave's death. We should never have blamed you."

Nick eased her away. There wasn't time for apologies, or any need for them either. "No harm done. Just promise to trust me from now on."

"I promise."

He cleared his throat and looked around at Rene, Anna, Cassie, Eve, and Pauline. A table in the middle of the room was piled with makeshift weapons and he picked up a replica hunting rifle from the midway shooting game. It would make a good club in a pinch- especially since it had been modified with a nine-inch nail wedged into the barrel like a bayonet.

The rest of the group armed up. They stood in a loose huddle, staring at each other apprehensively. Cassie looked the most nervous and was clutching a sharp blade against her chest like it was a crucifix.

"So, just fill me in one last time," Nick said. "Shawcross has Dash with him and they are going around killing people?"

"Alan is with them, too," Pauline said. "Maybe Jan and Michelle too."

"Shawcross has this crazy idea," Anna explained to him, "that the group's chance of survival is better if there're fewer of us. He's found the park's greenhouse and has stockpiled all of our supplies there. Apparently there isn't enough to sustain us all."

"So the crazy sonofabitch is trying to...what? Cull us?"

Crunch!

The group turned to the open window as the sound of cracking glass and shattering plates came from outside. Someone had breached the minefield, confident enough not to watch their step.

"They're here," Anna said, holding up a butcher's knife.

"Everyone keep quiet," Nick said, "and get down."

The group took cover behind the bar.

Minutes passed.

Nothing.

Then something came flying through the open window and thudded on the floor of the restaurant. It was a severed head.

Anna moaned as she stared at the disembodied skull. "Lily! You bastards."

"We've killed your precious friend, Anna," came Shawcross's nasally voice from outside. "If you don't surrender now, we'll systematically kill every one of your precious animals at the zoo."

Anna started to cry. Nick could see that the threat wouldn't work on her, wouldn't make her give up, but it was upsetting her a great deal. It upset him, too.

"You'll kill them anyway," she shouted back. "So don't take me for a fool."

"That's the last thing I take you for," Shawcross said. "You're a smart, rational person, Anna, so if you come out peacefully I'll rethink things and let you live."

"You're fucking crazy!"

"I've never been saner. I am strength and endurance. I am leadership and intelligence. I am survival for all those who follow me."

"You're batshit insane is what you are," Nick shouted.

"Ah, Nick. Is that you? I take it that our darling, sweet Anna has emancipated you? Just another transgression she'll later come to regret."

"Just give this up, Shawcross," Nick shouted from behind the bar. "You're not hurting anybody else tonight."

"I beg to differ."

There was silence for a while. Nick again made eye contact with Anna as the two of them tried to figure out what was happening.

Eve moved from her position by the soda fountain and joined Nick at the bar. "Do you smell that?" she asked him.

Nick smelt it: petrol. It came in through the window and pooled on the wooden floor of the restaurant.

Pauline and Cassie realised what was happening and looked at Nick like frightened mice.

"Come out," Shawcross demanded, "or burn alive."

"Bite me," Nick shouted.

"Do not test my resolve."

"You won't do it because, if you do, you'll be as screwed as we are."

"And why is that?"

"Because you know that fire attracts them. You set fire to this restaurant and you bring a shitload of death up the hill. The dead and infected will be up here within the hour, not to mention the fact that you could end up incinerating the whole park. I don't think the Royal Fire Brigade is operational anymore."

There was silence outside. Nick knew, of all things, Shawcross was a careful man. He was a planner above all else. He wasn't about to set fire to one of his biggest assets. He wouldn't scorch the earth he wanted to claim.

"I think you need to find a Plan B," Nick said, "and if it involves you coming anywhere near us, I'm going to kill you, Shawcross, you fucking weasel. Understood?"

"You'll regret this, Nick."

"Not before you do."

There were sounds of a discussion outside, the tone heated and irritable.

"What do you think they're doing?" Eve whispered to Nick.

"I don't know, but we're sitting ducks in here. Sooner or later they'll come up with a plan to get us out, or kill us where we stand."

"What do we do?"

Nick thought about it for a moment. "I think we should leave here, but on our terms, not theirs."

"What do you mean we should leave?" Anna said, scurrying over to him.

"All we're doing at the moment is giving them time to think. I say we hit back now when they least expect it."

Pauline shook her head. "Oh, bloody hell. I don't like the sound of that."

"Me either," Cassie said.

"You're right not to like the sound of it," Nick said. "It's dangerous and could get us killed, but what choice do we have? Shawcross put us in this position. Are we going to let him win? After surviving for this long, after all that we've been through, are we really going to let an arrogant pig like Shawcross determine our fate?"

"Hell fucking no," Eve said.

"Maybe we should just surrender," Cassie mumbled. "They haven't tried to hurt me or Pauline. Eve might be safe as well."

Nick shook his head. "You can do whatever you want Cassie. No one's forcing you to do anything. Just remember, Dash is with them. Remember when Dash tried to force you to do things you didn't want to do?"

Cassie's eyes brimmed with tears. "That's not fair."

"No, it's not, and neither is you refusing to pick a side. It's time for you to shit or get off the pot, Cassie. You have to pick a side, right now. Go out and join them or stay here with us. Once you pick, though, that's it. This is about survival – not just about tonight, but for whatever comes next."

Cassie wavered for a moment, turning towards the window and then back towards Nick. Eventually she sighed, her shoulders dropping. "Okay, I'm with you guys."

"Glad to have you," Nick said.

"So how do we get out there without being seen?" Anna said. "If we try to funnel out the window they'll pick us off easy."

Nick rubbed his forehead and formulated a plan as quickly as he could. "We deal with Shawcross the same way I dealt with those brain-dead zombies at the bottom of the hill. We distract him."

CHAPTER 39

"**W**E'LL MAKE HIM pay for Lily," Nick said to Anna as he knelt beside her and rubbed her back. Before them lay the severed head Shawcross had tossed through the window.

"It's not Lily," she said.

"What? It's an orang-utan, isn't it?"

"Yes, but it's not her. It's Brick."

Nick frowned. "Brick?"

"Lily's mate. He died when all this started. They obviously cut off his head to make me think it was Lily. This one has been rotting for weeks, though. The skin has almost turned to dust."

Nick straightened up and sighed. "Shawcross has lost his mind. What is he even fighting for?"

"The self-esteem he's always lacked," she said. "He was a worthless wretch before all this. This is his chance to finally be somebody, one of the Lords like the ones who used to live in Ripley Hall. He's starting as he means to go on. Power is not given, it is taken. That's truer now than it's ever been."

"Then I guess it's time to go to war," Nick said. "We're all clear on the plan? Does anybody need to go over it again? No? Good. Let's do this."

Rene handed Nick the bundle of keys he'd found beneath the bar. Nick was counting on one of the keys unlocking the hatch in the cellar. The rear of the building led into a fenced-off yard that hadn't been barricaded or paid much mind to. It was a clear route out of the back of the building.

He bid the others goodbye and headed down into the cellar. Heart beating fast, he climbed up the rear stairs and examined the steel lock fixed the door. There was one key made of a similar tarnished-grey as the padlock and he inserted it into the lock. It was a relief when it turned easily and he was able to shove the hatch cover upwards.

The night flooded over Nick like a living creature, a cold black mollusc clinging to his skin. He quickly eased himself over the back fence and dropped down on the other side, wincing as his feet struck the pavement.

He could hear Shawcross and his cronies conspiring around the front of the building. Nick crept away. If the plan was going to work, he needed to put some distance between himself and Shawcross.

Coming up on his left was the park's rollercoaster, the Hood. Its walled-off surroundings would provide good cover. There was a park bin nearby and kicked it over. The lid came loose and spun across the pavement, making an almighty clatter.

"Shit!" Nick shouted as loud as he could. "Come on, they'll hear us. Run!"

He quickly hopped over the waist-high fence that surrounded the queuing area and crouched down beneath the elevated steel track.

"They've escaped," Shawcross shouted from the front of the restaurant. "Come on, I hear them over there."

Nick stayed hidden as he listened to the footfalls of his pursuers get nearer.

"You a dead man," Dash shouted. It really was him.

"You're supposed to be the dead man," Nick shouted back. "I watched you die, blud."

"Can't kill me, honkey. Hit a dozen branches on the way down, but I walked that shit off like a gangster. I lost my eye, though, and somebody needs to pay for it. You tell Jan he's got it coming too."

Nick peered through a gap in the fence. Was Jan not with them? Then where was he?

"He's inside the rollercoaster enclosure," Shawcross said. "The others must be with him somewhere."

Nick grinned. That's right, you arrogant fool, do exactly as I expect you to.

"Hey, Dash. When I'm through with you this time, you'll stay dead."

Dash sucked his teeth, the sound cutting through the air. "Come on down, hard man. Let's see what you got!"

Nick laughed. "While I'm outnumbered? Don't think so. When I take you down, it's going to be just you and me."

"What do you mean...outnumbered?" Shawcross said.

Nick bit his tongue. Had he really just given himself away so soon?

There was a moment of silence before Shawcross shouted, "He's not with the others. He's distracting us. Back to the restaurant."

Nick had to do something. He shot out from his hiding place and sprinted after Shawcross. Dash was standing in his way, accompanied by Alan and Michelle.

Michelle spotted Nick first and shouted a warning, which led to Alan leaping out to block him. Nick swung his rifle and clubbed the man out of his way. He had to push through to Shawcross.

But before Nick got to the man he wanted, Dash hopped out and smacked him around the head with a shovel.

Everything went dark for a moment and Nick found himself flat out on the ground.

Dash loomed into view. "I'm not impressed, honkey."

Nick turned his head and spat a mouthful of blood onto the pavement. He felt a tooth come loose and spat it out. "Y-you pussy."

Dash broke out in laughter and stopped only long enough to raise the shovel so that it hung over Nick's neck, ready to take his head off.

Nick closed his eyes and waited.

"Get it over with," Shawcross said.

"Say night, night, Honkey."

Thump!

Dash staggered sideways, tripping over Nick's prone body before slumping to the ground.

Nick sat up and discovered Jan holding out a hand to him. "Get up, brother. Looks like you're having a party, but no one invited me to dance."

Nick took Jan's arm and leapt to his feet. He was dizzy from the blow to the head, but he was ready for a bloody good fight.

Dash recovered and scrambled to his feet. There was a screwdriver sticking out of his left shoulder and he'd dropped his shovel.

"Are my eyes deceiving me," Jan said, "or is that ugly, one-eyed motherfucker, Dash?"

"It's him," Nick said.

"Survived so I could take you bitches out," Dash grunted at them, making a grab for his fallen shovel.

Nick tried to stop him, but Dash grabbed the shovel and backed off. Instead of fighting, he made a run for it, heading straight past Shawcross and disappearing into the shadows.

Alan, Michelle, and Shawcross grouped together, keeping to a triangle and clutching their weapons tightly.

Nick picked his weapon back up off the floor. "Just give it up, guys. It's over."

"Nothing's over," Shawcross said. "There are three of us and only two of you."

"Maybe," Nick said, his words slightly slurred as his mouth had started to swell, "but Jan counts as two, so we're evenly matched. No one else needs to get hurt here, if you just give it up."

"You are the ones who should give up. You cannot win."

"I disagree," Anna said, hurrying up from the restaurant. Pauline, Cassie, Eve, and Rene were with her, all armed. "After the day I've had, I'm quite happy to kill you fuckers right now."

Nick grinned at Shawcross. "I don't think the Geneva Convention exists anymore, so if you want to be treated like human beings, I suggest you three put down your weapons."

There was a standoff for a moment, the air tense and vibrating. Then Michelle and Alan threw down their weapons and put their hands above their heads. Shawcross, however, kept a firm grip on his pitchfork and looked as defiant as ever.

"Give it up, Shawcross," Anna said. "It's over. Michelle, Alan, grab a hold of him."

Michelle and Alan turned anxiously toward their former leader. "Come on, mate," Alan said, reaching for the pitchfork in Shawcross's hands. "We're finished."

"Get off me!" Shawcross shoved the pitchfork at Alan and buried it right in his stomach.

Alan rocked backwards, clutching his torso as it began to bleed. Michelle screamed as her friend's bodily fluids spurted out onto the pavement. She reached for the pitchfork and yanked it free, but that only made the bleeding worse. Alan fell onto his side and let out a gurgling moan.

Shawcross took off like lightning, taking advantage of the chaos. Nick, Jan, and Rene gave chase while Anna and the others tried to help Alan.

Shawcross headed towards the front of the park. Nick did his best to keep up. The wishy-washy feeling inside his head prevented him from running full-speed and Jan, being so large, wasn't a great sprinter. If they weren't careful they were going to lose Shawcross. Luckily Rene seemed to be keeping pace.

They chased Shawcross around the front of the park's office block and past the open doors of the warehouse. Beyond was Ripley Hall.

"He's heading for the manor," Nick said.

"Isn't it full of infected?" Jan said.

"He's got no place else to go. Let's not corner him into doing anything stupid."

Nick didn't like increasing Shawcross's chances of getting away, but he was out of breath. Against his better judgement, he allowed himself to slow down. "Where were you anyway, man?" he asked Jan. "You saved my arse back there in the nick of time."

"A man spends long enough in a prison, he starts to appreciate solitude. I was just walking in the woods, enjoying the quiet."

"I understand," Rene said.

Jan looked at his fellow prisoner, dumbfounded. "You...you talk?"

Rene shrugged. "Of course."

"Long story," Nick said. "I'll fill you in later."

"Fair enough."

Shawcross was out of breath. His running had slowed to a panicked stagger. In front of him was the dark spectre of Ripley Hall.

"What are we going to do with him when we catch him?" Jan asked.

"I don't know. We'll figure it out once we have him."

They entered onto the lawns of Ripley Hall and stuck close to the trees. Shawcross kept glancing back at them over his shoulder, but made no effort to increase his speed. He seemed broken and unable to flee from them any faster.

Nick got close enough not to have to shout and said, "It's over, Shawcross. You're done."

Shawcross turned around to face them from the steps of the house. "It...would appear so...wouldn't it?"

"No one else needs to get hurt, brother," Jan said. "Just surrender."

Shawcross shook his head and gave them an icy stare. "You really think I'm stupid enough to do that? You'd just kill me. You have no choice after what I've done."

"No more killing," Nick said.

"Then what? What do you plan to do with me?"

Nick had no answer.

Shawcross nodded slowly. "Exactly." He took another step upwards towards the door.

"What are you doing?" Nick said. "Get away from there."

"I've looked after this house like it was my own for ten years, did you know that?"

Nick shook his head. "No, I didn't. We'll get it back one day. We'll make it safe."

"I was in charge of a piece of history," Shawcross continued as if he hadn't heard Nick. "Lords have lived here, cousins to kings and queens. Powerful men with royal blood running through their veins. My job was to walk in their footsteps and respect their memory."

"Where are you going with this, Shawcross? What's your point?"

"My point is that you all fucked it up! You brought death to Ripley Hall. You tarnished its legacy and now you scuttle around like rodents, disrespecting the history of where you are, disrespecting my position as guardian of this place. You knocked me down, you violated me, you reduced me to your level. You have no respect for anything."

Nick shook his head and pitied the man. "It's just an old house and a shitty amusement park, Shawcross. A cash cow. The integrity of this place was lost long before we arrived."

Shawcross took several more steps upwards, almost at the door. "Hold your tongue, peasant."

Nick put his hand up and started after Shawcross. Rene and Jan went with him. "Get away from there. The whole place is full of infected people."

Shawcross shrugged. His eyes were droopy and tired. He looked like a mad man and spoke in a faraway, dreamy tone. "It is full of my guests, and I would be grateful if you referred to them as such. I should go tend to them now, make sure things are in order. It's check out time."

Shawcross headed up the few final steps to the house and placed a hand on the door.

"Shawcross, just get back from there, please."

Shawcross laughed pathetically. "Do you know what I think, Nick?"

"No, Shawcross, I don't know what you think, but we can talk about it, okay? Just step down from there."

Shawcross shook his head and smiled grimly. He was no longer listening, talking only to himself. "What I think is that we are all fucked, and if that's the case, I think I'd like to be with my house. It's where I belong. I'm the manager, you see. Ripley Hall needs its manager."

Shawcross pushed open the door.

"NO!" Nick shouted, sprinting forward even though it was already too late.

The dead flooded out like pus from a pinched wound.

They sprawled on top of Shawcross and pinned him to the ground on the steps. His flesh was mercilessly torn away by a dozen hungry mouths, but Nick didn't hear the man scream. Shawcross remained silent as they tore him to pieces, but the look in his eyes was one of sheer terror. It looked like he was afraid of whatever came next. He had never managed to make it back inside his precious house.

Nick grabbed Jan and Rene by their collars and shouted. "Run!"

CHAPTER 40

"**H**E'S DEAD," ANNA told Michelle. "I'm sorry."

Alan had bled out quickly. Anna suspected his celiac artery had been severed. Michelle was distraught.

"Help me get her up," Anna said to Pauline. "We need to help Nick. Who knows what Shawcross will try next?"

Pauline and Anna each grabbed one of Michelle's arms, while Eve and Cassie stood nearby.

"Just leave me with him," Michelle begged.

"We're going to look after you, Michelle."

They half-dragged, half-carried Michelle as they headed back towards the restaurant. There were noises coming from somewhere in the park.

Eve flinched. "What's that?"

"I know what it is," Cassie said. She sounded close to hysteria and was clutching her knife close to her chest again. "I know what it is."

It was the moans of the undead.

"The infected are here," Eve said, terror in her eyes.

"No," Cassie said. "The infected scream, the dead moan."

"Who gives a shit? If they're here then we're screwed."

Anna struggled to hold on to Michelle, who had fallen into a catatonic state of shock. "Not necessarily," she said. "The dead are slow. We might be able to cope with them as long as there's not too many."

"We need to find Nick," Eve said. "He might be in trouble."

Anna nodded and reaffirmed her grip on Michelle. "Okay, let's get a move on."

They headed over to the restaurant, calling out for Nick and Jan along the way, but they found neither man and continued onwards. The moans of the dead persisted in the distance.

"They sound closer," Cassie said.

"It's coming from the house," Anna said. "Somebody has let them out of Ripley Hall."

"Shawcross," Eve said.

"Probably. He's crazy enough."

Up ahead were the park's office building and the warehouse. The doors to the warehouse were wide open and sounds came from inside.

Pauline stood still. "Is it one of them?"

Anna wasn't sure. It could be Nick, so she called out to him.

There was no answer, but the noises abruptly stopped. Bradley's truck was parked in front and prevented Anna from getting a clear view of the warehouse's interior.

"Hold on to Michelle," she told Eve, then headed around the truck. The first thing she noticed was that the crates of fireworks, and some of the remaining petrol cans. The second thing she noticed was...

"Dash!"

Dash was bleeding from his shoulder and the stains on his tracksuit looked black in the moonlight. The half-healed wound of his blinded eye glistened.

"Hey, baby," he said. "You just in time for the show."

Anna stared down at the fireworks and then back up at Dash. "What are you doing?" she said. "Come out of there."

"No can do, sweetheart. You fuckers blind me and stab me. They gunna be payback."

Dash pulled a lighter from his pocket and sparked it aflame. "From the gift shop," he said. "Blinging, huh?"

The flame seemed to hang in the air indefinitely, flickering in the darkness and lighting the shadows in a small cone of light.

Anna stepped towards Dash. "You light those fireworks and every monster at the bottom of this hill is going to start making its way upward. They'll come from miles around."

Dash grinned at her. "That's the idea, sweetheart. If I can't have this place, neither can you."

The lighter fell.

Anna stood in stunned silence, as split seconds seemed to pass like minutes. Eve and Pauline screamed from somewhere behind her.

The flame tumbled through the air, landing inside one of the crates. For a couple of seconds, nothing happened.

Then all hell broke loose.

Dash dove to the ground just as the first firework exploded. A split second later, a hundred more went off, some flying upwards and lighting up the starry sky, others whizzing around the warehouse like flies in a jar.

Beneath the sounds of exploding gunpowder and igniting petrol, Dash cackled like a hyena. He sounded ready to die, so long as he took others with him.

Without realising it, Anna had hit the ground too. She lay facedown, her nose mere inches from the pavement, afraid to move.

Less than a minute later, the final firework hit the sky and fizzled out. There was near silence, save the soft crackling of flames beginning to take hold of the warehouse.

Anna shook, her stomach hot, her heart aching. She waited for the inevitable.

And then it came.

Hungry moans filled the air from all around; not just from Ripley Hall, but from the bottom of the hill and distant villages. The moans carried on the wind from miles around.

The dead were coming.

All of them.

Anna leapt to her feet and spun a panicked circle. Pauline and Eve joined her, but Michelle remained slumped in a foetal position on the ground.

Dash made a run for it.

Anna headed straight after him, unwilling to let the bastard get away with what he had just done. With the loss of blood and his reduced vision, Dash was easy prey. She clattered into him from behind and took him roughly down to the ground. She grabbed a hold of his injured shoulder and made him scream in agony, but he surprised her by striking back with his elbow, catching her in the eye socket. The blow rocked her and Dash used the opportunity to transition off his back and climb on top of her. He smashed her in the mouth with his fist.

"Told you I was gunna get you, bitch."

He hit her again, splitting her lip. The blood in her mouth was hot and salty.

"I gunna make this last all night." He hit her again.

"Get off her, you son of a bitch," Cassie shouted.

Dash turned just in time to see the knife coming, but was too surprised to avoid it. The blade went in under his chin and slid up into his skull. He was dead before he could make a sound.

Anna kicked Dash off of her and watched him slump onto his face. Cassie had left the knife embedded in his jaw.

"Are you okay?" Anna asked her.

Cassie was trembling. Anna put an arm around her, tried to console her, but was quickly pushed away. "I-I killed him," she said, as if she couldn't believe it.

"It was him or me, Cassie, and I'm glad you chose me."

"We all are," Eve added. "You did nothing wrong."

Cassie shook her head and sobbed. "I-I stabbed him in the face." She bent over and vomited. When she was done, she straightened up and ran from them

"Cassie, come back," Anna shouted. She was going to give chase, but Pauline grabbed her arm. "You won't get to her in time."

"Cassie, look out!" Eve shouted.

In all her despair, Cassie had run headlong into an approaching group of the dead. They fell over her like a moving wall, their rancid, sticky bodies moving shoulder-to-shoulder. When Cassie collided with a tall brunette woman, she fell to the ground and screamed.

The dead woman fell on her, biting into her face. Blood spurted into the air as Cassie's nose was chewed right off her face.

Anna couldn't help herself. She started forwards to help her, and this time both Pauline and Eve grabbed hold of her. "She's already dead," Eve said. "You know that. We have to get out of here."

Anna closed her eyes as the dead ripped Cassie apart. She gave her fear only one more moment, then shook it away. "Okay," she said resolutely, "let's get our arses off this bloody hill while there's still a chance."

"How?" both women asked.

Anna reached into her pocket and pulled out Bradley's keys. "We take that truck," she said, "and drive over anything that gets in our way."

The dead were currently occupied with Cassie's half-eaten corpse, but more came from the house.

"Pick up, Michelle," Anna shouted. "We have to go now."

The three of them grabbed Michelle who was still a catatonic mess.

"Dump her in the back. We don't have time to make her comfortable."

They hoisted Michelle onto the truck's flatbed and left her to flop onto her back. Anna hurried to the driver's side and put the key in the lock. The central locking engaged and the doors opened.

"Eve, Pauline, get in, now."

The two women did as they were told and Anna started the engine. The moment the vehicle came to life, she instantly felt safer.

The thought of being on the road, after having been cooped up so long, felt exhilarating.

She shoved the truck into reverse.

The dead came from the house in droves. Anna could hear more of them coming up the hill from the car park below. Soon, the entire park would be overrun.

"What about Nick and the others?" Eve said. "We can't leave without them."

"They're already dead," Pauline said.

"They can't be."

"They have to be," Anna said.

Then they all saw them.

"Jesus," Eve said. "Is that Jan?"

Up ahead, surrounded on all sides by the dead, Jan fought for his life. He battled the dead bare-fisted, clocking them with right hooks and snapping the necks of any who got too close. Fighting side-by-side with him were Nick and Rene. All three men were unarmed.

"They're going to get ripped apart," Pauline cried.

Anna gunned the engine and shifted out of reverse. "Not if I can help it."

The truck rocketed forward, accelerating quicker than Anna had expected. Panicked, she aimed the bonnet at the thick ranks of undead.

The first body she hit went clean over the roof and landed behind them in a broken heap. Blood splattered the windscreen. The second body went down rather than up and fell beneath the truck's thick tyres.

Anna stamped on the brake and yanked the steering wheel sideways. More bodies went down as the truck went into a skid, scooping them up like a plough. The windscreen finally cracked and glass shards fell onto the bonnet.

The truck came to a stop. The dead were all around.

Anna rolled down her window slightly, screamed through the one-inch gap. "Over here! Get in."

Amidst the roving shadows of the undead, the three men turned around. They saw Anna and the truck and ran towards it. They pushed and shoved at their attackers, dodging their grasps and avoiding their deadly bites. The truck was their salvation, and they were so near...

But the undead were just too many. Their reaching, clawing hands made a net impossible to escape.

Anna watched in horror, praying for her friends to make it, but there seemed to be no way through for them. A dead waiter knocked Jan sideways with an elbow. The big man's ankle twisted beneath him and he fell to one knee. Probing hands dragged him to the ground. He kicked out and caught a dead man in the chin, managed to snap the neck of another, but as soon as one body fell away, two others joined it. He couldn't fight them all.

Nick saw that Jan was down and stopped to help him, trying to push his way through all of the undead lying between them. Rene tried to help too, but the dead were everywhere.

Jan disappeared beneath a blanket of bodies. His angry shouting was the last thing any of them heard.

Anna shook her grief to the back of her mind and focused. She shouted through the window. "Nick, Rene, move!"

Nick shook his head in despair at the loss of Jan, but turned and ran. Rene went right after him.

A scream startled everybody sitting inside the truck. Anna craned her neck and looked through the rear window. Michelle had snapped out of her daze and was now standing and screaming hysterically in the truck bed. As soon as the dead spotted her, they headed for the truck.

"Damn it," Eve said. "They're all coming this way."

The dead bunched together, grabbing at Michelle's ankles. There was no time to do anything. Michelle tumbled into the hungry mob, screaming at the top of her lungs.

Nick and Rene made it to the truck, both men exhausted and surrounded.

"In the back," Anna shouted. "Get in the back."

The truck bounced on its suspension as the two men slid through undead's grasping hands and leapt onto the truck bed. The dead clawed at them, trying to drag them back out again, but the two men fought desperately.

Anna stamped on the accelerator.

The truck bolted forward.

And stalled.

"Shit, shit, shit!"

A body leapt onto the bonnet and thumped at the broken windscreen. Anna cursed and put the engine back in gear.

The truck bolted forward.

And kept on going.

Undead fell beneath the wheels. The truck whined unhappily under the additional stress, never designed to drive over bodies.

"Where do we go?" Eve said. "They're everywhere."

The dead were indeed everywhere, and these were just the ones from Ripley Hall. The ones from the bottom of the hill were only just arriving.

"We need to head for the access road past the house," Anna told them. "It leads down the hill and into the towns. It's how the staff and delivery drivers used to come and go."

She sped up.

In the rear-view-mirror she could see Nick and Rene fighting to hold on.

"Wait!" Eve shouted.

"What?" Anna said. "What is it?"

"We need supplies or we won't last a week."

"We have to go. We have no choice."

"What if we can't find food...or water?"

Something occurred to Anna, something that made her drive towards the woods. "Hold on. I know where we can get supplies, but we'll have to be quick."

She took the truck into the treeline at the edge of the park. It was hard steering the truck through the woods in the dark, but there was no choice but to drive slowly. She knew the dead would be everywhere within the hour. Eve was right. They needed supplies if they had any chance of surviving on the road.

She had to concentrate hard to remember the way to the greenhouse. When the truck broke through the trees and entered into the open area of crop fields, she knew her memory had served her well.

The greenhouse was full of supplies. The truck had a full tank of petrol. They might have a chance of making it.

Something jumped in front of the truck. Anna turned sharply to avoid it. The tyres skidded in the muddy ruts and came to a shuddering stop.

Eve groaned. "What the hell was that?"

"I don't know," Anna said, peering out of the side window. "There was somebody in the road, but I can't see anything."

A man leapt against the side of the truck.

"It's one of them," Pauline cried.

Anna felt her heart turn to stone as she recognised the man outside. It was Mike.

"Oh no," Eve said.

Anna stared out at the man she had been growing to love. The man who had made Hell almost liveable. Now his loving eyes were puffy and his lips swollen and cracked.

"Anna! Anna, thank God."

Anna stared at Mike with disbelief. "You're alive?"

Mike nodded. "Of course I am. I could use a doctor, though, or maybe a good vet. Do you know any?"

Anna opened her door and fell out on top of him, wrapping her arms tightly around his waist. "I thought you were one of them."

Mike winced. "Ow, ow. Easy."

Anna backed away and looked down at Mike's stomach wound. "How did you...?"

Mike pulled up his shirt to show a layer of blood-soaked magazines layered over his abdomen. "He still got me, but the armour took most of it. Just a flesh wound. The guy who jumped us gave me a right beating before he left, but I'm okay. It wasn't until I saw the fireworks that I even found the strength to move. I take it the undead are here?"

"Get in the back with Nick and Rene," she told the man she almost loved. "We're taking supplies and getting the hell out of here."

Mike hurried to the back of the truck where Nick and Rene helped him up. Anna hopped back in the driver's seat and put her foot down.

The greenhouse was just up ahead.

CHAPTER 41

T HE TRUCK PULLED into an area Nick didn't recognise. There was a large, rectangular greenhouse in the centre of a clearing and rows upon rows of planters either side of it. Even from the outside he could see the treasure trove of supplies.

The truck stopped and Anna got out. "Okay everyone," she said. "Grab as much as you can as quickly as you can. Who knows when we'll have a chance to get more?"

They all got to work. Nick went into the greenhouse before Anna, and together the entire group formed a line, passing out boxes towards the truck. There were plenty of bottled soft drinks and water, along with bags of dried seeds and nuts. What they didn't have much of was time. Nick had the least time of all.

Within ten-minutes, the back of the truck was fully loaded with supplies, enough to sustain them for a week or more. Nick stood beside the truck and waited for everybody to gather around, ready to go. Once again they all held weapons, gardening implements from the greenhouse mostly. Nick himself had armed up with a shovel.

"Okay," Anna said, opening the driver's side door and readying herself to get in. "This is it. Time to go see what's left of the world. I can't say we have much chance of making it, but we're going to do our best and at least we have each other. No matter what happens, I just want to thank you all for reminding me what family is. Before I met you people I had no reason to live. Now I have no reason to die."

Everybody stood in silence. In some perverted way, they were a family and they all loved each other as brothers and sisters.

Nick took his opportunity to say goodbye, as he wouldn't be going with them. He cleared his throat and moved to the centre of the group. "I just want to thank you all as well," he said. "You gave me something to live for after everything else was gone." He looked at Eve. "You especially, Eve. If I hadn't met you I probably would've given up before the first night was through. My son would have liked you." He chuckled. "My wife...not so much."

"Come on." Eve grinned. "That's enough sappiness for today. We have to get going."

"Not me," Nick said.

Eve frowned. "What are you talking about?"

"I can't go with you."

"Why not?"

Rene stood in front of Nick, cutting off the discussion before it had time to begin. He looked Nick in the eyes suspiciously, curiously, yet compassionately. "You have been bitten, my friend?"

"No way" Eve said, rolling her eyes and scoffing. Yet there was a tremor to her voice that heralded her deep concern.

Nick rolled up the sleeve of his jacket and revealed the ragged bite wound on his wrist. "They got me back at the house," he explained, "right before we lost Jan."

Rene had tears in his eyes. "I am sorry, Nick. Truly."

Nick sighed. "Yeah, me too, buddy."

Eve started crying. "I don't think I can leave without you."

Nick hugged her tightly. "Yes, you can. You have no choice. You're a survivor, Eve. That's why you're still here. You just keep on surviving, okay?"

She nodded, clearly trying to hold herself together. Her lips were pursed tightly as she fought with her emotions.

Nick took off his woollen jacket and wrapped it around her shoulders. "You take this," he said. "It's going to get cold soon."

"It smells like you," Eve said, tears spilling down her cheeks.

Nick waved his hand. "Now go. Get out of here before I try to eat you all."

Teary-eyed, but knowing what must be done, everybody climbed into the truck. Nick took the time to say a separate good-bye to Anna. He knew the group was in her care now.

"Sorry it went down this way, Nick," she said.

"Me too, but somebody has to stay behind to let the animals free anyway. Can't leave them caged up to starve to death, can we?"

Anna smiled. "I feel better knowing they'll be free. Thank you."

"You just look after everyone, you hear me?"

Anna snapped off a salute. "I promise. I'll miss you."

She got into the truck and started the engine.

Nick turned around to look for Pauline. He couldn't let her leave without giving her a hug too. She had come a long way from the shattered wreck he had met on the bus. She and Eve had been with him since the beginning.

He spotted her over at the edge of the woods, pulling up some carrots and dumping them into a sack. She had been in the crop fields while the others had remained around the greenhouse.

Nick saw the danger before she did.

Two dead men came out of the bushes and grabbed Pauline by her arms.

"Pauline!" Nick sprinted towards her, holding up the shovel he'd armed himself with. He reached the edge of the clearing and smashed it against the two dead men's skulls, one after the other. Both of them fell to the ground, no longer a threat. But the damage had been done. Pauline fell onto her side. Blood pumped from her neck and soaked the grass. Her wide eyes stared at Nick.

"I'm sorry," he whispered softly to her.

She smiled and went still.

Nick looked back at the truck and shouted. "Go! Get the hell out of here. More will be coming and you won't get another chance to leave."

They all stared sadly for a moment, but then Anna got the truck moving. She took it slowly at first, but eventually sped up and bounded into the woods. The sound of the engine was the last thing to go, leaving only silence in its wake.

Nick sat down on the grass alone. He was going to miss them all, but it wouldn't be for very much longer. Soon he would be back with Deana and James. There would be nothing to regret.

He lay back on the grass and gazed up at the stars, wondering what Heaven was like, glad to finally be leaving Hell.

EPILOGUE

NICK HAD NEEDED to work fast to get all of the animals free in time. A moment longer and the dead would have swarmed. They had finally made it up from the surrounding areas and taken the park for themselves.

The various animals had run wild as soon as Nick had let them loose, but the undead ignored them. It was as if anything other than a human being was invisible to them. Hopefully, the animals would find a way to survive. The world was there's now to reclaim. At the very least the world would now at least be better for the animals; no more humans to round them up to slaughter in their droves.

Once he'd finished opening up all the enclosures, Nick had climbed up onto the roof of the orang-utan exhibit where the dead could not reach him. Now he sat at ease, watching the dead men and women wander around aimlessly while he waited for the end.

He could already feel himself changing. A deep exhaustion had fallen over him and his vision had taken on an unnatural orange tint. His internal organs felt heavy in his chest and abdomen, as if all movement inside of him had ground to a halt. He felt dead already, and that his mind was merely slow in catching on.

Above all else, Nick felt at peace. He could finally stop running, stop fighting, stop surviving. Truly, his life had ended the moment James had died in his arms. Now he could finally move on to whatever fate had lined up for him next.

Thud!

Nick turned around. He didn't flinch or even worry. Nothing could frighten him anymore. Fear only existed with a possibility of loss. He'd already lost all he could.

Sitting on the roof behind him was Lily. She'd leapt from a nearby tree and hooted at him now as she shuffled closer. Nick saw that she held a carrot in her hand, which looked suspiciously like the ones he'd seen at the greenhouse.

Lily reached out and offered the vegetable to him, but he laughed and shook his head. "No, thanks, Lily. It would just be wasted on me. You eat it."

As if understanding, Lily sat beside him and took a hefty bite out of the carrot. Nick reached over and patted her fur.

"You can't stay here for long, Lily. I'm sick, and eventually I'll become dangerous. I think you understand that. For now, though, I'm glad you're here. I hope you make it out of this mess better than me."

There was silence for a while, Nick staring at the horizon. The sun was beginning to rise. It was his last morning on Earth and he was feeling pretty damn good. The very notion was absurd, but it was true. Death wasn't so bad when you embraced it. It was a relief to see the end in sight. The line at the end of a marathon.

"You think they'll be okay out there?" he asked Lily. He was thinking about Eve and the others. Their chances of finding safety seemed pretty slim, but at least there was a chance. "You think they'll keep on surviving?"

Lily hooted.

"Yeah. That's what I think, too."

With a smile on his face, Nick lay back and watched the sun rise. A few minutes later, he rose with it.

End

ABOUT THE AUTHOR

Iain Rob Wright is from the English town of Redditch, where he worked for many years as a mobile telephone salesman. After publishing his debut novel, THE FINAL WINTER, in 2011 to great success, he quit his job and became a full time writer. He now has over a dozen novels, and in 2013 he co-wrote a book with bestselling author, J.A.Konrath.

WWW.IAINROBWRIGHT.COM